BILLY-BOY

Billy couldn't take his eyes off Miss Prescott as she walked to a cupboard at the other end of the cabin, where the deeper shadows were. Because the long old-fashioned dress she wore swayed so much, it looked as though she might have floated there.

In the cupboard was an array of dolls in separate boxes. Each doll was a perfect replica of every child that Emma Prescott had ever killed.

Billy recognized the sweater his doll had on. It even had on a set of blue jeans and little sneakers just like his.

She put the doll that was him on his chest, tilting its head so that it was staring directly into Billy's tear-swollen eyes.

Billy struggled with everything he had left to free himself. His eyes never left the shiny knife in Miss Prescott's hands. It looked as though it was suspended in the darkness of the cabin's rafters, and that she was growing taller and taller with each passing moment.

"Say good-bye," she said to the boy. And the deed she had so carefully planned, so skillfully worked to bring about, was instantly done. To her collection would now be added another blood-splattered doll.

She thought she'd call this one "Billy-boy."

TALES OF TERROR AND POSSESSION

THE DOLLKEEPER

BY JACK SCAPARRO

ZEBRA BOOKS
KENSINGTON PUBLISHING CORP.

ZEBRA BOOKS

are published by

Kensington Publishing Corp.
475 Park Avenue South
New York, NY 10016

First printing: February 1987

Printed in the United States of America

To Rose Montana, who understood and helped. And to my son, Marc, who is a patient teacher.

PROLOGUE

The terror caught in Billy Chadwick's throat like a hot coal. He didn't know how long he had been in the smelly burlap sack that the old woman had wrestled him into. She had tied his hands and feet with rope, and his mouth was sealed with a broad swatch of tape. He could hardly breathe.

Why, the eight-year-old boy wondered. He hadn't done anything wrong. Had ol' Miss Prescott gone crazy? Why was she doing this to him?

Emma Prescott took her eyes off the narrow road for a moment and turned to the cracked rear window of the battered old pickup she was driving. Rain had begun to fall and the first flash of lightning briefly lit the darkness. In the bed of the grinding pickup she could see the burlap sack twist wildly. "Tied you in there too good, sonny!" she shouted over the roar of the engine. "You ain't goin' nowhere. Not anymore!"

She couldn't wait to get to the isolated cabin at the end of the old logging trail. That's where all the fun begins, she thought. That's where all the little boys and little girls become my very own.

When she thought of what the rest of that stormy night held in store, the deranged woman jammed her foot all the way down on the accelerator until it hit the floorboard.

She didn't want to miss a moment of it.

PART ONE

CHAPTER ONE

By the time she got up to the cabin with the boy the rain was hissing down along the hood of her battered old yellow pickup like a chorus of angry snakes. Emma Prescott smiled. She liked a good heavy rain on a night like this. It made her feel clean, almost important, as though all of nature had risen to applaud the deed she had come so far up into the hills to commit. And when the lightning flashed, revealing the isolated log cabin that stood in the blackness of the clearing before her, she glowed as brightly as the electricity that crackled through the stormy night.

The old woman was pleased to have made it there. At one point on the journey up the mountain the front wheel of her pickup had hit a rock and the tire momentarily jogged off the narrow trail. Beneath it, the embankment dropped off sharply toward a brook at the bottom of a steep ravine. But Emma Prescott was a surefooted driver. She quickly recovered the road. She wasn't going to let a narrow, slippery trail keep her from where she was going. Not tonight.

The sound of the boy banging his heels against the bed of the pickup did not disturb her. They were five or six miles up in the hills, where the grown-over old logging trail came to a shabby end. The small patch of land on which the pickup was now parked had once been used for farming. It was surrounded by tall forest pines that were over a hundred years old. Toward the far end of the clearing there was a cabin that had been abandoned by a farming family more than three quarters of a century ago, when the invention of the Model-T made it more practical for a farmer to live closer to the main road. Not far to the side of the cabin there used to be a barn. It collapsed not long after the family had abandoned the place. Fragments of its slate roof had fallen everywhere, most of it having landed upon and crushed an old set of farming wagons that had been used for gathering hay. Most people in the valley towns below didn't know that the cabin or the trail that led up to it existed anymore. For Emma Prescott, the cabin's remoteness was not its only joy.

She jerked the hood of a blood-red slicker over her head, stepped out of the cab of the pickup, and stood there in the downpour. A blinding flash of lightning lit the darkness. The cabin, which was less than thirty feet from where she stood, looked like a dream. Ever since she was a little girl, ever since she could remember, she had been attracted to this lonely place. It was the only place where she had ever felt totally herself.

Emma Prescott was almost sixty, but when the adrenaline was pumping in her veins, like it was tonight, she felt like a nineteen-year-old. Nothing could stop her!

She lowered the gate on the back of the pickup and a sudden fall of water gushed out, causing her to take a quick step back. It had startled her at first, but now there was a worried expression in her pale, watery eyes. It was only when she saw that the sack was still moving that she relaxed. Can't let the little fella drown, she thought. Not when I have a better way for him to go! She laughed and grappled with the dripping sack until she had it on her shoulder. It wormed so much that she almost dropped it before getting it to the porch of the cabin. There, protected from the rain by a dilapidated shed-roof, she placed it on the weathered floorboards and prepared to open the door.

It wasn't easy opening the door. She had first to undo the booby trap. If she weren't careful, a heavy broadaxe, sharpened to a razor-edge, would swing out of the rafters once she took a step inside and plant itself in her head. She often wished, upon returning to the cabin, that she would one day find the body of an unwary intruder with a split skull. The thought was a comfort to her.

She reached down through a space in the floorboards until her cold fingers came upon an iron rod that was no bigger around than the thickness of her thumb. She drew it out and held it with one hand above her head like a spear. With the other hand she felt for the hole above the doorjamb into which it was to be inserted. Once the rod was fully in and she could feel the far end of it slide into the bend of the J-shaped metal bracket she had mounted on a rafter inside, the booby trap was disarmed, preventing the axe from swinging down. She then lifted the scuffling burlap sack, carried it inside to a low wooden table, and laid it down.

"You better quit all that fussin' about in there," she said to the boy inside the sack. "You're on a narrow table and I have a floor full of snakes in here." There was some storm light flickering in through the open door, and she could see that the sack instantly froze at her words. She suppressed a childish giggle. There were no snakes on the floor. As a matter of fact, there were hardly any snakes in Vermont at all. But her warning had always managed to get a sack to hold still when she wanted it to. She liked that.

Emma Prescott slipped out of her shiny red slicker and hung it on a peg beneath a shelfboard by the door. The almost windowless cabin was damp and she needed more light. The lantern and candles would help to dry things out too. She had never lit a fire in the old stone fireplace. Folks might see the chimney smoke snaking up through the treetops and come all the way up there, wondering what was burning. She didn't want that.

She removed a tin canister from the shelf above the slicker and fumbled through it with her bony fingers until she found a match. As she touched its lighted end to the wick of a sooty kerosene lamp, lightning flashed and illuminated the sharp broadaxe that hung in the darkness of the rafters like a poised pendulum. If it weren't for the iron rod that she had pushed into place from outside the cabin, it would now be hanging down, a few steps inside the doorway, silhouetted by the light of the raging storm outside.

She shut the door and slid an old wooden crate into place beneath the axe. Then she stood on it and very carefully reached up and removed the iron rod so that the axe was now free to fall upon anyone's head if they tried to enter the cabin. Even though she knew everyone was fast asleep in the towns and villages that surrounded the peak of Tweed Hill, where the cabin was, she was never the one to take any chances.

Emma Prescott now began to light her candles, one at a time, by holding their twisted wicks above the chimney of the kerosene lamp. The interior of the dingy cabin became brighter and brighter with each candle she lit. There were dozens of them flickering and sputtering by the time she was through. They sounded like a bunch of snakes, and when she saw that the sack on the low wooden table began to move again, she knew that the boy inside must have been having the same thought. She walked to the sack and stroked it for a moment before untying the top.

Billy Chadwick's head popped out of the sack like a loose ball. His eyes were hot with fear. There was no sound in the cabin except for the muffled cries that came from beneath the broad swatch of tape that covered his mouth.

"There, there, little fella," Emma Prescott crooned. "Don't waste yourself with strugglin' like that. You're not goin' anywhere. Not tonight. I gotcha good! So why don't ya just settle yourself down and enjoy it, like I'm gonna do."

Her words only made the boy squirm more vigorously. She laughed as she quickly wound a thick rope about the narrow table and tied him to it firmly. "I told ya, I gotcha good! Didn't I? So quit it now and have yourself a good look at all the nice things I do up here."

The crazed woman placed one hand behind Billy's neck and lifted his head so he could see what she was pointing to with her other hand. What he saw caused a shivery wetness to clamber up his spine. The old woman was pointing to a doll—a doll that looked exactly like him! It was about two feet tall and stood in an upright wooden box with a glass cover. The box had been made of old barn boards. There were other boxes too. He couldn't count how many. Each one had a couple of thick candles dripping wax down its sides. Only the glass fronts had been scraped clean to reveal the dolls that stood inside. Billy recognized who some of them were—children about his own age who had been missing for a long time. He now thought something that everyone in the valley below had never even dreamed of: Miss Emma Prescott, the nice town librarian, had killed all the missing children, just like she was going to kill him!

Beneath the tape that sealed his mouth, he soundlessly struggled to form the words: "Please . . . please don't kill me!" His tears blazed down on icy cheeks.

The candlelight flickered across Emma Prescott's toothy smile like the lightning that bolted through the storm outside. She was pleased. A perverse glow of pride radiated from her contorted face. "You know?" she asked the boy. "I can't help myself. I have to do the things I do. Some folks are just that way." She lowered his head back to the table as though it were an object she had found by a roadside—an object that was no longer worthy of her attention.

Billy couldn't take his eyes off her as she walked to a cupboard at the other end of the cabin, where the deeper shadows were. Because the long old-fashioned dress she wore swayed so much, it looked as though she might have floated there. She paused when she got to the cupboard and placed her hands on her hips, as though she were trying to make up her mind about something. The boy could faintly see that the cupboard was filled with old tools and paint cans. There was a broad worktable in front of a window beside the cupboard. On it, when the lightning flickered outside, he could see the forms of what his uneasy mind imagined were a pile of naked children.

Emma Prescott finally removed something from the cupboard and walked back out of the shadows to where he could see her better. He now saw, only too clearly, that what she had taken from the cupboard was a knife. It had a wooden handle that was carved in the form of a doll—a doll that looked just like the wicked old woman. His reaction to it was as involuntary as the tears and mucus that flowed from his eyes and nostrils. He couldn't help himself. He did something in his pants that he hadn't done since he was a baby. In his eyes there was an out-of-place note of regret, almost apology. He couldn't help that either.

"Now, now. Don't you fret about that," Emma Prescott said. Her tone was almost . . . motherly. "Lots of fellas, bigger 'en you, have done that very same thing, right here." Her words in no way comforted the eight-year-old boy. His eyes were riveted to the knife. She casually, almost absentmindedly, placed it on the table beside him, not too far from where his hands were bound inside the sack. She then went to the box that contained the boy's doll and removed it.

"I made this little fella with my own hands, Billy-boy. Looks just like you, doesn't he? Saw you listening to those stories being told by that library lady in the schoolyard one time. Said to myself, Now there's a little boy I just have to have for my collection." She leaned closer to the boy, closer to the knife. "Want to know why I go collectin' like I do." It wasn't a question. Her tone was that of one confiding a secret. "Well, I'll tell ya," she continued after a slight pause. "Ya gotta understand that when you're gone, this doll will have your life. Just like all the rest of your little friends here." She swept her free hand in a broad arc toward the array of dolls that stood in their separate candlelit boxes. For the first time Billy noticed some rust-brown stains on the clothes the dolls were dressed in. He thought he might know what those blotches were, but his panic-stricken mind blocked any further exploration of the thought.

Each doll was a perfect replica of every child that Emma Prescott had ever killed. There were about a dozen of them, each dressed in the clothing she had made for it—the same style, cut, and color as the original clothing the children happened to have been wearing at the time she made the decision that they simply had to be a part of her very own collection.

Billy recognized the sweater his doll had on. It even had on a set of blue jeans and little sneakers just like his. He knew it was the same clothing he had been wearing the same afternoon that the town librarian had visited his school and read stories to his class in the schoolyard.

He studied the face of the old woman as closely as his troubled mind and memory would allow: the pale eyes, the sharp nose, the skinny chin, the gray hair. Even the dark spot in the corner of one of her eyes was the same. He remembered how he had watched it moving as she read to his class that day. She's the same Miss Prescott, he thought. Why doesn't she know it? If it weren't for the tape across his mouth, he could tell her. Maybe if she knew who she was she'd stop what she was doing.

Something in Emma Prescott changed when she saw the boy's eyes searching hers so intently. She rested the doll beside him on the table, not far from where the knife was. Her eyes suddenly brightened and became shiny. "You're just like the rest of all your little friends here," she rasped. "Think you're so smart? Think you know everything? Well, I've got something to show you, little Billy-boy!"

She turned and walked briskly to the worktable that was in front of the only window in the cabin. Outside the storm boiled and a flash of lightning momentarily revealed the objects she had gone to fetch—three large wooden dolls that had not yet been completed. They made a bizarre armful as she carried them out of the shadows and back to where the boy was. Their disjointed bodies had not yet been fitted with clothing, and the detailed carving of their hands and feet had yet to be finalized. But their faces were perfect. She placed the dolls, all together, on the caned seat of an old ladder-back chair and took a step back. It looked as though three naked children were sitting there, silent witnesses to the horror that was about to be committed.

Billy knew exactly who the dolls were. They were Kathy and Kevin Adams, the sheriff's two children. Seated between the brother and sister was the replica doll of Jennifer Lineham, Kathy's best friend. Kevin Adams was two years older than Billy, and the girls, Kathy and Jennifer, were about two years younger. Billy quickly turned his head to the boxes that held the rest of the dolls. He had seen it before, but it hadn't registered on him. There were three empty boxes off to the side of the one that his doll had been in.

"That's right, sonny. Your little friends here are next. Just as soon as I can get them finished up. Has to be all done before the first snow comes, ya know. Can't use the road up here then. Now, doesn't that make you feel a whole lot better, knowing that you'll be having your friends over for company real soon?"

The old woman was about to laugh when something caused her to turn around—something about the way the rain was hammering on the old roof. To the boy it sounded as though buckets of loose nails were falling out of the sky. But to Emma Prescott it sounded like something else. Her eyes rolled up into her head until only the whites showed. And when she finally spoke, it sounded as though her voice were coming through her flared nostrils. "Is that you listening, Mother? Are you watching me again? The way you always did?"

As though in response, the rain stopped. The cabin grew still. The only movement came from the darting shadows that were cast by the shifting candlelight. Emma Prescott broke the stillness with a screech of laughter and snatched the knife from the table. Holding it high in the air by its intricately carved wooden handle, she proceeded to dance with it before the terrified boy as though he were an object of ritual sacrifice. She cackled and shrieked and poked the knife into the shadows above her head. It waved wildly in her hand as she stamped her heavy boots on the dusty floor and hollered like a banshee. Sparks of candlelight reflected off its shiny blade and hurtled about the dim cabin like a storm of shooting stars.

Billy Chadwick began to pray. He prayed for his mother and father to come save him.

When Emma Prescott stopped her dancing, she was breathing heavily. The boy could smell her foul breath as she lifted his doll from the table beside him and placed it, face down, upon his chest. Then she tilted its head back so that the doll's face rested on its chin, making it look as though it were staring directly into Billy's tear-swollen eyes.

The boy's Adam's apple worked furiously when the demented woman positioned her knife in the air above his throat as though she were taking aim with it. Both her hands were gripped tightly around its handle. There were stains on it, and he now realized what those splotchy rust-colored stains on the clothing of the other dolls were . . . *blood*. Dried up old blood. The other kids had been killed the same way that he was about to die—with the dolls ready to catch the life that splattered out of them.

"That's right," Emma Prescott said, reading the boy's thoughts. "You got it figured good. Doesn't he, Mother? His little life into my little doll." Her eyes clouded for a moment and appeared to focus on the infinite darkness that raged within her ravaged mind. "Do you hear that, Mother?" she shrieked. "That's why my dolls are better! Better than anything your feeble mind could ever imagine! Are you listening?"

Her hands were trembling and her eyes had once again rolled to white as the knife rose higher and higher into the air above the boy's throat. Through the dark vault of her shattered mind, something swift and angry suddenly set itself ablaze like a blinding light.

Billy struggled with everything he had left to free himself. His eyes never left the shiny knife in Miss Prescott's hands. It looked as though it was suspended in the darkness of the cabin's rafters, and that she was growing taller and taller with each passing moment.

"Say, good-bye," she finally said to the boy. And the deed she had so carefully planned, so skillfully worked to bring about, was instantly done. To her collection would now be added another blood-splattered doll.

She thought she'd call this one "Billy-boy."

CHAPTER TWO

Ten-year-old Kevin Adams sat straight up in the darkness of his bedroom and screamed. The nightmare that had awakened him was so vivid that for a few moments he thought he might still be in the woods, being chased by a menacing figure. Kathy, his six-year-old sister, was in the dream too. So was little Jennifer Lineham, his sister's best friend. In the dream he couldn't tell if the figure that chased them was a man or a woman. Yet, there was something familiar about it, like he knew who it really was but couldn't remember. That's what made it so scary. He knew the figure must have been the mad child-killer that his father was trying to catch. But why did he feel that he knew who it was?

Outside, the storm that had been raging when he fell asleep had stopped. In its place moonlight filtered in through the curtains and washed his room with a pale glow. It should have been reassuring, but the dream was still there, springing out at him from the shadows of the room like the flickering images that still darted through his mind.

The killer had scuttled after them through the woods like a beastly forest creature hunting prey. Little

Jennifer was caught first, then Kathy, and later Kevin himself. They had all been scooped up in the killer's strong arms and carried off to a haunted cabin, deep in the woods. There, Jennifer was somehow turned into a doll. There were other dolls in the dream too. Kevin knew who some of them were, and it seemed that he and his sister were about to become the next victims of the terrifying abductor. Just before he woke up, the killer shoved a doll in front of his face. It was a doll that looked exactly like him. That's when he screamed.

Jeff Adams arrived at Kevin's room no more than five seconds after he heard his son's scream. He knew what it was. Almost every kid in Tweed Valley had been having bad dreams lately. The disappearance of Billy Chadwick earlier that evening didn't help matters.

The first thing Adams did when he entered his son's room was to switch on the lights. He wanted to be sure that the windows were still locked. They were. Ever since some of the children had started to disappear from the valley he had installed locking devices on all the downstairs windows. Kathy's window was double locked. His bedroom was right next to hers. He had been looking in on her when Kevin screamed.

"What's the matter?" he asked when he got to the boy's bedside and took him in his arms. "Did you have a bad dream?"

Kevin quickly shook his head no. He wanted to be big and brave about it, like he knew his father would be. No dream, no matter how real it seemed, was going to scare him. One day he was going to be a sheriff, just like his dad.

Adams held the boy so he could examine his face. He spoke soothingly. "You can talk about it," he said.

"Dreams are dreams. Sometimes there's even a reason for them."

"It wasn't a dream," the boy lied. His lips went thin. No dream would ever make him cry out like that.

Adams knew where that stubborn streak came from. The boy's mother had had it good, denying the thing that was killing her right up until the very moment she passed away. Her last words to Adams were, "I'm sorry I took sick on you." It was the first time she had ever admitted, even to herself, that anything was wrong. She died in his arms.

A lump of memory rose in his throat. "I'm sorry," he said, relaxing his arms about his son. "I just thought you hollered because you might have been having a bad dream." The lump quickly cleared. "So what was it?" he finally asked. "You can tell me."

"I fell asleep on my arm," the boy responded without hesitating. "When I woke up I—I thought it hurt."

They stared at one another for a moment. Kevin knew his father could hear a lie from a thousand miles away. He didn't know what to say. He was glad his dad did not press the issue and just held him in his arms, more tightly than before.

Over his father's shoulder, Kevin gazed at the framed photograph of his mother on the dresser across the room. It showed her hugging him and Kathy at a baseball picnic. The small towns that were scattered about in the bowl of Tweed Valley had separate teams. Each year there were play-offs. The picture had been taken the year Kevin's team won the championship. That was the same year his mother died, about three years ago. His sister Kathy hardly remembered her anymore.

Kevin finally took his eyes off the picture and awkwardly pulled himself back a bit so that he could look directly into his father's eyes. "I lied to you before," he said in a low voice. "It was a dream. I just don't want to talk about it. Okay?"

Adams never ceased to marvel at the things his son could say and the courage it took to say them. It had a lot to do with his wife, he thought. She had given the boy a good start in life. He was now trying to do the best he could with his daughter. At that moment, in his mind, his dead wife seemed only an instant away, as though she might have stepped out of the room for a moment and was about to return. He could almost feel her hand on his shoulder.

Something cold whispered across the back of his neck. Someone was standing in the doorway. He turned. It was his daughter, Kathy. "Daddy," she said, rubbing her eyes sleepily. "What's going on? You forgot to read me a story." Willie, the stuffed giraffe she always slept with, dangled from one of her hands. In the other, she held a bit of her nightgown off the floor so that she wouldn't trip over its hem as she walked into the room. Adams gathered both of them up in his arms and held them close. He was with his children and they were safe, they were sound, and they were loving. It was the best feeling a parent could ever have. He hoped, prayed, that it would last forever.

Jeff Adams didn't sleep the rest of that night. He sat out on the back porch in his winter coat, smoking Camels, until the nearly full moon slipped out of the black sky. And now he watched as the sun began to push its gray light up behind the distant hills of the valley. There was something soothing about it, something that helped him forget the difficult day he was about to face.

Tweed Valley stretched out before him, a broad patchwork of Vermont farms and orchards. It looked like a quilt, and when the grasses were high and the wind made herringbone patterns through them, it looked like a cloth of woven tweed. A thick white river, fed by pure mountain brooks and streams, flowed through the heart of it. Folks in the valley called it Tweed River, but once it got out of the valley and began to bend eastward, toward Connecticut, it was known as The White River. After a dry summer, like the one that had just passed, it wasn't so white anymore. Boulders that had been submerged by the swiftly moving waters of early spring now protruded from its lazy bed like the huge stone heads of ancient Olmec statues. Last night's storm had left the quartz and garnet deposits in the stones glistening like polished gems across the foreheads of the giants.

In Vermont, where Jeff Adams had spent his entire life, except for his three years in Vietnam, late autumn could quite easily be mistaken for winter . . . if it weren't for the foliage. Like flames shooting from a campfire, scarlet and yellow sparks had dappled the woodlands less than three weeks before. Now, between the cold and last night's storm, it was all gone. The maples, poplars, beeches, and oak had lost their autumnal brilliance. Every shade of orange, yellow, and brown now drifted and spiraled in the wind, waiting for the rake. It was only a week into November and the season's first snow was expected to come and cover them up any day now. But even then a fallen poplar might hold a few of its golden leaves above the powder until they could go skating on the ice once it had formed. And then there were the pines, running in every direction like rivers of green through the hills that surrounded the valley.

Adams loved Center Hollow, where he lived. He wanted his children to grow up there, live there, raise their own children there, and . . .

He suddenly saw graves in his mind, mounds of them, frozen swells on the forest floor that had been covered with a soft blanket of snow. He didn't know how many children had been killed. No one knew that. Of the almost one dozen children that had been reported missing from the valley, no one could really say how many of those had either been abducted by an estranged parent, a person known to the family, or had voluntarily run away. The only thing that Adams did know was that during the past six weeks the body of one of the missing children had been found: mutilated.

Pomfrey, where the body of the missing girl had been found, was about ten miles from where Adams sat. If the light was any better he might be able to see the spiked white spire of the town's church through the naked branches of the trees further down the valley. Other children had been reported missing from the same area, and in Norfrith, which was about eight miles to the north of him, there were even more. Some of the missing children also came from the tiny villages that branched off from the three major towns of the valley. Billy Chadwick was the first child to be reported missing from Center Hollow, where Adams lived.

Many searches had been conducted for the missing

children, and enquires had been sent out to friends and relatives in different parts of the country. Nothing had ever turned up. Some of the kids had been missing now for almost a year. Why here? Adams thought. Why so sudden? He didn't know what to make of it.

Just two weeks ago he had received a call from the state capital informing him that they were going to send in their own man to investigate the one known murder. Through a friend in the lieutenant governor's office, Adams was able to borrow a piece of time. He now knew that if he couldn't come up with a solid clue in the next couple of days, the state was going to move in. They had no choice. He knew the man they wanted to send in, too. He was an arrogant lawyer from the attorney general's office, looking for his big chance. In two short weeks he would be up for election to a seat in the state senate. Now, with the disappearance of Billy Chadwick, it looked as though the state might move in the direction of sending him a lot sooner, especially if a body was found, confirming that the boy had indeed been murdered.

Adams found himself secretly wishing that if any harm had come to little Billy, the body would not be found . . . not right away . . . not until he had a chance to catch the killer and nail the goddamn bastard to a tree.

Adams reached for another Camel in his coat pocket but found the package empty. He crumbled it in the palm of his hand and tossed it into a wooden box where he kept some kindling for the fireplace. On the back lawn, just beyond the porch, was a disorderly pile of two-foot pieces of round hardwood logs, about four cords of it. He hoped he would have time to get it all split and stacked up neatly beside the house before the snow came. Kevin, who was only ten years old but as tall and as strong as any twelve-year-old, was already beginning to help him with such chores.

Adams walked to the rail of the porch and could feel the temperature coming up. The pale light that had been behind the hills was now almost to the top of them. It wouldn't be too long before it peeked over the edge and lit up the valley. He inhaled deeply and smelled the aroma of cooking being done.

Next door, in a small frame house with hardly any lawn, Betty Lineham was already up and fixing breakfast for herself and her little daughter, Jennifer. Something about the familiar smell of home cooking made Adams feel easier about the long day he had ahead of him. He was the elected sheriff of Tweed Valley. Its three towns and seven villages shared one school, one library, and one sheriff—him. He had two deputies who had been out all night looking for the missing boy. He expected the phone or his police radio to start up any minute. Before going back inside Adams glanced in the direction of Betty Lineham's house. Something like a chill trickled into his heart. He didn't know why. He liked her.

Betty Lineham was new to town, moving there less than a year ago when the factory she had worked at down near Bennington relocated to Mosstown, about a one-hour drive from where she now lived. She had just divorced her alcoholic husband and decided to make the move with the company. It wasn't that difficult a thing for her to do. Jennifer had not yet started school, and Betty had always liked the northern part of the state a lot better than where she was.

Betty Lineham was a native Vermonter, just like Adams. The only time she had ever left the state for any period of time was when she moved to Wyoming to get married. Her husband had been a rodeo man. One day the van they were driving got a flat. He left her on the road with little Jennifer, who was less than a year old, and said he was going to walk into town to see if he could get it fixed, since there was no spare. He never came back, instead getting himself drunk and kicked in the head by a horse at some local fair. It took almost two years to nurse him back to health. By then Jennifer was almost three. When her father was better, he went off again. That's when Betty moved back to the state where she had been born.

Adams had learned all this in a few minutes one afternoon when he was out in back of the house changing the oil in his fifteen-year-old Peugeot. He always did his own work on the car, and as he installed a new oil filter—the same week Betty moved in—Emma Prescott had stopped by and filled him in on his new neighbor. The town librarian had welcomed Betty with a home-baked cake and stayed to have some tea. Emma was always doing for someone. People trusted and loved her. Adams regarded the information she had offered about Betty as nothing more than some good-natured gossip. He had hardly paid any attention to it at the time, but now that he knew her better the story had more meaning. He had grown to like his new neighbor, not in a romantic way, but as one would like a person of strength, someone who could cut her own way, with either a hard or a soft edge. She never talked about herself or about where she had been or where she was going, another of the qualities that Adams liked in people.

On school mornings Betty Lineham would bring Jennifer over to his house so that her daughter could walk with Kevin and Kathy down to the post office, where the school bus made its stop. Betty had to be at work early and she didn't want Jennifer waiting at the stop before any of the other children got there. Getting to work early was good for Betty, and it was good for Adams too. It meant that she could leave early enough to pick up Jennifer and his own children after school. The kids would then stay around Betty's house until he got back. Sometimes, like last night, when he was out late because of the missing boy, Betty would fix dinner for his kids too. She never seemed to mind. She liked children and had wanted to have more of her own, that is, until she realized what a bad marriage she had gotten herself into.

Jeff Adams had just plugged in the Silex when the phone in his kitchen rang. His teeth came together tightly when he thought his deputies might have found Billy Chadwick's body. He got to the phone before it rang a second time. "Hello?"

The voice at the other end was not one of his deputies. It was Mrs. Chadwick. She apologized for calling so early but wanted to know if there was any news about her son. Just as Adams could never listen to a lie, he could hardly ever tell one—or even give an evasive answer.

"No," he responded. "Nothing yet, but Ben and Arthur have been out on it all night." He didn't tell her that he; too, had been out with them until the storm started. His deputies had insisted he get back home and retrieve his own children from Betty Lineham. They both had wives at home taking care of theirs. He had been out with them on so many fruitless searches in the past that he decided, reluctantly, to do what they had suggested. He would leave his police radio on all night in case they needed him. When he got to Betty's his children were asleep in the living room. He carried them back home, one at a time, as Betty made the trip back and forth beside them with an umbrella to protect them from the downpour.

"That's okay, Mrs. Chadwick. You can call me anytime, either here or at the office." He paused for a moment, listening to the boy's mother at the other end. It sounded as though she was beginning to cry. "We'll be in touch," he said, knowing that she wasn't listening anymore. When the phone clicked off in his hand he stared into its mouthpiece for a moment before replacing the receiver. He wished there were something he could have said that would have made her feel better. But there wasn't. He knew anything he said would have sounded like a lie.

He had fixed them a breakfast of eggs and toast. They were almost finished with their milk when he thought he should say something to them about being careful, about making sure they didn't wander away from their friends and go off alone somewhere. But he didn't know how. He didn't want to frighten them or destroy their natural sense of joy and playfulness. Having been both mother and father to them for the past three years, he felt a different kind of bond to his children, stronger perhaps than if his wife had not passed away.

Now, with his back turned away from his children, Adams stood at the kitchen counter where he was making sandwiches for their lunch. When Kevin saw that his father wasn't looking, he quickly spread a small mound of jam on his last patch of toast and waved it before Kathy's lips. She had already finished hers, and that one last morsel he tempted her with looked real good. As she opened her mouth and moved toward it, Kevin slowly pulled it back until she had both her hands on the table and was standing on the rungs of her chair. He was just about to pull it farther away when she grabbed his hand in both of hers and snatched the toast between her teeth. Her milk almost toppled over in the process, but she swiftly steadied the glass and prevented a spill. It was all a great accomplishment to have achieved over her older brother, and she sat back down with pride and chewed the toast with a broad grin on her face. Kevin was about to tweak her nose when Adams looked over his shoulder.

"Quit the foolin' now," he said as he placed their sandwiches in baggies. He wasn't cross; as a matter of fact, he was pleased to see Kevin had apparently forgotten about the bad dream that had awakened him in the middle of the night. Kathy, too, showed no indication that she remembered having been up.

No, Adams decided. He couldn't bring himself to warn them about being abducted. The stories had been all over town and he knew that some of the teachers at school had spoken to their classes about it. So they knew. But there was still something he wished he could say. He simply didn't know how to go about it without causing a harmful jolt of terror to enter their everyday lives.

"Be sure you don't miss that ride back home with Jennifer's mom after school today," he finally said. "And stay with her until I come to pick you up." He placed the sandwiches in their separate lunch boxes and tucked an apple and a small candy bar into each. "Now clear off the table and get yourselves ready to leave." He wondered why Betty wasn't there with Jennifer yet. She usually was by now.

Kevin and Kathy went to the sink with the dishes from the breakfast table and prepared to wash them. Kevin helped his sister into one of their father's old white shirts. It fit like an artist's smock over her jeans and soft green sweater. She rolled the sleeves up and pushed her blond hair back beneath the collar of the shirt so that it wouldn't fall into her eyes as she stood on the stool in front of the sink to do the dishes. Kevin was going to do the drying and putting away today, so he didn't have to roll up the sleeves of his red flannel shirt; its tail dangled from the back of his faded blue jeans like the tongue of a stuffed lion. They both wore sneakers.

Halfway through their chore at the sink Kevin had to go down to the cellar for a fresh rubbish bag. He was not in the kitchen when Betty Lineham and Jennifer entered from the porch. Adams had poured Betty a half cup of coffee from the Silex when he saw them coming. It was now waiting for her, steaming. He pointed to it as she helped Jennifer out of her checkered wool jacket.

"Oh, I can't," Betty said as Jennifer went to greet Kathy at the sink. "Spent so much time getting Jennifer to try on these new boots that if I don't hurry I'll be late for work." She held the box out as though he would understand. "Have to return them today after work.

It's the only time I can do it."

"You'll still be able to pick up the kids?" he asked.

"No problem," she answered, half out the door and on her way. "I should be able to get it all done before school lets out."

He held the door for her and followed her out onto the porch. "I'll try to pick up Kevin and Kathy earlier today if—" Betty took a step back to the bottom of the porch steps where he was now standing, in the cold. She knew what it was that he couldn't finish saying. "Has there been any news yet?" she asked. "About Billy?"

It was not gossip she was after, Adams knew that. He could tell by the troubled expression in her warm eyes. It was that she feared for her daughter, the same way he did for the safety of his own two children.

"No," he answered, lowering his eyes to the tip of his walking boots. "Nothing yet."

They stood there for a moment in complete silence, neither of them able to accept the absolute terror that existed in their hearts—a terror that insisted the worst possible thing anyone could ever imagine had already happened to little Billy Chadwick.

Adams didn't return to the kitchen until he watched Betty drive off down the road in her blue Volkswagen. When he stepped back inside, he saw something that . . . that frightened him. Kevin, having returned from the cellar with a new plastic rubbish bag, was now standing in front of Jennifer and staring at her as though he had never seen her before. It wasn't only that, but his face was pale.

"Daddy, Daddy," Kathy said when she saw her father. "What's wrong with Kevin? He's been standing there like that ever since Jennifer said hello to him."

Adams looked at Jennifer and the little girl shrugged. "I don't know," she said. "He came upstairs from the cellar and I just said, 'Hi.'" Her large dark eyes had the same troubled look in them that her mother's had only moments before.

"Kevin?" Adams said, holding his son by the shoulders. "Are you all right?"

The boy's eyes immediately refocused. "Sure," he said, looking somewhat puzzled. "Why? What's wrong?" He walked to the sink and fitted the fresh rubbish bag inside the plastic pail below. He didn't know what all the fuss was about. Neither could he understand why his insides were churning as though he were about to lose his breakfast. He swallowed hard to keep it down. Then he remembered. The dream. Jennifer being turned into a doll. He and Kathy being chased through the woods.

Adams told the girls to get their jackets on and their books ready for school. While they were busy with that, he went to Kevin, who was still at the sink. His son tried to smile. "I'm okay," the boy said, trying to be bright about it. "I was just foolin' around."

Adams didn't like it. Not only that, but he knew it was a lie. Something had definitely scared the boy. He looked at his son in a way that was just the same as speaking.

"I'll tell you tonight," Kevin said quietly. He didn't know how to go on with the rest, but knew his dad wouldn't let him leave it at that. "It's about that dream I had last night," he finally said. And that was his final offer. Adams knew that no matter how hard he probed, the boy would offer nothing more, not until that night.

Kevin's bright, well-scrubbed face showed no clue as to what he was really feeling. But there was something eating away at his insides, something that struggled mightily to be spoken out loud. It was a warning. He wanted to warn everyone about something. But what? About being turned into a doll!? He knew how crazy that was. Anyone would laugh if he even mentioned it. Yet, as he left the house with Jennifer on one side of him, his little sister on the other, he wondered why it all seemed so real—like everything was really going to happen just like in the dream.

CHAPTER THREE

It was almost dawn when the shovel in Emma Prescott's hands sliced into the hard earth out behind the cabin. Her breath hung in the air like an icy ghost before vanishing into the pale light that was beginning to awaken the valley below. Billy Chadwick's lifeless body remained in the burlap sack in which he had been killed only hours before. It rested on the ground not more than two feet from where she was digging a hole for it. She liked to think of the clearing out behind the cabin as a place where the little children slept, a private cemetery for all the innocent victims she had killed. There were no markers, no headstones, only a dozen or so mounds of soil on the floor of the small and gently sloping clearing. Some of the graves were newer than others. A number of them were overgrown with scrub and almost indistinguishable from the rest of the softly rolling ground. The riprap she was turning out of her shovel had once been fertile farm land. Now, potato-size rocks had taken over most of it. They smouldered in the cold air after having been gouged out of the earth. Vapors rose from the heap and mingled with the mist of her own heavy breathing as she buried her shovel repeatedly into the earth.

It's hard work getting rid of bodies, she thought. There's a science to it, that's for sure. First the hole has to be deep enough, at least five or six feet down, so that when the frost comes it won't heave up what's in the grave and leave the children standing there, upright, like a bunch of fence posts in the middle of a field. Then there's the matter of the red pepper, a whole fifty pound sack of it. It has to be spread over the body, just the right way, and mixed in with the covering soil once the child is in the ground. That's to keep the hound dogs and other critters from digging up the grave. And it isn't so easy buying a whole sack of pepper, either. Just try it once and people will go asking you a thousand stupid questions.

Emma Prescott stole the pepper she needed from the loading dock of a wholesale spice plant that was over in East Hartfield, almost seventy miles from where she now shoveled the earth out of the ground. Beside her was a bulging fresh burlap sack of it. The name of the company from which it had been stolen was stamped in large red letters in a blue diagonal field that ran down the long way across its front. FIFTY LBS. NET was stenciled across it in bold black letters. Beside the sack was the other, less-filled burlap that contained the body of Billy Chadwick. Its contents had been used for a previous grave. She was always careful to wash the pepper out of a used sack first. She didn't want any of the children she abducted choking themselves into a fit while they were still alive. It was a detail she prided herself on.

"Another foot or so and you'll have a nice place to sleep for all the rest of time," she said to the sack that contained the boy. "Then I'll cover you up with a nice warm blanket of earth so you'll be real cozy."

As her shovel sliced into the rocky soil she began to hum a tune that soon fell into cadence with the rhythm of her work. In her head the words sang out brightly:

> Billy's in his grave
> His doll is in its box
> He's mine to keep and touch
> To play with as I choose
> For ever, ever, and ever . . .

There was something else besides the song in her head, something that seemed always to be there—a soft, well-reasoned voice. It marched right along with whatever she happened to be doing or thinking. Most of the time she didn't even know it was there. It spoke to her in a well-reasoned tone and appeared to know more things than she did. How this voice ever got to be a part of her thinking she could never guess. It seemed that ever since she could remember it was always there, fussing at her. When she was much younger the voice seemed to have more force to it. It made her do things like go to church and care for her old demented mother, whom she despised. It also caused her to read a lot of worthless things out of newspapers and books, things she couldn't remember one moment after reading them. It was as though the words went in and immediately disappeared down the dark and twisted passages of her mind. But as time passed, she seemed better able to ignore the voice. She was now at a point where it was, at times, almost nonexistent. Whenever it did manage to leak its way back into her thoughts she would merely sing or talk or dance and wave her arms about. That seemed to drive the voice back into the stillness from where it came. But lately, within the last few months or so, an uneasy chill lurked at the boundary of her dark consciousness. No amount of singing or dancing could set it to rest. All she knew was that she had to hurry with the dolls before that pestering, self-righteous voice rose to the surface again. This time it might win out and make her stop doing the things she liked best, just like when she was a girl. Then she'd have to go back to church and reading, and be forced to do all the other dreadful things she hated. It was as though time were running out on her, as though if she didn't hurry and get her dolls finished before the first snow fell, she might never be able to again.

Her arms began to work more vigorously along the handle of the shovel as beads of sweat oozed from the creases in her furrowed brow like salted pearls. Across her shoulders a fume of vapor rose into the cool air from her heated body. She didn't know how long it had taken her or how long she had been singing and stamping her feet about. She stopped and stood back only when a cool breeze, disturbing with its pungent scent of impending snow, swept through the thin branches of the trees that circled the clearing. What few remaining leaves clung to them scattered about in the brightening sky like a flock of disoriented pine warblers.

When she looked back down again, the grave had somehow been completed. Billy Chadwick had been placed inside the hole and it was now covered over with the peppered soil. The empty sack with the red and black lettering was on the ground where the sack that contained the body of the boy had been. She had no recollection of having gotten that far along in her work. If she ever lived to be a thousand, she told herself, she would never know how such things like that could happen. But it wasn't anything new or something that alarmed her. It had happened many times before.

The feeling gripped her again. Hurry, hurry, she told herself. There was something more that had to be done before the sun fully came up above the hilltops. Another doll had to be completed. There was also the new pepper sack that had to be washed out and made ready. "Things to be done," she intoned sweetly as she scuttled through the small thicket that separated the cabin from the small clearing where the graves were. "Who's going to be my little doll today?"

CHAPTER FOUR

It looked like any other house in any other town. Its white paint was fresh and bright, its green shutters were tied back and not dangling, and its windows sparkled in the early morning sun that had just come up over the ridge of hills to the east. It was only after pulling off the main highway and parking on the graveled turnaround in front of the small frame house that a person could see the sign that informed him he was parked in the driveway of the sheriff's office. If he had business to conduct there that day, he would walk around to the side of the building where the main entrance stood; if he did not, like some motorists who were not from these parts—and sometimes found themselves a bit lost—he would gingerly scoot out of the turnaround, thinking that some small-town sheriff might be itching to issue him a summons for violating something he knew nothing about. If Jeff Adams or either of his two deputies happened to be in the office when such a thing happened, they'd break into a quiet grin, knowing what the misplaced motorist was probably thinking as he carefully nosed his automobile back onto the main road.

Ben Jenson and Arthur Winston were already in the office. Both deputies had been out most of the night searching for little Billy Chadwick. They decided not to go home, where they would be certain to wake their families, but to go instead to the office, where there was a shower and a small kitchen in which to fix a pot of coffee and get some sandwiches. They had even started a fire in the iron stove to warm up the front office.

Adams saw the smoke coming from the chimney before he pulled off the highway. He was glad his deputies were already in and felt a beat of relief to realize they had not found the boy. If they had, they would have already contacted him on the police radio he kept at home. He pulled his old Peugeot into the small parking area at the back of the building and parked next to the police cruiser that Ben and Arthur had been using the night before. It had been purchased with state money, and there were so many reports to fill out and restrictions on its use that he hardly ever used it.

Inside, Adams greeted the deputies and was quickly filled in on the fruitless search of the night before. The men had not been able to come up with a single clue as to what might have happened. They had traced and retraced every known movement the boy had made right up until his sudden disappearance: from the moment he left his house in Center Hollow to go to school that morning, to when friends said he just went off into the woods to take a pee after school and said he'd be right back. That was the last time anyone had seen him. The only unusual thing that Ben and Arthur had discovered in the woods out behind the school was an unusual quantity of red pepper on the ground near where the boy had wet against a tree. They couldn't figure it out at first. But when they brought the boy's dog to the spot, hoping that it would pick up a scent, all it could do was howl and choke.

"Pepper?" Adams asked.

"Crushed red pepper," Ben repeated. "The dog buried its snout so deep into it that we had to take him over to the vet in Hannerville. The hound's nose got swollen to twice the size by the time we got it there." Ben stood up and showed Adams a tear in the sleeve of one of the still-wet uniform jackets hanging from a coat stand that had been brought over to the wood stove so the garments could dry. "The hound tried to bite me, too," he said after running his fingers through the hole for dramatic effect. "Lucky I saw it coming and got my hand up in time."

Arthur shuddered. "If he didn't get his arm in the way, that hound was going to take his throat out," he said with a wince on his face.

Adams shook his head. He waited a moment, then asked, "How much pepper did you say was on the ground?" He wondered if this were a new development, a clue that might finally lead somewhere.

"Don't know," Ben responded. "It got raining so hard after you left that most of it was washed off by the time we got back to the spot."

"Had to be a lot of it," Arthur put in. "If it hadn't been, it would not have caused the hound to go so crazy."

Adams massaged his earlobe between his pointing finger and thumb. He was puzzled. "I know this probably won't lead anywhere, but I'd like you to call around to some of the big supermarkets. See if they can recall anyone buying large amounts of pepper," he finally said to Ben. "And, Arthur, you call that vet to see if the boy's dog is better. With all the rain last night, we don't want that hound to lose the scent."

Even though both his deputies wore a standard uniform, Adams did not. He had been issued one almost a year ago but never wore it. No sheriff in his time ever had. But when the state finally decided to take over and abolish the office of sheriff throughout the state, he would have no choice in the matter. He'd then be a state police officer, of slightly higher rank than his deputies now were. The pay would be a whole lot better, and so would be his pension. Yet, even with all that, his deputies looked forward to that day more than he did. He didn't know why, but he always preferred to do things his own way. It meant more to him than the salary.

Arthur sat at a desk that faced the door leading to the one-room detention cell. No one had ever been held there overnight. There were two cots, a small table, and no bars on the only window. Wires had been stretched across it in a pattern of squares, but it was easy to see they wouldn't keep anyone from getting out in under five minutes. If there were someone who needed a secure lockup, he would be driven over to the state jail in Winslow.

Adams poured himself a half cup of black coffee from the pot on top of the wood stove. By the time he got back to his desk with it the phone rang. Ben picked it up. "It's the state," he said to Adams, trying to conceal the sudden worry in his voice. He covered the mouthpiece with his hand and motioned with his chin to the phone that was on Adams's own desk by the front window. "They want to know about the Chadwick boy," he said softly.

Adams frowned as he took a sip of coffee before reaching for the phone. He was wondering how the state knew about the missing boy so soon. Ben replaced the receiver on his extension when Adams finally picked up. "Hello?" he said. The coffee he had taken a sip of to clear his throat was so hot that he winced and sucked cool air in between his teeth as he listened.

It was Reid Hatcher, the rotund attorney who wanted to take over the case of the missing children and solve it in a hurry. If he could, his goal of winning a seat on the state senate would be assured. The election for state officials was coming up in a couple of weeks and his name would be on the ballot, prominently. Adams knew how he would solve the cases, too. Hatcher would come in for a few days, push his ponderous weight about, and arrive at the conclusion that all the children who had ever been reported missing from Tweed Valley had voluntarily run away from home! And somehow he'd have a whole lot of evidence to back it up—evidence that he and several of his influential reporter friends would have everyone in the valley believing . . . everyone, that is, except the families, friends, and neighbors of the missing children.

Hatcher greeted Adams with a summary of weather conditions in and around the capital, which was a three-hour drive farther north than Tweed Valley. It was snowing up there, Hatcher reported, and it looked as though it might be headed in the direction of where Adams was, maybe later that day or for sure tomorrow. Adams looked out the window and saw that the sun was warming everything up nicely. There had been a taste of snow in the air before dawn, but that had all been burned away by the time the sun climbed up over the hills. He thought Hatcher's prediction about the weather was close, but he wouldn't bet on the first snow coming for another two or three days yet. His thoughts came back when he heard Hatcher wanting to know as much as possible about how the search for the missing Chadwick boy was going.

"How did you hear about that so soon?" Adams asked.

Hatcher told him that he had friends all over the state who knew what was going on. Now that he was running for election to the state senate, those friends seemed to have multiplied a thousandfold. He actually used the phrase "a thousandfold." Adams shook his head. As soon as someone thinks he's become a god, he thought, he starts to talk like the Bible. And as though to confirm what he had just thought, the next thing out of Hatcher's mouth was, "You know, Jeff, the wolf hath sometimes to lie down with the lamb. We've never had any great love for one another, you and I, but if you invite me to come in and help you out with the investigation, we could have the whole matter cleared up in a couple of days. You're sitting there with two local boys who think they know how to be detectives. I can come in with a couple of highly specialized state troopers who know what they are doing. Why wait for what the governor is going to let happen in another day or two anyway? Wouldn't it look a whole lot better if you asked me in rather than the governor having to *send* me in?"

As Hatcher was speaking, Adams's eyes had followed Emma Prescott's battered yellow pickup as she passed by on the highway. She was headed in the direction of the town library, where she lived and worked. There was a small apartment just above it that she had occupied ever since her mother died. If it weren't for the anger that Hatcher's words had built up inside of him, Adams might have wondered what she was doing up and about so early. But the thought never crossed his mind. He liked Emma. Everyone in the valley did.

The less Adams said, the smoother and quieter Hatcher's tone became. "So how about it, Jeff? Are we going to do it my way, or do I have to start swinging my weight around?" He waited a long time for a response, but Adams didn't offer one. Hatcher knew he was still listening because he could hear Adams breathing at the other end of the line. "You know I'm shortly going to have a seat in the senate," Hatcher blurted out in a tone that was less smooth, less quiet than before. "Does that happen to mean anything to you, Jeff?"

"No," Adams responded simply. "Not a blessed thing. Should it?" He waited several moments and then quietly replaced the receiver as Hatcher was about to speak again. He wanted to smile but couldn't bring himself to it. He turned away from the window and spoke to his deputies. "Ben, Arthur," he said, drawing their attention. "That was Hatcher from the attorney general's office. He's probably going to be here in another day or so to take over the investigation. If he does, no one here is ever going to make an easy transfer to becoming a state police officer." He pulled the corner of his upper lip into his mouth before going on. "But there are other reasons why we have to catch the killer soon. We live here. We know the victims. And the lives of our very own children are at stake. If we can't break this case in the next couple of days—"

His voice trailed off and ended in the silence that seemed to take over the small room in which they sat. The only sound to disturb that silence came from the fire in the wood stove. One of its doors was loose and never did sit properly in the groove of the housing that was meant for it. A crack of red flame licked out of it and ran up the edge of the stove until it hit the thick top-pan on which the coffee pot rested. Adams looked into the bright cherry blaze inside the stove as though it held some special meaning—a meaning he neither understood nor wanted to understand. He only knew that the glow caused something inside of him to suddenly shift, as though it were a warning of something more terrible than anything that had as yet transpired. Looking at him, his deputies could feel it too.

CHAPTER FIVE

Emma Prescott forgot what she was doing. She had just taken her morning bath and, dressed in a wool robe, had wandered downstairs from her apartment above the library and found herself standing in front of a locked closet that was under the polished stairway. She couldn't imagine what she was doing there nor what she had possibly come downstairs into the library at that early hour to do. She stood there, naked beneath her loose robe, and shivered in the early morning chill. She hadn't even put her slippers on.

A trail of shiny puddles, left behind from her bare feet, gleamed like pools of silver in the sunlight that ribboned in through the beveled glass panes in the library's vestibule door. She could see how the tracks made a turn from the bottom of the stairs, crossed in front of the doorway that led to the children's special reading parlor, passed the sun-filled vestibule area, and gracefully avoided the Empire sofa that stood against the side of the old mahogany staircase. The footprints stopped where she now stood, before the locked closet door at the back of the staircase.

Emma had never bothered much with that closet. A

long time ago she had used it to store some of her gardening tools. Then, when she had the shed built out back, closer to the small garden she always kept, the closet was emptied and the key somehow misplaced. There was never any real need for that cramped wedge-shaped space at the back of the stairs. As she remembered it, the closet was only a foot or so deep, and the back of it slanted down so sharply from the angle of the stairs coming from above that it hardly held anything at all. Besides, the door to it was so low that she'd have to get down on her knees to reach what was at the back of it. So she never bothered trying to find the key or even attempted to have another one made, which wouldn't have been an easy thing to do, since the building in which the library was housed was almost a hundred and fifty years old.

It felt as though her feet were about to turn to ice, so she stepped away from the closet and sat herself down on the couch to lift them from the floor. She rubbed them with her strong hands to get the circulation going again. If it weren't for the fact that the thermostat controlling the furnace had been moved upstairs during the renovation, she would have moved the needle of it down so it would fire up and begin to warm the library. Upstairs was always warmer than it was downstairs. That's why she lived up there, and that's why the furnace hadn't clicked on yet. She thought she might one day have another thermostat control installed right downstairs where she was.

Her arms and shoulders ached, and so did her legs. It was as though she had been out all night chopping wood or something. She didn't like the feeling. Neither did she like the scent of pepper she detected in the air.

For some reason it troubled her. She couldn't imagine where it was coming from.

Through the archway that led to the main library, just opposite where she sat, she could see the sun warming a large braided rug on the wide-board floor. There were tall narrow windows on three sides of the large room and oak bookcases rose up to the ceiling between them. The books kept the large room comfortably protected from the outside cold, even in winter, and the sun that now raked in through the lacy rose pattern of the Victorian curtains added another stroke of warmth to the library. It looked so inviting that she decided to remain downstairs for a few minutes and warm herself in the sun-filled room. The moment she rose from the couch, the floor beneath her feet came to life with the familiar tremor of the furnace coming on. The comfort and warmth it promised was enough to make her forget the uneasy feeling she had about being downstairs so mysteriously that morning.

She entered the library through a broad wooden archway opposite the side of the staircase where the couch was. The carved oak columns attached to the walls on either side of the wide passageway concealed the openings through which there once ran a set of sliding oak doors. They had been removed during the renovation and taken upstairs to the small apartment that had been remodeled for her. They now served as sliding doors to a wall-to-wall closet that had been built there. She walked quickly across the book-lined room to a reading nook that was flooded with sunlight. There, she sat in her favorite captain's chair and placed her cold feet on a hot air register in the floor. The heat from the furnace was already beginning to come up.

Her teeth sparkled for a moment in the sunlight as her feet warmed. She couldn't imagine how they had become so cold in the short period of time it had taken her to come downstairs from her apartment. She now wished she had brought a cup of tea along with her. It would be perfect, she thought, sitting there in all that peaceful sunlight and warmth. But if she couldn't remember having come downstairs, how on earth could she have remembered to bring a cup of tea with her? The question ate at her.

But try as she did, Emma Prescott couldn't trick herself into remembering what it was that she had come downstairs for the first thing that morning. The harder she tried, the further her mind wandered. Maybe it had something to do with the locked closet under the stairs, or the way all the wood in the house now creaked like an old schooner as the heat rose up into it. She didn't know. But for some curious reason her thoughts began to focus on the old library-house in which she lived and worked. There was something about its history that appeared to be related to the unidentifiable grip of uneasiness she felt about herself.

The small Greek-Revival-style house, with its Doric columns out front, had once belonged to Lewis B. Olcott, Emma Prescott's great-uncle. A large portrait of the man hung across the room in a tarnished gilt frame above an oak table with a marble top. Emma studied the faded likeness from where she sat. The gentle expression in his eyes told her more about the man than some of the local histories that had been written about him. If there ever were a man she could have fallen in love with, it was Lewis B. Olcott.

Emma let her head go back until it gently touched

the wall behind her. There was a faded spot on the flower-embossed wallpaper, where her head came to rest. It attested to the frequency of her sitting there over the years. Her eyes slowly closed as the sun and heat began to pull the chill from her aching muscles.

The room in which she now dozed had once been Olcott's "favorite reading parlor." He was the valley's first adventurer. Ever since he started reading in the early days of his boyhood, he was tormented by an urge for things remote. But he had been forced to work the local mill, which made wooden handles for tools. The mill had been in the family ever since the days of his grandfather. He had no choice in the matter. His widowed father was ailing and his two sisters had married and moved off to another part of the country. When his father died in 1849, Lewis was in his mid-twenties and had never been anywhere besides the Vermont village in Tweed Valley where he was raised. Gold-rush fever tormented his soul. News stories about it appeared in the local papers every week. He decided to go. There was no longer anything to keep him back. But instead of heading west with a pickaxe, he went with a railroad boxcar that was filled to the roof with over ten thousand pickaxe handles—all that his mill could possibly produce in the short period of time it took him to set matters in order before leaving. He figured that with all the digging going on out there, there had to be a mighty number of men in need of pickaxe handles—once the ones they had brought along with them broke. He made them of hickory, black cherry, maple, and any other hardwood he had curing at the time. They were the best, and he sold every last one of them for one silver dollar each, in less than a week after he arrived. That was the beginning of his fortune. The next two trips he made were with boxcars filled with flour, sugar, pots, pans, and anything else his brief visit west instructed him might be useful to the settlers who flocked there. In one year he made more money than he would ever need for the rest of his life—even, he figured, if he lived to be three hundred years old! He traveled a lot after that, collecting books wherever he went. He had first-person handwritten accounts of pioneer journeys across the country, old maps, local histories and, curiously enough, one of the largest collections of books on ancient Egypt owned by a New Englander. He had mummies, too, and other things he had carried home with him from visits to foreign lands. In all, by the time he passed away, he had accumulated a vast and valuable collection, most of which Emma had since donated to the state university, for preservation and safekeeping. The rest of his collection, whatever hadn't been donated, went to the library. Money to get it all started came from a family trust that Olcott had established over a hundred years ago. By the time Emma finished with the renovation, there was very little of it left. The state now pitched in with some funds to cover her modest salary and to expand the library's current collection.

One of Olcott's sisters had a daughter who came to live in the house after he passed away. Her name was Jenny . . . Jenny Prescott. She had been married to a man who went mad. There had been craziness in his family, but no one had ever told her so until he had to be taken away one day in a tied jacket and put in an asylum, where he shortly killed himself by bashing the back of his head against the stone walls of his cell.

When a daughter was born to her, Jenny named the girl Louise, feminizing the name of her deceased uncle Louis, whose home she had inherited and was happy to live in. As Jenny feared, but was no longer around to see, her daughter Louise Prescott, when she was almost sixty years old, went mad herself and had to be put away, just like her father. Louise had never married but did leave a grown daughter, fathered by an itinerant farmhand who had moved on when he saw the madness coming. Some said it was out of revenge for being abandoned to raise the child alone that Louise treated the girl so badly; others said it was because she was crazy all along, like her father had been. It was a puzzle to almost everyone when the girl, who had been named Emma, turned out to become one of the most respected residents of Tweed Valley. Even the old-timers had by now forgotten the twisted history of the librarian's past. She was a useful and trusted member of the community, there to offer help where help was needed, and the first to bake a batch of cookies for the parents of a newborn child—a tradition she seemed to have created all on her own.

A chill swept into the library and suddenly opened Emma Prescott's eyes. They searched the stillness of the room for any sign of movement. There was none. Just her imagination, she thought. Then why was the seed of darkness she felt earlier beginning to spread throughout her thoughts in a most uncomfortable way? She sat upright in the old captain's chair and stared through the archway of the library to the Empire couch that stood against the stairs opposite it. It was almost as though someone were sitting there watching her. It wasn't unusual. She'd felt it before. This was an old house, she told herself. Everyone who lives in an old house feels such things from time to time. None the less, she wanted to get out of there, back to her rooms upstairs, where everything was friendly and comfortable.

As she rose from the chair she couldn't free herself of the thought that it was her dead mother that had been watching her from the couch. Guilt, she told herself. Plain and simple guilt. The guilt she suffered for leaving home and allowing the demented creature to die alone in an asylum while she was away at college. She hated her mother. The first thing she had done after being graduated from library school was to rid the house of every vestige of her mother's existence. The doll collection went first. Into the fireplace, one at a time, until the last of them had been devoured by the acrid blaze they produced. There had been dozens of them, crowded about on tables and shelves in the small downstairs sitting room her mother had lived in during the last few years of her life, so she could be closer to her precious dolls. Emma despised and detested every last one of them. As a child, she had never once been allowed to touch or play with any of them. They were her mother's pride and joy, and the crazed woman kept them all to herself. She would whack Emma across the face with her bony hand if the child ever so much as stopped by the forbidden room to gaze at them from the doorway.

When Emma left the archway of the library, her nostrils flared. There was that peculiar whiff of pepper in the air again. But this time it brought the chill back into her bones. Something about it made her think of death, horrible and unnatural death. She hurriedly sidestepped past the Empire sofa and rounded the corner to the foot of the broad stairway. There she froze. She had been about to take her first step up when something made her turn to the side. She glanced into the room that had once been her mother's downstairs sitting room and could have sworn that it was exactly as it had been before she burned all the dolls. They were still there! Every single one of them, dressed in the exact silk and lace clothing that her mother had made for them. Her mother was there too, sitting before the fireplace in her favorite rocker, grinning out at her with a toothless smile. The vision quickly faded and was replaced by the familiar surroundings of the room that Emma had long ago converted into a special reading room for little children.

The dark feeling that had earlier touched at the edges of her consciousness now shuttled through her heart like pounding lead. She raced up the stairs as quickly as she could and slammed the door shut behind her. The vision acted as a confirmation of something she had only recently begun to feel. It had been lurking about in the dark corners of her troubled mind like an unspoken thought that was about to be pronounced. She knew the words before they barreled out of the inner darkness and screamed themselves into her head like a crash of thunder. The words pronounced themselves in the same tone that her mother would have used. They told her she was going mad—as mad as her mother and grandfather before her had been.

Then it laughed.

CHAPTER SIX

Puddles left by the rain the night before had all but disappeared from the grounds behind the school where the children were just being let out for recess. They erupted from the double door of the one-story schoolhouse like a hundred pent-up engines, all going in different directions at the same time; some skidded dangerously close to colliding with one another. The sun was high and had warmed things enough so that many of the children didn't have the need for coats. It was a sweater afternoon, and that was just fine with the group of boys who wrestled themselves into a large ball over near the equipment box by the baseball diamond. They were choosng sides.

The girls did other things. The more active of them played volleyball, some played tag, and others read. There were others, too, who just whispered and giggled every time their eyes cautiously rose to meet those of a passing boy.

The oldest children in the school were between the ages of nine and ten. They were always let out of the building first lest they trample the younger grades, which now flowed more quietly into the schoolyard from the same double door. When all together, there were no more than two hundred children in the whole lower school. Some knew Billy Chadwick; most did not.

Kathy Adams and Jennifer Lineham held hands and went with a small group of first graders to a sunny bench beside the school building. A teacher came and spoke to them quietly. She told the group that the town librarian was due to arrive at school in a little while. She was going to read stories and tell them about books. Their bright little faces lit up at the news.

Kevin saw the teacher turn her back when she stooped over to talk to the group of children his sister was part of. He took the opportunity, as did two of his friends, to steal out of the schoolyard through a small slit in the chain-link fence that surrounded it. They headed directly for a shrubby knoll that was a few feet from the fence and disappeared into a cluster of trees beyond it. In all, it took them no more than three seconds . . . a great adventure! There they opened their pants and peed, with great force, on the gnarled roots of an old dead tree. They called it the "killer tree." It rose from the ground like the embodiment of evil itself, stretching its bare limbs threateningly to the three boys who urinated against its withered trunk. Their eyes averted, at that close range, the wicked leer that spread from a chink in the large gnarl, which capped its uppermost part like the head of a demonic monster. It gave them shivers to think that its twisted branches might come alive and grapple them up as they finished their pee and shook themselves off.

There was a large heart cut into the tree, about five feet from the ground. It wasn't put there by anyone proclaiming their love for anyone. Deep gashes, some freshly made, some older than the others, splintered the area of the heart as though a bear had clawed it. Only a few gouges had entered directly into the center of it.

After their pants were all closed up again, Kevin reached beneath his sweater and pulled out his hatchet. The other boys immediately began to count off the usual fifteen paces—the only fifteen paces in the small cluster of trees that had a clean line of sight to the tree. The rest of the trees that started behind the schoolyard raced uphill until they became part of the forests that converged with the White Mountains. The only way the boys could be discovered where they were would be if a car pulled into one certain spot at the very end of the teacher's parking lot out front. But nobody ever did, as it was too far from the main entrance to the building.

"You first," Kevin said to one of the boys, the one with a runny nose. "Kill the killer." He handed his hatchet to the boy, handle first. Kevin was a good scout. His father had even taught him things like first aid. The other boys looked up to him.

"Thanks," the boy said. His name was Peter, and before raising the hatchet into the air behind his right ear, he wiped his nose on the sleeve of his sweater. He was only nine years old. The boy took aim, ran his tongue out of the corner of his mouth, and let the hatchet fly. It cartwheeled through the air, end-over-end, seeming as though it was going to strike the tree dead center but missing—by a considerable distance.

"That's getting better," Kevin said. "Seen your folks about getting you some glasses yet?"

The third boy, Josh, who wore thick eyeglasses,

laughed at Kevin's remark. So did Peter as he ran to fetch the hatchet back. He knew Kevin had meant no malice by what he said.

"Your turn, Josh," Kevin said after Peter returned with the hatchet.

"Don't get it lost in the woods!" Peter added with a grin as he handed the hatchet over to Josh.

Again they all laughed, but this time there was a bit of a strain to it. Josh hadn't ever hit the tree squarely. He was an intense little boy, about the same age as his two friends, but as with everything he did, he tried harder—or at least it looked that way.

As Josh took his place at the firing line his face grew stern. In spite of the thick glasses he wore he could see fairly well, but he liked to squint. It made him feel better. His face wrinkled up too—and he was only getting started. Neither of the other two boys bothered him about it; it didn't pay. Josh would do it the way he wanted to and there was no use trying to change that.

By the time Josh let go of the hatchet his face was a rage of expression. His eyes had closed down to slits, his teeth were bared and glistening with saliva, and his countenance had gone entirely red. But it was all worth it. He hit the "killer tree" in the heart, as squarely within its carved boundary as anyone ever had. "That's for Billy," he said, drawing in a deep breath.

The boys were quiet after he said that. Although everyone there knew that Billy was missing, no one had spoken a word about it that entire morning. Kevin lowered his head for a moment. The vaporous tendrils of the dream he had the night before still clutched at his thoughts like sticky fingers. He wanted to push them away.

The hatchet didn't come out of the tree smoothly. Kevin had to give it a good tug to get it loose. He never knew Josh to have the strength to throw anything with such force. "Your turn again," he said, handing the hatchet back to Josh. The rule was you kept your turn until you missed. Josh waved it away, not wanting to so immediately spoil a perfect score.

Kevin nodded and took his place at the line. He was taller than they were and a stronger thrower—probably better than anyone around—yet there was something disturbing him today. He seemed to lack the confidence and concentration he usually felt. He didn't know what it was, but today it seemed terribly important for him to score a perfect hit, as perfect as Josh had just done. It wasn't that he felt challenged by his classmate, it was something else, as though it all had something to do with last night's dream.

And as though in a dream, Kevin leaned himself way back with the hatchet, raised one foot in the air in front of him—as if he were about to hurl a baseball from the pitcher's mound—and side-armed it smoothly, like a sinker, from the palm of his relaxed hand. It went hurtling off his fingertips sideways and spun like the blades of a helicopter, parallel to the ground. It looked as though it were headed directly for the heart, but before anyone knew what was happening, it slowly began to curve upward from the mark in a graceful arc. The blade finally struck, imbedding itself with such force into the gnarled *head* of the "killer tree" that it knocked the spooky-looking gnarl clean off its top.

"Wow!" his two friends shouted at the same time. They stood there with their mouths open as Kevin tried to figure out how it had happened.

They weren't the only ones amazed by what they saw. Emma Prescott, who had pulled into the end space of the teacher's parking lot—so she could walk around back into the schoolyard where she knew the children were still at recess—watched from the cab of her yellow pickup as Kevin had hurled his hatchet at the tree. At first there was a smile on her face. Then, as she left the pickup with her storybooks and approached the path that led to the back of the school building, something unspoken whispered through the cortex of her thoughts. The voice was a familiar one. She had heard it go rattling about during those quiet moments of the night when everyone else in the town was asleep. "Save Kevin for last!" it said. "He's gotta be done special!"

Emma never knew what the words meant when they came, but today—after what had happened to her in the library that morning—they caused her to quicken her steps on the narrow footpath alongside the school. The voice quickly faded, and she was smiling her usual warm and familiar smile by the time she rounded the corner of the building and saw the children playing in the schoolyard. A group of the smaller children, seeing her approach, ran to greet her with hugs and tugs at her clothing. Some wanted to carry her books. Emma Prescott forgot all about the voice and stooped down to return the hugs of the little children who now circled about her. They were the sweetest, dearest things on earth, she thought. And she found herself offering a silent prayer that nothing would ever harm them.

Kathy Adams and Jennifer Lineham sat with the rest

of the first graders on the floor of their classroom. They were gathered about the kindly town librarian, who also sat on the floor, just like their teacher, Miss Jones. Everyone used a "sit-upon"—a handcrafted pad made by weaving broad strips of newspaper that were covered with a sheet of clear plastic—for comfort and warmth. Each child had made his or her own, and there was always several extra for guests.

The windows of the room were decorated in anticipation of the coming of Thanksgiving toward the end of the month: construction-paper turkeys and Pilgrim children with Bibles being led to church by their fathers, who carried rifles to protect them from Indians. There were also a few remnants left from Halloween: witches on brooms, pumpkins with smiles, and a cluster of pointed black hats with stars and crescent moons pasted to them.

Emma Prescott had been reading for almost an hour, but the children were still captivated by her ability to tell a story. Kathy Adams sat with her legs crossed and her elbows resting on her knees as the librarian read. Jennifer Lineham, sitting close to Kathy, was leaning way back with the weight of her upper body resting on the palms of her hands. Others had their tiny faces in their hands, and some rested their chins on the closed fist of one hand, while the other hand cupped their elbow. Without exception, everyone's eyes were focused on the nice librarian who had come to school that afternoon to read them stories and to tell those children who hadn't already done so how to visit the library and borrow books.

As the librarian's final words were spoken, a lingering silence hung in the atmosphere of the room like a single, unspoken thought. It was felt by everyone, and there were no words to express it. The children had been touched—touched in a way that would last in their hearts for a very long time. Although it was beyond their reading level, Emma Prescott had just finished reading to them the closing passages of *The Yearling.*

The silence that followed had even touched Miss Jones. "That was beautiful," the first-grade teacher said after gently clearing her throat. "Simply beautiful."

Emma Prescott smiled. Her almost sixty years had not yet burrowed deeply into her features, and at moments such as this, with the late afternoon sun slanting in through the windows, she looked radiant. The glow not only came from her face, but from within. She had managed, once again, to capture the hearts and imagination of a group of little children—children she felt certain would one day grow up to appreciate reading more than if she had not bothered coming to school for them that day.

None of the children made a motion to stand or to replace his "sit-upon" in one of the cubbies beneath the row of windows. They just sat there. Kathy Adams, who was closest to Emma Prescott, leaned forward and rested her head against the librarian's shoulder. "Thank you," she said quietly. And the rest of the children began to applaud without any coaxing from their teacher. It sounded like the quiet pelt of rain on the roof of an old farmhouse.

All the fears and all the doubts that Emma Prescott ever had about her sanity melted in the glow of that warm and gentle patter of applause. The fulfillment she felt at that particular moment made up for all the years of doubt and loneliness, years in which she sometimes thought of nothing else but moving away and looking for a husband—just so she could have children of her own.

As Emma Prescott sat and answered the children's questions about the story of *The Yearling,* Arthur Winston, one of the deputies, walked out into the woods behind the schoolyard. He was alone. The other deputy, Ben, remained in the police cruiser to pick up any radio calls that might come in. He was parked in the teacher's parking lot, right next to the town librarian's old pickup, working on reports. He didn't see the movement of a patch of burlap that the breeze waved at him from the tailgate of Emma's pickup. If he had, he might have figured it was part of something bigger that had accidentally been caught in the rusted flap when it was slammed shut. Having gone that far, he might also have left the comfort of the police cruiser and gone out to see if he could fix it for ol' Miss Prescott. But he didn't. He was busy doing reports while he waited for Arthur to get back. They were then going to drive into Rutland to see if anyone had purchased a large amount of red pepper lately.

When Arthur walked past the "killer tree," on his way to the woods, he stopped for a moment and noticed the small footprints in the soft soil around the twisted roots of the tree. They seemed to go off in a hurry, up over a small knoll and back toward the schoolyard. He remembered how Billy Chadwick's dog had brought them to a spot that was further up in the woods and wondered what the boy might have been doing way up there. He started to make his way up the steep hill. Maybe there *was* something up there that they had all missed the night before.

When he got to the spot where the dog had picked up its strongest scent and buried its nose in the ground, he saw that most of the pepper had been washed away in the heavy rain last night. He hoped and prayed that the boy's scent was still there. He had called the vet earlier and was told that the dog was going to be fine, just as soon as the swelling of its nose went down. It would probably be out of the animal center in Hannerville later that night or first thing tomorrow morning. There was no use trying to get a dog in from the state in that short amount of time, as it usually took about a week for such a request to be cleared. Besides, the best dog for the job would be the boy's. Even the sheriff had agreed with that.

He circled the shrub just as he and the dog had done the previous night—before the animal got its snout full of pepper and almost took a piece of Ben's arm off. Arthur wondered if that was the spot where the boy had been taken or if he had been further up over the ridge of the hill—a hill he suspected some schoolboys would like to climb, just because it was there. He and Ben had not made it up there because of last night's commotion with the dog. There might be something up there that's worthwhile, he thought. He was about to start up when he saw some movement out of the corner of his eye and stopped. A dark-brown string had caught on a bush beside him and was fluttering out in the chilly breeze like a long worm. He examined it carefully before reaching out to remove it. It could

lifted the binoculars to his eyes, but the pickup had already disappeared behind the edge of the school building and he couldn't see it anymore. He didn't know what it was, but it made him think of the scrap of brown thread he had so methodically removed from the bush. He touched it lightly through his shirt pocket. It was still there.

Naw! he thought, moving his hand away from his shirt pocket. That's stupid. Just because a brown piece of something flaps from the tailgate of a pickup doesn't mean it has anything to do with anything, he told himself. But . . .

Arthur was caught in a maze of bewildering thought when the final dismissal bell sounded. He realized he'd better hurry back down the hill so that he and Ben could get out of there—before the children started to swarm out of the building with all their questions.

CHAPTER SEVEN

Betty Lineham pulled smoothly into the teacher's parking lot at precisely the same moment that the two deputies were preparing to leave. When she first saw the police cruiser she had hoped Adams would be in it. There was something she had to tell him. She hadn't been able to leave work early enough to exchange Jennifer's new boots. Not only that, but in her haste to be on time to pick up the children at school, she had forgotten the parcel with the boots at the factory. With snow predicted for as early as tomorrow morning, she ought to get the errand done tonight. She would have to drive back to the factory, about an hour away, get the parcel, then drive another half hour into Lambertsville where the store was. That meant she wouldn't get back home with the kids for over three hours if she rushed—which was something, after a full day's work, that she'd rather not do. And as long as she was going to be in Lambertsville with Jennifer anyway, she thought, she might as well make sure the boots really fit her this time and also get her daughter that winter coat that had just gone on sale. If Kevin and Kathy had to be dragged along on such a trip, they would be fidgety and bored.

As she pulled up alongside the cruiser that had just begun to pull out of its parking space, Betty rolled down the window of her Volkswagen and asked Ben, who was driving, if it was possible to reach Adams on the radio.

It wasn't like Ben to tell her that Adams was at the office and she could reach him by using the pay phone in the school's lobby, so he stopped the cruiser and motioned with his hand for her to come on over.

"Thanks," she said, a bit out of breath. "I would use the phone inside the school but it's been broken for about a week now. I didn't want to take the chance that it might still be out of order and miss calling Jeff."

Ben was glad he had not suggested she use the pay phone. "Something urgent?" he asked.

"No. It's just that I want to know if it would be okay to have Kathy and Kevin go home on the school bus today. Something's come up and I can't get them straight home like it was planned."

Arthur, who was sitting beside Ben, depressed the call button of the radio and handed the phone across Ben's nose and into Betty Lineham's hand. "Try to make it quick," he said to her in a tone that was not unkind. "We have to get into Rutland before it gets too late." He returned to his side of the front seat and saw that the doors of the school were just beginning to open. The kids would be out any minute now. Both he and Ben slouched down slightly as Betty began to speak.

She told Adams what the situation was: She'd be happy to take the kids along with her, which she really meant, but the trip might be too long for all of them. He told her to see that they got on the school bus okay and to tell them to stay around the house until he got back home, which would be soon.

She felt a measure of relief work at the tight knot that had developed at the back of her shoulders. Adams seemed to be one of the most easygoing men she had ever met. She liked that very much.

"Thanks," she said, handing the phone back to Ben. "I hope I haven't kept you too long."

Arthur and Ben looked at each other, then at the children who had started to stream out the front doors. As swiftly and as dignified as he could, Ben maneuvered the cruiser out of the parking lot and onto the main highway. Both men let out a quiet sigh of relief as the school building, with all its milling children, receded further and further into the distance.

"Mommy, Mommy!" Jennifer called to her mother as she came running out of the school with Kathy. "Look what Miss Prescott gave to me today." It was the same copy of *The Yearling* that had been read to the class that afternoon. "She said I'll be able to read it all by myself soon."

Betty smiled and examined the book. "That's lovely," she said. "And in the meantime, maybe I can read some of it to you too."

Jennifer hugged her mother as Kathy looked on from a short distance away. She wanted to hug her, too. The only recollection that Kathy had ever had of her own mother was being hugged. She went over and stood beside her friend Jennifer. Betty looked up and circled her arms about the girl, just as though Kathy were her own child.

"And how was school for you today?" she finally

asked Kathy.

"Just fine," the girl responded, close to Betty's ear. "I read the story too."

Betty knew Kathy had meant to say that the story had been read to her too, but she didn't correct her. "Well," she said, standing back up. "We'll all read it together again sometime. Would you two grown-up young ladies like that?" Both Kathy and Jennifer rapidly bobbed their chins up and down in agreement.

"What's keeping Kevin?" Betty asked, looking in the direction of the school bus that was beginning to fill up. "He's usually out by now." Some parents were already pulling out of the parking lot and on the way home with their children. She was beginning to worry that they might miss the bus. If that happened, she'd have to drive Kevin and Kathy home before going to Lambertsville. That could easily put another half hour on the trip to change the boots.

While Betty took Kathy and Jennifer over to the school bus, where she could ask the driver to wait a few minutes if it became necessary, Kevin and his two friends Peter and Josh were out in back of the school where the "killer tree" had been "beheaded" during recess.

"See, I told you," Josh said to Peter as he squinted through his thick round glasses at the gnarled "head" lying on the ground. "It's still here."

Earlier, Peter had insisted that it had picked up and rolled off into the woods as the boys ran back to school. It might have, Kevin thought. That's why they were all there, to investigate. When Kevin had pulled his hatchet out of it earlier, the "head" moved and jerked in such a way that it looked as though there might have been some life in it. They lit out of there in a hurry after that, and they all had a good chance to think and make up things about it in their minds as they sat in class the rest of the afternoon. While Peter had remembered the head rolling off, Josh thought he saw it spin like a top and bury itself in the ground. The tender sprouts of a vengeful new "killer tree" had already begun to take root in his mind as they all ran back to class.

As for Kevin, he wasn't talking about what he thought he saw. It made the fine hairs on the back of his neck stand out and twist. He thought it had sneered at him as he yanked the hatchet out of the gnarled "head." Josh had screamed at that precise moment, and the sound combined with the eerie movement of the thing and the loud gong announcing the end of recess. After that the three boys had run like a bunch of frightened rabbits back to the sanctuary of the schoolyard where the "head," no matter what it did, couldn't get them.

Now, the three boys stood around and looked down at it. It didn't look spooky at all, not to Peter, nor to Josh. Only Kevin had a peculiar feeling about it. That gaping chink of a mouth still sneered at him contemptuously. It was as though, even if he *had* cut the "head" off, it was still an evil thing to be contended with—if not now, then at some other time of its own particular choosing. He wondered if it would come at him in a dream.

Betty was at the point of going into the school to ask about Kevin when he and his two friends came bounding from the path that led to the back of the school. Peter and Josh saw that the bus was about to close its doors and made a beeline to it. If they missed it, they'd have to try and get a lift home with some classmate's parent. And the only cars left in the lot were Betty Lineham's blue Volkswagen and the station wagon that belonged to Mrs. Bently, the principal. She never went home until after dark.

The boys were out of breath by the time they reached the bus where Betty was now standing. She motioned to Kevin that he should hurry too. He came up right behind Josh and Peter with a puzzled look in his eyes.

Betty held her hand to the door so that the bus driver would know not to leave until she had said something to Kevin. "I spoke to your father a few minutes ago," she said quickly. "He said you and Kathy should stay around the house until he gets home, which should be almost as soon as you get there." There was no time to explain anything further. The driver, though patient, had started to hit the air brakes. It sounded as though the bus were about to roll—ready or not.

"Something came up and I can't take you and Kathy home today," she offered in response to the boy's puzzled expression. "Okay?"

Kevin looked at his sister who was already climbing aboard, then to Peter and Josh who were smiling at him from a window near the front. Their fists were raised in a sign of victory, indicating there was a good seat that he and his sister could squeeze into beside them. He wasted no further time in getting inside the bus.

"Well," Betty said to Jennifer as the bus was pulling away and as they walked toward the Volkswagen, "It's back to the factory to pick up those boots. Then into Lambertsville to get them changed for the right size and then—then we go to McDonald's for something to eat and later we'll see if we can get you that new winter coat we saw on sale in the papers yesterday."

Jennifer's jaw dropped open. New boots, a new coat, and McDonald's too! That, and the copy of *The Yearling* that the nice librarian had given her, made the day seem super-special. "Is today my birthday?" she asked.

Betty Lineham smiled and helped her buckle up her seat belt once they were in the car. "No, you silly," she said, smiling at her daughter. "On your birthday you get more than a trip to McDonald's!"

When they pulled out of the lot and were headed down the main highway, they saw Emma Prescott's yellow pickup coming toward them in the opposite lane. Jennifer picked up the copy of *The Yearling* that was on her lap and pressed it excitedly to the inside of the Volkswagen's windshield with one hand; with the other hand she waved. The librarian passed them by without a nod or any indication that she had even seen them.

"Why didn't she wave back, Mommy?" Jennifer asked. There was a touch of disappointment in her voice.

"That's okay, honey. Sometimes people get to thinking when they drive and they don't see everything."

"Oh," Jennifer said, as though she completely understood. She then opened the book in her lap and pretended she could read it as well as a grown-up . . . as well as the wonderful librarian had read it earlier that afternoon.

Betty Lineham had never seen the factory parking

lot so empty. She knew it must have been because the night shift had not yet arrived. Those few cars that were parked next to the main door belonged to the early birds.

"You stay here for a minute while I go inside and pick up the boots," Betty said to Jennifer as she pulled in as close to the front door of the factory as she could. "And don't you open the door for anyone, no matter who. Understand?"

Jennifer nodded. "I'll just stay here and read my book" she said. And she picked up *The Yearling* beside her and reopened it on her lap.

Betty made sure that both doors of the car were locked when she got out, and that she had the key to get back in. She didn't want to take Jennifer into the factory for something as simple as picking up a parcel she had left on the counter by the time clock. If anyone was around when she did, there was bound to be all sorts of necessary introductions as they admired the pretty little girl. It was getting late and Betty wasn't up for anything like that. Not only had the driving back and forth fatigued her, but it showed in Jennifer's tired eyes too—and there was still so much yet to be done. Better her daughter should stay in the locked car for a minute while she ran inside to get the boots, she thought. She had left the parcel on the counter just inside the front door, no more than ten feet away from where the car was parked.

No sooner had Betty entered the factory than Emma Prescott's old pickup rolled up to a silent stop right alongside of the Volkswagen. Jennifer didn't notice it, nor did she notice that the town librarian was glaring down at her from the window of her yellow pickup with a very peculiar grin.

Inside the factory the parcel with the boots wasn't where Betty had left it. She couldn't believe that anyone would have simply walked off with it. Such things rarely happened there. She was about to go and find Walter, the day shift foreman, to see if he knew anything about it, when she spotted the parcel on his desk inside the glassed-in cage where he usually stayed late to catch up on paperwork. He wasn't inside. She began to feel a bit . . . peculiar. Maybe it was all the quiet. The mill had not yet started up for the night shift and there was a disturbing absence of noise. The lathes and sanders stood silent, as did the huge blowers that sucked the sawdust out of the plant through a large overhead duct. Something made her think of Jennifer, of going out to see if she were okay. But she had only been gone for a minute, and the child was probably still "reading" her book. It was probably the strangeness of the plant being so quiet that had unnerved her for a moment, she thought. She quickly walked behind the counter and reached for the brass knob on the door to the foreman's cage.

Emma Prescott was standing beside the Volkswagen now, holding something behind her back and grinning in through the window at Jennifer, who still hadn't noticed her. She tapped the window lightly with the fingers of her gloved hand, and when the child finally looked up at her, she smiled. But there was something about the smile that wasn't familiar to the girl. Although she returned the smile to the librarian, there was something inside of her that frowned, especially when the librarian motioned that she should roll down the window.

"I can't," Jennifer shouted through the glass. Her breath fogged it for a moment. "My mother said I shouldn't."

The child's words didn't seem to bother the librarian. She simply shrugged and showed the girl what she had been holding behind her back. It was a doll—a doll that looked exactly like Jennifer. It even had on a little checkered wool jacket, just like the one the child was wearing. The little girl's eyes grew as large and as bright as the headlights that were beginning to pierce the darkness of the highway that skirted the factory.

The door to the foreman's cage was locked. "Damn!" Betty muttered to herself. She was headed for the exit door to get Jennifer out of the car when she saw the foreman walking toward her from the long, narrow corridor that led from the main machine room where Betty worked a wood-turning lathe. She caught his attention and made a frantic twisting motion with her right hand extended in front of her, as though she were turning an invisible key in a lock. He nodded, indicating he knew what she meant, and held up a set of keys he unclipped from his belt. She had had one hand on the large metal door and was about to leave when she had spotted him. He was now only a few feet away from her. Her impulse to leave could wait another second or two while he opened the office for her.

Jennifer remembered her mother saying very distinctly that she shouldn't open the *door* for anyone. She hadn't really said anything about rolling down the window. The doll that gazed in at her from the other side of the glass made the funny feeling she had about the nice librarian completely disappear. Her tiny hand toyed with the knob of the window opener as she pressed her face to the glass. As she did so, Emma Prescott touched the tip of the doll's nose to the window against which, on the inside, little Jennifer puckered her lips.

"I never lock the cage," Walter told Betty as he pushed the key into the lock. "No one here takes things, but I thought I'd better lock it up safely until tomorrow since I don't know most of the people working the night shift all that well. Never can tell what folks might be up to these days." He was a kindly man who took his time about most things, and Betty didn't want to snatch the package right out of his hand and run—which was exactly what she felt like doing once he began to ramble on about all the wooden bowls, cutting boards, and trays they were behind that month.

"I have to go," she quickly interrupted. "My daughter's waiting in the car outside and we have to get into Lambertsville before the stores close."

Walter pursed his lips thoughtfully, signifying he understood her haste. He handed her the parcel and was going to escort her to the door but she reached it long before he could come out from behind his desk.

"Thanks," she called back from the exit door. "I'll see you in the morning." Then she stepped outside and froze at the top of the metal stairs that led to the factory parking lot. At first she thought some kind of bizarre joke had been played on her. A car was pulling into the lot toward her Volkswagen, and in the beam of its headlights she could see that the window on Jennifer's side of the car had been smashed in. The door was open and there was no other car near it.

"JENNIFER!" she screamed. "Somebody's taken my child!"

The parcel she had been holding went tumbling out of her hands and down the stairs ahead of her as she bolted for the car. The last thing she remembered after tripping on it and striking her head against the metal railing was the sight of the boots spilling out of the parcel ahead of her. They landed at the bottom of the stairs a fraction of a moment before she did. A circle of light fell from an outside roof lamp and highlighted them like the beam of a spotlight. It would later be determined that Betty had been inside the factory for no more than three minutes. For her, it would always seem like a lifetime.

CHAPTER EIGHT

In the middle of the same night that little Jennifer Lineham was taken from her mother's car, Emma Prescott sat up in the darkness of her bedroom above the town library and looked around. Something had startled her from a sound sleep. The moonlight filtering in through the windows filled the room with a wash of pale gray tones. The first thing she noticed was that the bed was icy cold. She thought she might have been awakened by a bad dream but realized that couldn't be it. She hadn't had a dream in years.

She reached across the bed to a small table lamp and switched it on. What she saw in the light that spilled from it disoriented her, as though she might have woken in a strange house. The bedroom, always as neat as she could possibly keep it, was in complete disarray. She couldn't imagine what had happened. It couldn't have been a burglar. She was too light a sleeper and would have heard something.

A noise at the window caught her attention as a stiff chill swept into the room and parted the curtains. A couple of books she hadn't remembered removing from a low bookcase beneath the window were fluttering like a pair of disjointed birds whose feet had been nailed down to the broad sill. She knew if she had been reading before going to bed the books would have been returned to the bookcase, or at least neatly piled on the small table next to her bed.

The next thing she focused on was the enormous closet opposite the foot of her bed. Its sliding oak doors, which had been removed from the downstairs library during the renovation, had been left wide apart. All her clothing, usually hung with an orderliness that only she could manage, was scattered about on the floor as though someone had pulled every garment from its hanger and trampled it with muddy boots. And there was more.

Pictures on the walls had gone askew, the lace doily on her dresser had been yanked off with all the hairbrushes, pins, and bottles that had been on it, and the drawers of a small writing desk—which had been set into a windowed alcove overlooking the garden—had been removed and their contents strewn about. Everything that should have been closed was opened, even the door that led to the tiled bathroom to the side of her bed.

She always closed things before going to bed. That was the way she was. If things had been left opened, whether they be closets, drawers, books, doors, or even windows, she would close them before retiring no matter what, summer or winter. What was going on? she wondered. She knew no burglar could have done all this without waking her.

She looked again at the flapping books on the wide sill beneath the opened window. She couldn't believe the calm she felt. Was it the calm that comes when one has finally gone mad? Like her mother? But she knew that wasn't it either. Her mother had always been a terrible person. People knew, long before she had had to be put away, that the woman was a lunatic—keeping dolls at her age, cherishing them above all else. No, Emma Prescott thought as she contemplated her own sanity. She was far from mad. But just how far? She quickly buried whatever response might come from such a queasy question by forcing herself to imagine that a burglar had indeed been in her bedroom and had indeed been responsible for the disarray about her. But . . . *in my own bedroom?* she thought after thinking about it for a moment. Without waking me up? The edges of her mouth pulled in and she shook her head. Impossible! She was too light a sleeper. Besides, nothing like that had ever happened in the valley before. It had to be something else. But what? She wondered if she should call Sheriff Adams at home. Wake him up in the middle of the night and have him come to investigate? she wondered. It was almost 4 A.M.

Emma Prescott decided that before calling anyone she'd better have a good look around the rest of her apartment. The darkness that came down like a curtain beyond her opened bedroom door seemed still and quiet. Thank goodness for that, she thought as she pulled the covers to the side and swung her legs over the edge of the bed. Instead of her feet gliding gracefully into the soft slippers that were usually there, her toes brushed against a pair of old barn boots that she used for gardening. They were cold and slightly damp, as though she had recently been wearing them outside. Another impossibility. The boots were always kept downstairs, in a cabinet near the back door that led to the garden. There was no reason for her to wear them upstairs and track all that mud and dirt through the house. She stared down at them with deep furrows in her brow and began to feel the cold. There was something else, too. When she went to close the window, she noticed that her body ached. Her legs and arms were sore, like the other morning when she found herself downstairs in the library, wondering what on earth she had gone down there for. It was as though she had been carrying or dragging something heavy. And when she saw a bright red bruise on the knuckles of her right hand, she cringed. It looked like she had rammed it into a wall or something. But the skin wasn't broken, as if she might have been wearing gloves when it happened. It even throbbed.

Without warning, tears began to fall from her eyes. It wasn't that she was in pain, and it wasn't that she thought there might have been a burglar in the house. It was something else; something, she reasoned, that had to do with the voice. It had been intruding more and more upon her thoughts these days. It was beginning to confuse and terrify her. Maybe she *was* going mad. She was almost the same age her mother was when they had had to take her away.

She looked at herself in the large oval-shaped dressing mirror that was mounted on an oak stand. The image that came back to her looked more like someone else, someone she didn't quite know. It was more distressing than the disarray of the room. Her eyes were red, as though some irritant had been working at them, and the tone of her skin was ghostly, the only way she knew how to describe it to herself.

She pulled the sleeve of her nightgown up to her pale cheeks and blotted away the hot tears that streaked them. It was then that she noticed how badly she had begun to tremble. Her body quivered inside her loose nightgown like the plucked string of a cello.

She began to feel that the voice was going to start at any moment. She couldn't face anything like that right now. She abruptly turned from the mirror and headed for the darkness that hung beyond her bedroom door. Keep busy, she told herself as she raced into it. Keep doing things. That way the voice can't talk to you.

It took her no time at all to go through the house. After turning on all the lights, she checked all the doors and windows. Everything downstairs was locked and closed, just the way she had left things before going to bed. Back upstairs, the only room that had been disturbed was her bedroom. The small kitchen, the tidy dining area, and the sitting room, which held a small collection of her own antique books, had all gone undisturbed—which was a disappointment to her. She had hoped to uncover the undeniable signs that a burglar had indeed been at work. When she did not, she thought of the next best thing to do: carry on as usual, put everything right, and . . . and . . . She didn't know what to do after that. By then it would probably be dawn and, hopefully, things would have sorted themselves out.

The first thing she did when she got back to the bedroom was to walk briskly to the window and close it. The books that had been fluttering about like disjointed birds suddenly fell still. They were quickly closed and returned to their places in the low bookcase beneath the window. She noted, with some wonder, that the books were about crafts: how to make things with wood and cloth. She wasn't in the least bit interested in woodworking or sewing. The only reason she kept several shelves of useless books beneath the windowsill was that it helped insulate the drafty outside wall. The books that really mattered to her were kept in the sitting room, where they were better protected from such things as drafts, and where she could comfortably sit and study them anytime she wanted. They were mainly books on magic—books that had once belonged to her great-uncle, Lewis B. Olcott. She had never donated them to her alma mater, the state university, because she didn't want anyone to think the man was mad for having accumulated such a vast and curious collection of bizarre books.

Her quick movement about the room, as she began to put things back in their proper places, was making her feel better. If only she didn't run out of things to do before the sky outside her window filled with light, she would be fine, she told herself. Then she remembered that she hadn't been into the bathroom to inspect it yet. She stopped what she was doing and headed for it.

Nothing prepared her for the sight that met her eyes once the light switch in the tiled wall had been flipped. The bathtub was as filthy and grimy as though a field animal had been washed in it. Towels were scattered about, soiled and trampled upon. The medicine cabinet was opened too, and things had been pushed from its glass shelves and broken in the sink. She wondered if the mirror that was mounted on the front of the cabinet door, which was opened in such a way that she could not see it, was broken too, and she cautiously reached to swing it closed.

It was then that she screamed. The horror she saw in he mirror was a confirmation of her innermost fear. It was not so much the image of her standing there, screaming and trying to pull her face off as though it were a grotesque mask. It was something far more horrible. There were words scrawled across the mirror n the bright red color of her only tube of lipstick.

DEMENTED BITCH! it said.

And it was written in her own unmistakable handwriting.

CHAPTER NINE

As Emma Prescott stood before the bathroom mirror at 4 A.M. that morning, Jeff Adams was in the parking lot of the factory in Mosstown. It was out of his jurisdiction, but the county sheriff there let him conduct an investigation of his own once he found that Adams knew the little girl who had been abducted from her mother's car. The sheriff also knew that Adams had children of his own, and that his daughter and the missing child were best friends.

When the county sheriff and his men left, Adams stood in the empty parking lot, entirely alone. The night shift had been cancelled, and the day people weren't due to arrive for another couple of hours. Betty Lineham wouldn't be among them. She was still in the hospital at Copely where the head wound she had suffered in her fall down the metal stairs was being cared for. The doctors said she had suffered a mild concussion and they didn't want to take the chance that it would develop into something more serious. They planned to keep her there for the night and release her in the morning if everything went well.

When Adams visited her earlier, Betty had been so heavily sedated that he wasn't sure she knew what had happened. It was only when he got to the factory and spoke to Walter, the day shift foreman, that he learned of Betty's scream from the top of the factory stairs before she fell. Walter said it sounded as though she had shouted something about her daughter being taken from the car.

He looked at the Volkswagen. The county sheriff had some of his men build a clear vinyl casing about it. It looked like a transparent garage whose supports of strip-wood from the factory were plainly visible. An overhead lamp had been strung from the factory and suspended from a strip of wood that supported the roof of the plastic covering. The light that filtered out of it into the deep shadows of the parking lot made Adams shiver as he approached. There was something unsettling about the sight of the Volkswagen inside the plastic housing. It puckered and swelled in the wind like a living thing. He was glad his deputies weren't there. After returning from Rutland with nothing to report about a recent purchase of any unusual amounts of crushed red pepper, Adams had sent them home to their wives and children. He had even asked each of them if they'd be willing to care for one of his own children for the night. Kevin went with Arthur and Kathy with Ben. There was no problem with that. As long as he was not in charge of the investigation himself, Adams knew he would not be hurting anyone's feelings if he remained behind to be on his own—no reports, no calls from the state, no pressure. Just the simple investigation by a fellow sheriff who had been granted permission to look things over once those in charge had done their work. He had been allowed one hour. After that the local sheriff was coming back to remove the car to a pound where it would be gone over one last time and stored until Betty Lineham could claim it.

Adams approached the vinyl casing and peeled away one of its overlapping flaps so he could enter. The first thing he noticed was the small amount of shattered glass on the ground outside the car, as compared with the piles of it inside, all over the front seat and floor. There were blood stains, too, splattered across the open pages of a copy of *The Yearling*. He froze when he saw it. Earlier that afternoon his own daughter had mentioned how the nice librarian had given a copy of the book to Jennifer. Kathy had even asked him to get a copy for her, too. She wanted to start reading it for herself, just like Jennifer was going to do.

It took a great effort for him to examine the blood stains splattered across the open pages of the book. Although he doubted it, Adams hoped the stains belonged to the person who had abducted the child. Samples had already been taken and it would soon be known whether or not the blood belonged to the child. He looked again to the shattered window in the door, which had been left opened, exactly as it was found. The county sheriff had said before leaving that no prints belonging to an adult other than Betty Lineham had been recovered anywhere on the car. He reasoned that the kidnapper had worn gloves and either used his fists or a heavy object to smash the window in. He opted for the gloves. There was something too brutal and too spontaneous about the appearance of things. He further reasoned that Jennifer didn't know the person who had abducted her. If she had, she would have rolled the window down or even opened the door. A child could always be tricked into doing something like that if the person is known to them. A stranger, he concluded.

Adams went back to his Peugeot and removed a large police lantern from the trunk. As he scoured the area with the light, it looked as though the full moon had fallen from the sky to pierce the swirling mist that rose from the pavement of the parking lot. He looked into every corner before heading toward the back of the factory itself, where he knew the county sheriff had not yet been. Halfway around, where the pavement ran out and a graveled slope leading down to the river began, he stopped. There were tire tracks all over the place. They belonged to cars, bikes, motorcycles, and pickups, all jumbled together. It would be impossible to identify any of them. A scent dog wouldn't be able to pick up a clean scent either. He played the strong beam of his lantern down the trail to see where the tracks led. They all disappeared behind a stand of tall trees, where he could hear the river running strongly. The tracks were probably made by fishermen and kids on their way to the river, he thought. Then, for a moment, he considered something that might possibly be a clue.

He knew there was absolutely nothing to indicate that the person who had abducted little Jennifer from the parking lot had spent more than a minute or so doing it. Whoever the kidnapper was, he knew what he was doing, Adams thought. He might even have ducked behind the factory to hide until everything out front quieted down. Maybe that's why no one saw anything out of the ordinary. It was just a short drive—probably less than two or three seconds—from the spot where Betty Lineham's car was parked to where he now stood. If the kidnapper were a psychopath, there might be some clues back there. Adams knew from his training as an MP in Vietnam that psychos usually left clues all over the place, as though something deep within them wanted them to get caught. But so far there hadn't been any clues in the investigation besides the crushed red pepper—a hard thing to trace. He tried to remove the negative thoughts from his mind as he followed the trail that led to the river.

There was something about the stillness there that gave him an uneasy feeling. Suppose he found little Jennifer's body? What would he do? How would he react? Would he go to pieces? Could he handle it? He thought of his own little daughter and his insides began to quiver. At that point he wasn't sure he could handle anything.

He heard a noise that sounded like someone snapping a twig beneath his feet. He quickly turned his lantern off, crouched down in the darkness like some forest creature, and waited for the sound to repeat itself. The water rushing over the rocks in the river masked everything, as did the pounding of the blood in his head. He thought he might have been hearing things. But as he rose and flipped his lantern on again, a fluttering noise from the branches of an overhanging tree made him duck as though something were hurtling down at him. When he looked up, the beam of his lantern caught the flight of a great white owl that had been startled by his presence. A piece of meat from some prey dangled red from its beak. He was about to breathe an inner sigh of relief when something else caught his attention. High up in the tree where the owl had been feasting, there was a bundle of something larger than the bird could possibly have carried up there. It was balanced precariously on a forked limb that still shuddered from the owl's sudden flight.

He took a quick step back when several drops of blood fell from it and splashed against his face. The suddenness of it made him cry out as though he had been hit by a bullet. His shout echoed in the darkness and returned to him from the other side of the river like a hollow scream. He looked down at the blood on his shirt and wiped away the drops that had fallen on his face. Holding the lamp so that he could examine his blood-stained hand, he could almost smell the scent of terror that rose from it. It was many moments before he could bring himself to approach the tree again and position himself beneath the object for an unobstructed view. His heart almost gave out as more drops of blood glittered through the beam of his lantern as they fell from above. He felt the anguish of a tortured soul raining down about him.

Adams knew what was up there, had known from the moment his hammering heart had started its wild racing. It was little Jennifer. And, as though to punctuate the horror that had so suddenly materialized before him, the child's body slipped from the fork of the branch and fell, snapping and crashing its way through the clusters of thinner branches on its way down. He dropped the lantern and tried to catch her, but everything went black the moment the lamp hit a rock and went out. As long as he would live, Adams would never forget the sound that little Jennifer's body made as it struck the ground, not more than an inch away from where he had stretched out his arms to catch her.

CHAPTER TEN

And she dreamed. Horrible dreams. She twisted in her bed like a struggling animal attempting to free itself from a trapper's snare. She was a child again, listening to her demented mother warning her about the dolls. They belonged to her mother, and little Emma was not even allowed to go into the room where they were all kept. But she was there, in that special downstairs parlor, sitting in her mother's old rocking chair with a heap of dolls piled up about her. She read them stories and hugged them until they almost seemed to come alive in her arms. Why was her mother so cruel? Why couldn't she ever be allowed to play with the dolls like she was now doing?

There was sweet music coming in through the windows. It was summertime. A town band was playing a gentle march in the gazebo in the center of the village green. Lacy curtains billowed into the downstairs parlor like wispy clouds, carrying the scent of roses into the doll-filled room. The child rocked back and forth in her mother's chair and sang to the dolls in her little girl's voice. She couldn't have been more than six or seven years old.

That was the best part of the dream. But it didn't prevent Emma Prescott from twisting and turning as though she wanted to wake herself up. There had always been temptation, heavy doses of it. Her mother used to leave the door to the doll room wide open so Emma couldn't help looking into it as she went upstairs to her room. There was always a warning to the child as her mother left the house to do an errand. Emma could never resist. It was only when she grew older that she realized it was all a trap. Her mother never had to go and do an errand. She . . .

Little Emma rocked and sang and read stories, just as though the dolls tucked in all about her were real children—*her* children. She thought that when she grew up she wouldn't have dolls. They were useless for older people. What she really wanted was to have children of her own, children she could read stories to and sing lullabies to when they were sad.

A shadow crossed the room. It was as though the day had turned to night. The little girl who had been rocking the dolls in her mother's forbidden room looked toward the window. A familiar figure rapidly approached the house. Her mother hobbled up the steps to the front door and flung it open. Oh, how the child wished she had been smart enough to invent something that would stop her mother's mad rush into the house. Something she could rig up by the door that would slam her in the face when she opened it.

"And what did I tell you about touching my dolls?"

WHACK!

And in her troubled sleep Emma Prescott could feel

the stinging blow across her face. It burned as hot as any fire she had ever felt.

"How many times must I tell you!"

WHACK!

Her body twisted and trembled beneath the covers of the bed as though she were being tossed about by an ocean wave. Tears leaked from the corners of her tightly closed eyes. She was as hurt and wounded as she had been as a child, when her mother would set the trap, with the warning not to touch the dolls, and then go out into the dooryard until she knew Emma was sitting in the room, rocking the dolls and reading stories to them. Then she'd explode back into the house, returning all too soon from her "errand," and catch the child with the dolls. It was all a game. One that had been orchestrated as skillfully as a piece of music in the mind of her demented mother.

"Bitch!" Emma had once shouted out, once she had grown old enough and took to realizing that her mother was mad and had to be put away before she killed someone.

"DEMENTED BITCH!"

Emma Prescott sat up in her bed. She was covered with perspiration. Beads of it glistened on her upper lip. She was breathing so heavily that the headboard of the bed rapped against the wall behind her like a heavy fist on a door. Her eyes were large. She hadn't had such dreams in years. Why were they beginning to come back to her now?

She looked around the room as though there were something about it that she should remember. It was as neat and tidy as it always was. Dawn, breaking as peacefully as it always had through the branches of the trees outside her window, didn't reassure her. Something dark, something sinister lurked about her. She didn't like it. There was madness in her family. Her mother had it. So did her grandfather. And before that? Before that?

She rose from the bed, walked rapidly to the door, and swung it open, half expecting someone to be standing there. Nothing. Everything was as usual. In the hall she looked down the stairs to the front door of the library. The light was beginning to brighten the entrance vestibule. Just to the side of it was the special reading parlor for little children, where her mother used to keep the dolls. Everything looked as it should.

What was eating at her? she wondered. Had the dream been so real that she could actually feel as though she were a little child again and her mother were still alive, setting those childish traps for her?

And why did her arms and legs ache so badly? She hadn't been doing any heavy work in the garden for weeks and weeks now. It felt as though she had been climbing trees or carrying buckets of coal up from the cellar, things she hadn't done since she was a little girl.

She massaged her arms. A hot bath would do her good, she thought. Then a soothing cup of tea. That's what she needed. And after that, it would be off to the school, where she had made an appointment with the first grade teacher to read more stories to the children. She was already beginning to feel better.

Back in the bedroom she stood before the window for a moment and pulled the curtains aside. The distant hardwood hillsides looked like a pencil-line sketch of slopes and skinny trees. Deep shadows clung low to the ground. And, in the sky, there hung the threat of snow, just like it had been predicted on the radio. But why did that bother her so? She always liked the first snow of the season. It made everything look so clean, so much like a fairy tale. Sometimes she would even get out and throw snowballs with the children after school. So why did the thought of it begin to make her stomach churn, as though there were something that desperately needed to be done before the first snow fell?

Before the dark feelings had a chance to return, she walked briskly to the bathroom and stooped over the immaculately clean tub to turn on the hot water. The chilled room immediately began to fill with steam. As she removed her nightgown she couldn't help looking into the mirror of the medicine cabinet. As it began to cloud over with steam it looked as though something had been written across it—written across it with something waxy, like a candle.

She took a step closer to the cabinet and examined it. Her eyes widened. Something red in the edge of the chrome frame about the mirror caught her attention. It looked like blood. She poked her fingernail into the tight crease between the chrome and the mirror and scraped it out. When she brought it closer to the light for a better look, she saw it was a scrap of lipstick: her lipstick! It was as though something had been written on the mirror with it and later wiped clean. Only that thin red line had remained trapped in the edge of the chrome frame.

She looked at the mirror again. What could possibly

have been written there? she wondered. In my own lipstick!

Then, automatically, as though being directed by a mind that was not her own, she raised a trembling finger to the mirror and wrote something on it through the coat of steam that had built up. The words puzzled her at first. She had never used such language. Then she remembered. They were the same words she had hurled at her mother so many, many years before.

"DEMENTED BITCH!" was what she had written through the steam on the mirror.

At first, the words didn't frighten her or even chill her. It was as though she were still dreaming the dreams of the night before. Reality and dream became a jumbled mass of confusion in her mind. All she knew was that she wanted to rid herself of every vestige of it.

She lifted the palm of her hand to the mirror and wiped away the words. In the moment or so that it took before a fresh coat of steam formed on the glass she thought she saw her mother staring back at her! A chill shot through every bone in her body. It was then that she felt sure that she was going mad—as mad as her mother and grandfather before her had been.

Well, she calmly said to herself. What are you going to do about it? And, as though in response, the telephone beside her bed began to ring. It sounded like a buzz saw cutting its way into her thoughts. It took her a moment before she could bring herself to pick it up.

"Yes?" she answered, swallowing a cold lump in her throat.

It was Sheriff Adams. He wanted to know if she were available to take care of his children for a few days. He didn't tell her about finding little Jennifer Lineham.

She'd find out about that real soon, he thought, right along with everyone else in the valley.

"Why . . . *yes,* Jeff. That would be no problem at all," she responded, trying, with everything she had, not to make her acceptance sound as out of place as she herself felt. "I can start any time you like."

PART TWO

CHAPTER ELEVEN

The first snowfall of the season hadn't arrived as predicted, and because little Jennifer Lineham had been killed outside of Tweed Valley—and outside of Jeff Adams's jurisdiction—the people up at the state capital had not yet linked the child's death with the disappearance of the other children from Tweed Valley. Adams knew it was only a matter of another day or so before they would. Reid Hatcher would then come crashing in to take over the entire investigation. The thought of it troubled him as much as his failure to uncover a single scrap of evidence at the murder scene in Mosstown last night.

And now there are *two* known deaths among the missing children, he thought: the little girl his deputy Arthur had discovered in Pomfrey, and that of six-year-old Jennifer Lineham, his own daughter's best friend.

He took a swallow of coffee he had just poured from the Silex at his kitchen table. Outside the sky was beginning to brighten. Adams had been out in Mosstown the whole night, and when he returned home, which was no more than twenty minutes ago, the first thing he reached for was the coffee. Just time enough to dash some water on his face and fix the coffee. That first swallow was so hot and his mind so distracted that he almost choked on the coffee when it reached the back of his throat.

"Jeez it!" he said aloud. He was thankful the house was empty. His children were still at the homes of his two deputies. From there they would be driven directly to school. The second sip of coffee was more cautiously swallowed. It stung his palate, but it tasted good. He undid the wrapping on a fresh pack of Camels and lit one up. As he exhaled that first puff, he thought of Betty Lineham. He was shortly going to pick her up at the hospital and drive her back home. What was he possibly going to say to her? He could have had her taken home by either of his deputies. Even the local sheriff in Mosstown had volunteered to do it. Why had he been so obstinate about doing it himself?

He looked about the empty kitchen and then to the door that led to the porch. It was only the morning before that Betty Lineham and her daughter Jennifer had walked through it and into his kitchen. As sheriff of Tweed Valley for the past twelve years, he never ceased to wonder at how fate can sometimes fall from nowhere and twist the lives of good and honest people so badly that the knots of it take almost forever to untie.

He lowered his head and stared into the blackness of the coffee cup in his hands, as though it were a crystal ball with answers. The only useful thing he could think of doing was to devote as much time on the investigation as he possibly could. After bringing Betty home, he planned to return to Mosstown and go over every inch of territory around the factory. That would take a lot of time . . . time he'd have to be spending away from home.

He looked at the kitchen clock on the wall beside the phone. Although it was still very early, he knew that Emma Prescott would be up. It was then that he had called her about taking care of his children.

When Emma Prescott replaced the receiver on the bedroom phone after talking to Adams, her mind surged with a jolt of pure energy. It was like coming back to life. The vulgar words and image of her mother in the bathroom mirror faded from her mind just as easily as she had earlier wiped them away with the palm of her hand. Just as easily, taking care of Kevin and Kathy would wipe away all those dreadful doubts she was having that morning about her sanity. She couldn't wait to begin.

She'd pick the children up after school, bring them first to the library where, while she attended to her usual job, they could do their homework, then she'd take them home and fix their supper. Afterward, if Adams were not yet home, she'd see to it that they brushed their teeth before going to bed—just as though they were her very own children.

Emma liked that part best. She'd then alternate herself between their bedrooms to read stories. Kathy, of course, would be first because she was always so impatient to hear one; then would come Kevin, who by now probably considered himself to be too old for such things, but Emma knew the boy liked the sound of her voice. He had even told her so once, saying she sounded like his mother used to. She also knew the boy liked the special way she treated him.

And there *was* something special about Kevin, something that Emma had first observed in him about three years ago. He seemed to know things, as though he possessed the seeds of a curious magic. She had made this discovery quite by accident one afternoon while he and Kathy were staying with her at the library, where they were waiting for their father to come and pick them up. That was right after the children's mother had died. Kevin was only seven then, Kathy three.

On that particular afternoon, Kevin and his sister were sitting in the special reading parlor for little children when the boy suddenly looked up from the book he was attempting to read and asked Emma if the room had ever been used as a nursery. She smiled and shook her head no, of course not. It wasn't until later that night that she thought more deeply about what the boy had said. Dolls, she thought, sitting upright in her bed. What Kevin had either "seen" or "sensed" in his mind was the presence of all the dolls her mother used to keep in that room before they had been burned.

Emma had heard about such baffling things like that before, having once read that such events were sometimes triggered by a traumatic experience in the lives of little children. The loss of the boy's mother, at that time, was certainly such an experience. She had wondered then if there were some way to expand that seedling of power but never considered it any further than that. It might be bad for the boy, she had thought.

Ever since that time, Emma had begun to periodically read more and more about such things in the old books that had once belonged to her great-uncle, Lewis B. Olcott. One of them, a book of ancient magic she now remembered, described a ritual for the awakening of such latent powers as the boy appeared to possess. When she had first read it, many years before, Emma never imagined that she would one day be thinking of actually performing it.

That was three years ago. But now, after having just finished talking on the telephone with Adams, she wondered about the ritual more intently then she had ever done before. If Kevin did indeed possess some hidden ability to "see," she reasoned, perhaps it could be developed to a point of being useful. The boy might even be able to "see" who the child-killer was and lead his father to the brutal savage.

Emma, just as much as any other person in Tweed Valley, wanted the disappearance and killing of innocent little children to stop. The murderer had to be caught and soon—before any more children disappeared. And it was with that thought that the ancient ritual she had once read came to mind.

And now, as she pulled her robe tightly about her body, all the bizarre events that had lately become a part of her own life suddenly flooded her mind like a tide pool of hissing foam. She recalled how she would sometimes find herself in different parts of the house, not knowing why or how she had gotten there. Then there were those sore and aching muscles of hers, as though she had been doing the work of a hired field hand. And the scent of pepper that seemed to be lurking about her these days. Why did it depress her so?

But nothing troubled Emma Prescott more than the dreams in which she was a little child again, being hit across the face and spanked by her mother for playing with the old woman's stupid dolls. It all seemed so real, she thought. To say nothing of the eerie image of her demented mother laughing at her from the bathroom mirror.

The realization that she might be slipping further and further into the same realm of madness that had claimed her mother and grandfather before her almost made her gasp. Was her infatuation with the thought of ancient magic just a manifestation of that madness? Did she really believe that little Kevin Adams possessed some hidden ability to discover who the childkiller was? And that she, possibly on the brink of losing her own mind, could help to bring it all about?

She thought she should probably be seeing someone—someone who might be able to help her. Dream and reality were becoming so closely intermingled that she sometimes had trouble distinguishing the two. But what if she could awaken some hidden power within the boy—if even for one fleeting moment—just long enough for him to catch a glimpse of something everyone else might have missed? Wouldn't that make it all worthwhile? Kevin could then lead his father to the killer. The children of Tweed Valley would then be saved from the terror—a terror that, for some unknown reason, had only recently begun to intensify.

Yes, she thought as she watched the sky grow brighter and brighter outside her window, it *was* worth a try. There was nothing to lose and she could probably perform the ritual in such a way that the boy wouldn't even know it was happening. But first she'd have to familiarize herself with it again. In her mind she could almost see the worn binding of the book in which the ritual was described. Just as soon as she dressed herself she would go to her private reading parlor and try to find it again.

CHAPTER TWELVE

Adams drove Betty Lineham away from the hospital in a pall of desperate silence. He wasn't sure he knew how to tell her about her daughter's death without choking on the words. Before having arrived at the hospital he had rehearsed the words. They all sounded hollow and meaningless against the grief he felt. He glanced to the side for a moment and looked at her before returning his attention to the road. She was staring straight ahead through the windshield of the old Peugeot as though she were focused on something far off in the distance. Her jaws were clenched.

Earlier, Adams had asked if anyone at the hospital had told her about her daughter. No one had. That was left for him to do. But he knew the words could not yet be spoken without an emotional catch. He paid close attention to the road, as though that would somehow ease the chaotic churning of his own troubled thoughts.

"Is she dead?" Betty Lineham finally asked. Her voice was quiet and seemingly far away. She examined his profile against the scenery that whizzed by in a blur outside the window on his side of the car. His lips were as firmly pressed together as hers. She quickly looked away, down at the twist of stark-white fingers she had knotted in her lap. "She is dead," Betty pressed. "Isn't she?"

Adams wasn't sure she was ready to hear it—or that he was ready to tell it—but he couldn't hold it back any longer. She had a perfect right to know what everyone else back in Tweed Valley already knew. He slowly began to give her the facts, omitting all detail: Jennifer *was* dead and, so far, there were no clues as to who the killer was.

He could hardly believe he had managed to keep his emotions in check. It was as though he had just told her about something that had happened to someone else, someone neither he nor Betty knew.

"I knew it," Betty winced, lowering her head. "Knew it from the moment I first saw the car's window smashed in like that." Tears spilled quietly from her eyes. As they drove on in silence Adams swallowed hard against the anguish he was feeling for her. Finally, Betty lifted her chin and stared straight ahead at the winding roadway. Her eyes still held tears and her cheeks were streaked with the wetness of those that had already fallen. She had the far-off look of someone who was attempting to remember something. The frightful memory of the night before had played itself over and over in her mind like an endless loop of film. She couldn't block it.

"I shouldn't have left her alone," she said after a long while. "It's all my fault."

Adams's shoulders tensed. It's all *my* fault! he felt like responding. If only he were a better sheriff, maybe none of this would have happened.

He saw the sign for a rest stop about a quarter of a

mile up ahead. When he reached it, he turned off the road and stopped the car. It was one of those desolated areas without facilities, just a painted-green oil drum with a black plastic bag for motorists to deposit their travel litter. But there was a view. A broad vista of fields and farms stretched out toward the horizon like a scene from a calendar. During foliage there would be at least a dozen cars jammed into that little space, and people with cameras. Both he and Betty were thankful for the wintrylike bleakness of the vista before them. They were the only two people there.

"They told me at the hospital that you refused to take home a prescription for some sedatives," he said. "Do you think that's a good idea? I mean, for right now?" He really wanted to say that she should be taking something until after Jennifer's funeral. Betty lived alone. He knew she didn't have any close friends.

She looked at him with the faint glimmer of something resembling a cautious smile on the edges of her full lips. "Thanks," she said. "I'll be all right."

"Not if you keep blaming yourself for what happened," he responded. "That can sink even the strongest person."

It suddenly occurred to him that he was speaking to her as though she were much closer to him than an ordinary neighbor. Within him, there had always been a special feeling for her. He wasn't sure what that feeling was, but at that moment all he wanted to do was to reach out with his hand and brush away the tears from her cheeks.

"When I get you home," he finally said, "I'm going to call Emma Prescott and see if she can come over and help you out. I've already spoken to her about taking care of Kevin and Kathy. Maybe she could spend part of the day helping you around the house. I know she'll be glad to do it."

Betty Lineham had had a terrible marriage. The man she had fallen in love with was a drinker and womanizer. It suddenly struck her that he had never once given her the same concern and warmth that Adams was now showing. And the man had been her daughter's own father! She found herself wishing he were dead. How was she ever going to muster the strength to try and locate him and tell him about their daughter? Would she be able to? Would he care?

"I won't be needing anyone," she finally said, responding to his suggestion about having Emma Prescott come over. The librarian was a good friend and neighbor, and would be a welcome comfort to her right now, but Betty had always been uneasy about asking for help. She sat up beside him and wiped her tears with a tissue from her handbag. "I'll be all right," she finally said.

Adams was sure she would be. There was a strength in her that plainly showed in almost everything she did. She was the only unmarried women in town who, knowing that he didn't have a wife, had never made a play for him. Yet he felt she had always had a special feeling for him—just as surely as he now realized he had for her.

Just as soon as they got back to Betty's house, Adams placed a call to Emma Prescott—against the halfhearted protests of Betty Lineham. She had cried most of the way back home, and he didn't want her to be left alone.

Emma was still at the library. She'd have to call the school and tell them that she wouldn't be able to keep her appointment with the first grade today. She never liked to break a promise, but Betty Lineham needed her more. Emma was more than happy to be of assistance to the grief-ridden mother of the little girl she had, only yesterday, read to in class and given a copy of *The Yearling*.

Emma arrived at Betty's house in less than ten minutes. Adams saw her pickup pull into the driveway and stop at the side of the small frame house. He went out to meet her.

"Look," he said quietly. "She's going to be fine. It's just a matter of time. But if you see that she's going to fall apart or something like that, call me right away. One of my men will be at the office and will know how to get in touch with me."

Emma gave him that understanding nod he knew so well. She was an intelligent lady and knew how to handle almost any situation. That's why he trusted her, even with his own children.

"We're good friends, Jeff," Emma said as they walked toward the house. "Everything will be fine. The only problem is that I'll have to leave her alone for a little while when I go to pick up Kathy and Kevin at the school this afternoon. I wouldn't want to take Betty along with me to do that. . . . Too many children for her to see right now, if you know what I mean."

He did. "Try to get her away from the window that faces the road when you come back with the kids. I don't think it'll be good for her to see all the children coming up the hill on their way home from school." He pointed to his house next door. "You can leave Kevin and Kathy alone in the house to do their homework. From Betty's parlor window you can see my front door and the living room windows, so it won't be like they are entirely without some kind of supervision."

When they reached Betty's door, Adams let Emma enter alone. He had to hurry over to the sheriff's office where he knew Ben and Arthur would be waiting for him to arrive. It was only 9 A.M. and, with having had no sleep the night before, he already felt as though he had put in a full day's work.

"Anything new on that pepper thing?" Adams asked Ben just as soon as he walked in the door of the sheriff's office. Ben looked at him and shook his head. Nothing. "I'm making some calls now to a couple of out-of-state wholesalers and things like that," he said.

Adams liked that. "That's probably what we should have done yesterday," he said. "From what you and Arthur told me yesterday, it sounded as if someone had dumped a whole sack of it all over the place."

Arthur's head bobbed up from the telephone directory he had been going through like a cork in a barrel of rainwater. He stood up and rubbed the back of his neck as though an insect had just stung him there. *Sack.* That's what was sticking out of the tailgate of the librarian's pickup yesterday. A burlap sack. But when he thought about it for another second or two, he almost had to laugh. Burlap sacks are not all that uncommon. People in these parts used them for all sorts of things. Besides, what would Emma Prescott have to do with anything like this! The thought was certainly a stray shot. They were *all* trying too hard to come up with anything they could. He sat back down and found what he had been looking for in the telephone book. It was the number of the veterinarian in Hannerville where Billy Chadwick's hound dog had been taken.

Adams hadn't noticed Arthur standing up and then sitting back down again. He was still talking to his other deputy. "Ben," he said. "You stay here in the office today. There's bound to be a mess of calls coming in about what's going on. I don't think the state is going to link the disappearance of the Chadwick boy with the killing up in Mosstown last night. Not yet. But Hatcher and his newspaper boys up at the capital are going to put it together, real soon. You can bank on it. We're going to have to come up with something real soon, otherwise—" He just let it go at that. Everyone in the office knew what he meant.

"I got the vet up in Hannerville on the line now," Arthur turned and said to Adams. "The boy's dog is fine. Says it can be picked up any time now. Should I tell him I'm on my way?"

Adams looked at him. Arthur seemed to be pushing to do just that. He had wanted to take him along to Mosstown so that they could both go over the territory around the factory and fine-tooth it if they had to. He hadn't thought about using the dog. Adams finally nodded his chin in a gesture of consent. From the way he pulled the edge of his upper lip into his mouth, Arthur figured that Adams considered it a good thing for him to have pressed for.

"Okay," he said to Arthur after the deputy finished speaking to the veterinarian. "After you pick up the dog, go over the area behind the school first. If you come across anything, anything at all, you call back here on the radio phone and tell Ben. He'll get in touch with me up in Mosstown. I'll probably be there the rest of the day." He looked at Ben to make sure he understood what had just been said. He did. Then Adams thought of something else and turned back to Arthur. "If you don't get a lead on something real quick, get in the cruiser with the hound and bring it on up to Mosstown. Maybe there's a scent up there it can follow. I didn't notice any pepper on the ground last night." Adams knew that the area of the factory parking lot and the slope that led down to the river behind it was so heavily trampled by people and vehicles that even a *trained* scent dog would have a hard time following a single trail, but it was all he had to go on.

When Arthur left the sheriff's office on his way to Hannerville, he had to drive right past the town library. He remembered the thought he had had earlier, about Emma Prescott and a large sack of crushed red pepper. He would have laughed out loud, now that he was alone, but he was doing over sixty when he zoomed past the library and had to negotiate the sharp turn onto the route that led to the interstate. He shouldn't have been moving that fast, not on that sharp curve. But Arthur liked that turn, having taken it at even faster speeds in the past. It took all his concentration to keep to his side of the roadway. Had he been going a notch or two more slowly, he would have noticed something on Emma Prescott's clothes line out behind the library. It was a sack. A large burlap sack. It billowed out and filled with the cold wind as though something inside of it were alive.

The first thing that Adams felt as he drove into the parking lot of the factory in Mosstown was the absolute normality of the scene. It was as though the tragedy of last night had not occurred. A full complement of cars belonging to the day shift people were all lined up properly in evenly spaced lanes. Betty Lineham's car had been removed, and Adams knew from having spoken to the local sheriff before starting to Mosstown that the Volkswagen was going to be impounded for another day or so before it could be released. Adams had asked the sheriff if he could have someone repair the broken window and clean up the inside of the car so that every time she got into it it wouldn't remind Betty of what had happened. The sheriff had agreed. There was no problem with that, he had said. The pound where Betty's car had been taken was also a garage. He would have someone look into it just as soon as all the necessary tests and photographs had been taken. And, no, the blood that was tested so far did not belong to anyone other than the little girl who was killed. Her body was still at the hospital mortuary, waiting to be picked up for the funeral. That was another thing that Adams had agreed to take care of.

When he got out of his Peugeot he went first to the area where Betty's Volkswagen had been parked. The vinyl casing that the local sheriff had erected was gone. There was another car parked where it had been. He got down on his hands and knees and looked beneath it. Nothing. Every scrap and shard of glass that had been there the night before was gone. So, too, were the small splotches of blood that had fallen to the ground. The place had been swept clean and scrubbed with a stiff broom and water. He knew it was useless looking for anything there.

Still on his hands and knees, he looked sideways beneath the rows and rows of parked cars. The light was even, and raking his vision along the ground at that low angle would have made anything unusual, like a weapon or tool, stand out clearly. But the only thing he saw, in any direction, were some small stones and a number of brown leaves circling in the cool breeze. Being that close to the ground somehow magnified the sound of the gushing river behind the factory. He slowly rose to his feet, dusted his palms against one another, and started for the trail at the other end of the parking lot—the trail that led to the spot where, not more than six hours before, Jennifer's mutilated body had tumbled out of a tree.

He didn't want to go at first. It was as though a pair of strong arms were holding his legs in place. He had seen all kinds of killing when he was in Vietnam, but none was worse for him than the slaughter of innocent children. There was plenty of that there. He had had a good deal of trouble handling it then, and that was well before he had any children of his own. Now, with his own daughter the same age as the two little girls who were known to have been killed, his insides quivered the same way they did whenever a concussion bomb had gone off in Saigon. He opened his mouth and took in a gulp of cold air to get his breath back. It took more than one deep swallow to do it.

As a military policeman in the army, he had learned

that in an investigation one has to look for relationships, similarities, individual characteristics, and possible motives that link events together. From these a picture, no matter how hazy at first, usually forms.

Maybe it was because of the lack of sleep or because he was so worn out and confused about the death of little Jennifer, but he couldn't come up with anything. All he knew was that he was after a killer who was insane, but not so insane that he was leaving clues all over the place. The pepper was the only thing so far, and Adams had hopes that Ben would come up with something on that before the end of the day.

Everything behind the factory looked much different than it had the night before, when he scoured the area with his police lantern. Now, with the gray light that fell from a sky that looked heavy with snow, it would be easier. He could see through the bare branches of the trees in any direction, an advantage the killer must have had before it grew totally dark last night. The river below roared about the rocks and boulders in its bed with such force that no one in the factory or the parking lot could possibly have heard the child scream out—if she ever had a chance to.

He went to the tree that the child's body had fallen from. He knew his own daughter's weight to be almost forty pounds. It must have taken a strong person to have hurled little Jennifer up there like that. He also knew that even underdeveloped psychopaths could sometimes muster a strength that was far beyond their expected capacity.

He lowered his eyes to the spot where Jennifer's body had landed. His mind involuntarily reproduced the sound of it hitting the ground in the darkness of the night before. He knew the memory of that sound would haunt him for the rest of his life.

There was not the slightest trace of pepper anywhere. Perhaps the killer was smart enough to realize that, with so many fishermen coming into the area, driving down close to the river with every sort of vehicle, it would be impossible for a dog to pick up a clean scent. He didn't like that. The fact that the killer was an *intelligent* psychopath chilled him to the bone. What would that kind of murderer do next?

Autopsies had determined that neither of the two little girls had been sexually abused. What then could the motive have been? Why the mutilations? It was almost as though the killer might be some sort of vampire, in desperate need of its victims' blood! He didn't like that theory at all. But it appeared to be the only one that even came close to fitting into the relationships, similarities, and individual characteristics of an investigation that was leading him straighter and straighter down the road to nowhere. The only hope he had at the moment was for his deputy Arthur to show up with something that Billy Chadwick's hound had led him to.

CHAPTER THIRTEEN

Arthur walked the dog out through the opening in the chain-link fence behind the school. It was part retriever, part something else—a mixed breed, just like most of the dogs that the deputy had ever known. It had broad floppy ears, and its golden coat was almost uniformly colored except for a white bib that fluffed out from its breast like a down pillow. Arthur wished he had remembered to get the hound's name. It might be useful.

The deputy had just given the dog a whiff of a shirt that Billy Chadwick's parents had provided. The hound immediately lit off at a full run up the hill to the spot where, the night before, it had filled its snout with red pepper. The dog froze. It would go no farther than ten feet of the spot. It circled about a shrub at the top of the hill behind the school, barking as though it saw something within the confines of the area that was invisible to human eyes and into which it could not be coaxed, no matter how hard Arthur tried.

Arthur knew it was the scent of the pepper and not anything else that made the dog refuse to go any farther. He wished the pepper hadn't been washed so deeply into the ground by last night's downpour. The dog certainly knew the scent of the boy. He must have been carried from the spot, Arthur thought. If the boy had left the area on his own two feet, the hound would have easily had the trail by now.

The deputy shook his head as he watched the retriever continue to circle the shrub. Its bark was so fierce that Arthur wondered if he could ever get it collared again. He was about to try it when the dog got its nose right down to the ground at the edge of the circle it had been making and stopped barking. Arthur thought the dog saw him coming with the collar and was holding still for him—a nice piece of training he hadn't expected in such a mixed breed. But before he could reach the hound it picked up a scent and began to follow it. The hairs went up on the back of Arthur's arms. It was the eeriest thing he had ever seen. The dog's floppy ears filled with protein and stiffened right up for a moment, actually pointing before they flopped back down again. He had heard of such a thing happening before but never really believed it. Not only that, but the dog stopped and looked up at him once, to see if the deputy had been paying attention. When it saw that Arthur had, it bolted down the hill like a fox chasing a rabbit. Arthur almost stumbled as he tried to keep up with it. His heart was pounding faster than his feet on the ground. He had to stop when he got to the bottom of the hill to catch his breath; that was at the teacher's parking lot, right where he had parked the cruiser. There wasn't much time to waste. The dog was heading out of the yard and racing toward the highway. It was a good thing traffic was light. Arthur realized that Billy had probably been taken somewhere by car, a car that had left the school parking lot and went in the same direction along the highway as the dog was now running. He got in the cruiser and sped after it as fast as he could, praying all the while that it wouldn't leave the road and race up into the woods that engulfed either side of it.

When he was almost up to the dog Arthur relaxed his foot on the accelerator and followed at a slower speed. Just as he was beginning to reach for the radio phone to tell Ben that it looked as though the dog had picked up a scent, the hound cut across the road in front of the cruiser and made its way up into the woods. There was an old logging trail that went that way, and Arthur didn't know if it was passible. He would have to try. There was no other choice. Where it led, he did not know. He only knew that the hill, which rose up beyond it, was called Tweed Hill and that long before he was born there had been farms up there.

There should be two dogs on a thing like this, he thought. One to follow the scent, and the other on a leash to help follow the hound that got the scent! He was having a hard time on that old back road. It twisted and turned and the cruiser's tires nearly left it whenever he pressed to pick up speed. The dog seemed *constantly* to be at the edge of a bend every time Arthur got to a place where he could see it. It was as though the dog kept checking to make sure he was still following.

A full-flowing brook appeared to one side of the road once they got higher along the trail. At one point, about five miles up, the dog left the narrow logging road and shot off down the ravine, swimming across the brook and scampering up the other side of it. Arthur stopped the cruiser and followed. He slipped part of the way down the ravine and thought he might have hurt his ankle, but the feeling came back to it just as his feet hit the cold water. It was up to his waist and it took some doing to push his way across to the other side without getting pulled off his feet. He had removed his gun from its holster to keep it dry, replacing it only when he reached the steep embankment the dog had scampered up. He would need both hands and all the strength he had to do what the dog had so effortlessly just accomplished. Its trail was easy to follow. The boy's dog had turned soil over with such force that its path shot like a furrow through the slippery brown leaves that covered the ground. Arthur found himself hoping against hope that the boy was still alive. If he could only find him, Billy would be the first missing child that had been recovered alive. Maybe the other children would be there, too. Maybe some crazy person just wanted to live up in the woods with a bunch of kids they could never have on their own.

He almost stopped dead in his tracks. Emma Prescott! he thought. The burlap sack! The dog had followed the scent right to the spot where the librarian's pickup was usually parked when she was at the school—like yesterday, when he had spotted something flapping from the tailgate of her pickup. He touched his shirt pocket. The single strand of brown twine he had plucked from a bush on the hill behind the school was still there. He pulled it out. Damn, he thought. That's *exactly* what it could be—a strand from a burlap sack. He cursed himself for not having first gone to the librarian's house, just to see if he were right. Whatever it was that had been flapping from the back of her pickup might still be there. Maybe it *was* a pepper sack!

Up ahead, he heard the boy's dog barking and growling at something. He hurried to the top of the embankment and unholstered his gun. The thought that he might come face to face with the crazed child-killer at any moment made the adrenaline pump through his veins like pellets of ice. There was also the fear of having to discover, once again, the dead body of one of the missing children—like the little girl he had found in Pomfrey, not more than half a mile from where he lived. The thought of it made his stomach tighten.

There was a clearing of some sort up ahead. He could see the dog through the naked branches of the low shrubbery that surrounded it. It didn't appear as though anyone were about. Just the hound, circling the small clearing like it had circled the spot out behind the schoolyard. Arthur approached it cautiously. When he stopped away from the bushes he saw that he was standing in a small clearing that sloped off in the direction he had just climbed. The floor of the clearing was irregular, as though someone had been digging it up, one small patch of it at a time. Some of the patches had been more freshly dug than others. They looked like . . .

Arthur took a step backward and almost cried out when he realized what he had just stumbled across. It was a graveyard. Not one with old markers that ran by the side of a picturesque New England roadway, but a new one. There were no markers. It could not have been more than a year or so old. He swallowed hard against the knot of dryness in his throat and tried to count the soft mounds of soil that rose from the floor of the clearing. There were almost a dozen of them, the same amount as the number of children that had been reported missing over the past year.

Billy Chadwick's dog had furiously begun to dig away at one of the mounds. The soil was loose, indicating to the deputy that it had been recently dug and turned in. He also saw that the dirt was mixed with red pepper. It flew like fire ants into the hound's eyes. Its snout was bleeding from the soreness of it. But the dog wouldn't quit. It had definitely found something. When it got to the sack that had recently been buried there, the dog let out a whimper, like it was about to die. It slowly began to tear and nuzzle its head into the sack, as though it had a mind to make certain who it was that had been buried there. Arthur knew it was the boy. So did the dog.

As the deputy came closer and stooped over to examine Billy Chadwick's lifeless form, the dog lunged at him. It had gone mad from grief and the pepper. Arthur rolled with it in a struggle to keep the hound from ripping into his throat. But the dog managed to nuzzle itself into the softness behind the deputy's ear and sink its teeth into his neck. Arthur was barely able to unholster his gun when the dog lunged at him again. This time its teeth sunk into the deputy's thigh. Somehow the gun in Arthur's hand went off. There was so much pain raging through his body that he thought he might have shot himself. The sound of the gun did something else, too. It seemed to have made the dog freeze. But that can't be, Arthur thought. His mind was a blur of pain but he was still able to reason that the hound was a hunting dog. It was used to the sound of guns blasting away. He pulled himself up on one elbow and saw what it was. He had shot it. There was a clean red hole in the white bib that covered the dog's breast. From the way that the blood pumped out of it, Arthur knew he had gotten the dog through the heart. The only consolation he felt as the dog's legs finally gave out and it toppled over into Billy Chadwick's grave was that if he hadn't shot it, it would certainly have killed him. He eased himself down on his back for a moment and covered the wound in his neck with his hand. It wasn't as deep as he had thought, but he was losing blood. He pushed the .45 back into its holster and rolled himself over so that he could get up and cover the wound in his neck with a handkerchief. It was only then that he felt the full force of the wounds he had just suffered. His neck and thigh throbbed hotly. His shirt and jacket looked like a red rain slicker, and his pants were no better. He knew he'd have to get some help up there before he lost any more blood. But the radio was in the cruiser. He didn't know if he had the strength to make it back across the ravine and up the other side to get it.

He heard the bushes rattling at the edge of the clearing behind him. He thought someone might have heard the shot and was coming to find out what had happened. But when he turned he saw that it was only the wind churning through the leafless bramble. Then he saw the old log cabin behind the bushes. He thought it probably belonged to whoever had dug the graves . . . the killer. If anyone had been inside the cabin, they would have heard the barking and the gunfire. They would have either gotten to him by now or fled. He assumed no one was there.

Arthur struggled toward the back of the cabin, leaving a trail of blood across the graves as he went.

There were no windows in the back, and from the looks of the place it appeared as though it might have been abandoned a hundred years ago. He pressed the handkerchief tightly to his neck with one hand, and with the other he gingerly touched the bite wound in his thigh. It seemed to have clotted against the heavy twill of his pants. Fine, he thought as he removed the .45 and cautiously stepped around the side of the house to see what was there. On that side, too, there were no windows. Neither was there a door. The logs that made up the cabin were old and split. The stone chimney that ran from the ground up past the pitch of the roof gave out no smoke. Another indication that there was no one inside. If there were, surely a fire would be going on such a chilled day.

He eased himself behind the house and retraced his steps to the other end of it to see what that looked like. It was the same. Nothing different. Nothing, that is, except for a small window in the side of it. He cautiously approached. His thigh throbbed so badly that it was a great effort for him to crouch beneath it. He wanted to take a good look inside before he went all the way around to where the front door must be. If this were where the killer lived, he thought, he'd burn the damn thing to the ground. That would bring help from the people in the valley, quicker than anything else. They'd come with an ambulance and fire-fighting equipment, too, if only they could make it up the old disheveled logging trail with them.

He was still crouched beneath the window and could have stood up and looked inside any time he wanted, but he had first to catch his breath and put the pain he felt out of his mind. There was also the matter of making sure that the clip of his automatic was fully loaded. When this was done, he listened for any sign of life from inside. When none came, he slowly pulled himself up to the window for a look. What he saw made him spin about and sit right back down on the ground, breathing as hard as if he had just seen a ghost. He had seen a naked little girl through the window. Or at least that's what he *thought* he saw. She had been lying on a broad wooden table that looked like a workbench or something. There were tools. And the child looked dead.

The memory of the little girl's body he had discovered in Pomfrey shuttled through his mind like a lonesome cry. He wanted to get out of there in a hurry and try to get in touch with Ben on the cruiser's radio. It was almost noon and he knew Adams would be checking in from Mosstown soon. But his legs wouldn't work. Besides, he had better make sure he really saw what he thought he had just seen.

When he lifted himself to the window again he was ready for the worst. But it didn't come. It was only a *doll* he had seen. He was relieved by that. He could now see that the cabin was empty except for a number of wooden boxes with dolls standing inside of them. There were unlit candles on the top of each box. The only thing he could figure was that the killer was using the cabin to make dolls. He frowned. Why? he asked himself.

Then, as his eyes lowered to the doll that was on the workbench just inside the window, he realized something about it that was, at first, difficult for him to accept.

He knew who the doll was.

Perhaps it was the loss of blood that was making him think things like that. He was getting weak, too. He didn't know how much longer he could stay on his feet. Yet, for some curious reason, the pain had stopped. He couldn't figure it.

He looked at the doll again. It was a lifelike replica of Adams' own little daughter, Kathy. The skin across the top of his scalp crawled. What the heck's going on? he wondered. The answer didn't come until he looked at the rest of the dolls that were further inside the cabin. Although the light was bad, he began to make out the features of the dolls' faces inside the boxes. His mouth was bone dry by the time he realized that they were accurate replicas of all the children that had ever been reported missing from the valley below—and that the reason Kathy's doll was there was that she was going to be the next victim.

"HELP!" he shouted. It sounded like the desperate cry of a wounded animal, but it was the only thing he could think of doing at that moment. "HELP ME UP HERE!" he screamed hoarsely. Then he calmed himself for a moment and emptied half a clip of ammunition into the air. He would have emptied the whole thing had he not caught himself and realized it was as useless as his shouting for help. No one in the valley below could have heard it through the thick pines that covered the hillside. But he had to try something.

He looked about. Although he had not yet been to the front of the cabin, he could see it faced the end of the old logging trail he had been on with the cruiser. Instead of cutting across the ravine on foot, he could have stayed on it with the police car. It led right up to the place. He cursed Billy's dog for having taken a shortcut. The scent had been so close at that point that the blasted hound had followed it in a straight line instead of sticking to the twisted trail.

Something made him suddenly realize that he wasn't going to die after all. The handkerchief he had pressure-pressed to his neck had clotted the flow of blood. His thigh, though it still stung, was carrying his weight without any further loss of blood, too. He was just a little weak, he thought. That was all. He could easily make it back to the cruiser. It was all downhill from where he stood. The old trail came up out of the woods on the other side of the clearing in which the cabin stood. It couldn't have been more than fifty feet away. Why, there might even be someone coming up it right now to investigate the sound of his gunshots. All he had to do was go inside and light a fire in the old stone fireplace. That would bring someone up even quicker.

He took another look inside and studied the interior as though he wanted to etch it into his memory for all of time. He now saw something that he hadn't seen before. Along the far wall of the cabin there was a pile of several burlap sacks—full sacks of what he was sure would prove to be crushed red pepper. He wondered if they would match the one that had flagged itself at him from the tailgate of Emma Prescott's pickup.

His heart was racing as he limped around to the front door of the cabin. He aimed his gun directly at the door and carefully lifted the latch to see if it was locked. It was not. There was a momentary silence inside the cabin as he entered. Then, something suddenly whistled at him from the darkness of the rafters like an angry hawk. Even as he lifted his head to see what it was, the heavy broadaxe that Emma Prescott had booby-trapped the front door with whizzed into his skull. He never knew what hit him.

CHAPTER FOURTEEN

Mrs. Bently, principal of the lower school, looked out at all the children who had been called to the auditorium to hear a special message. When the news of Jennifer Lineham first came to her, she had thought that speaking to the children would be a good idea. More than that, the parents expected it. She knew that many of them felt the need to caution their children but lacked the manner with which such a dire warning should be given. That's what most country people still think teachers and ministers are for, even in this day and age, she found herself reasoning.

The auditorium was less than half filled. Many of the parents had kept their children home this day, as though that would somehow protect them from the menace of the killer. Mrs. Bently had appealed to them that they couldn't keep their children home forever and, as an example, had sent her own three children off to school that morning as usual: one to the lower school where she was the principal, and the older two to the upper school in Woodville. But, for the most part, her argument hadn't worked. And Mrs. Bently could understand why. If she were not the principal she might not have sent her children to school that day either.

Her mind was numb. She didn't know how to begin. The children were as silent as they could be. They knew that Mrs. Bently had called the special assembly today to say something about what had happened to Jennifer Lineham last night. The news of it had overshadowed the fact that other children had been reported missing too—most recently, Billy Chadwick, just two days ago. Mrs. Bently thought that maybe she *should* go ahead and contact the state for permission to close the school until the killer was caught, just like a good many of the parents had been pressuring her to do. But they were the newer breed, like her, parents who had moved to Vermont from out of state to get away from crime in the cities. And we're still running away from it now, too, she thought. Without exception, those who had lived in Vermont all their lives had refused to keep their children away. When the suggestion was made to some, they couldn't imagine how that would change anything. There were a thousand ways for a child to die, they had countered. There were fires, car accidents, falls from trees, and an even greater variety of assorted farming mishaps. There were even drownings—in summer and through the ice in winter, too—and just last year a little boy was killed when his sled skidded off a hill and out onto the highway where a truck got him. Nobody liked any of it, of course. But to keep a child out of school because two children out of the thousand or so who lived in the valley had been murdered—and they hadn't even been at school at the time—well, that just didn't seem to make much sense, not to a lifelong Vermonter, anyway. The thing that had to be done was to catch whoever it was that was doing it!

"Children," Mrs. Bently began. Her tone was even. "I don't have to tell anyone here what has happened to one of our own schoolmates, Jennifer Lineham. . . ."

At the mention of her best friend's name, Kathy Adams, who was sitting next to the empty seat that had been assigned to Jennifer at the start of the school year, began to cry. She did it without making a sound. Tears rolled down her cheeks and gathered in the dimple of her chin until they dripped, one salty bead at a time, onto the folded hands in her lap. Kevin, sitting two rows in front of her but off to the other side of the auditorium, turned and saw her just as though she had called out his name. Something had made him carry his hatchet into the auditorium today. It was under the sweater he wore. He knew if he were caught with it he'd be suspended and kicked out of school for a week, maybe longer. His father would sorry him good for that! But he didn't care. He rubbed his hand against the lump it made beneath the sweater. Kathy turned her head and saw him looking at her. He jutted his chin forward a bit—a sign that she should be brave. She took a deep breath and wiped the tears off her chin with the back of her hand. Her teacher, Miss Jones, saw that she was crying and handed her a fresh Kleenex from a small cellophane packet she had been holding in her hands.

". . . She was a quiet girl, a conscientious girl, and one who had showed such great promise in the short time that she was with us," Mrs. Bently went on. She was about to continue, but something clouded her thoughts and she fought back tears. All she could think of at that particular moment were her own children and what it would mean to her if anything ever happened to them. She cleared her throat and swallowed before going on.

"I'm not going to go on and tell you that you must never leave the house alone or that you shouldn't play outdoors. That would be wrong. Simply keep in mind what I am sure your parents have told you about strangers or anyone else who might act in a way toward you that is unusual. You don't have to be afraid of hurting a grown-up's feelings if you think they are acting strangely, even if you know who they are. If they mean you no harm, they will understand, and so will your parents, your teachers, and anyone else you may want to tell about it. These are troubled times, but we must have the faith to believe that things will shortly be better for all of us."

It wasn't so much the skepticism, which faintly showed in the eyes of several teachers who were seated with their classes. It was that it also appeared in the eyes of some of the students, too. She could tell they hardly believed her. And why should they, she thought. She herself hardly believed that things would soon be better.

"Let everyone rise for a moment of silence, please. And let each of us, in our own special way, offer a prayer for our lost classmate, Jennifer Lineham."

The children stood as one and bowed their heads. Kathy prayed that her friend wasn't really dead and that she would find her alive and her usual self just as soon as she got home from school. And Kevin, clutching the hatchet beneath his sweater, prayed that his father would find the killer . . . soon.

At recess later that afternoon, Kevin ran laps on the

cinder track that circled the schoolyard. Each lap was about a quarter of a mile and he had, so far, almost completed three of them. He found that when his heart pounded as rapidly as his feet hit the track, it helped him forget things—things like the fact that his father had not yet caught the killer.

His friends Peter and Josh had chosen to remain behind in the gym, where they wanted to play one-on-one basketball with each other. Kevin was happy they had. He was only one of a dozen or so children that had opted to go outside today. The sky looked so loaded with snow that the boy could almost taste it. The first snowfall of the season was best. You could scoop it up and spill some maple syrup on it. "Sugar snow" is what his mother had called it the first time he ever had it.

He was just completing his fifth lap around the track when he saw that the teacher in charge of the yard was not looking his way. It was exactly what Kevin had been waiting for. The next time around he darted straight through the hole in the chain-link fence that led to the woods behind the school. As soon as he got to the other side of the knoll he leaned against a scrubby tree and tried to catch his breath. It vaporized in the cold air like steam from a hot engine. When his breathing returned to normal he walked around to where the "killer tree" was. It looked as wicked as it had the day before, when he had clipped its "head" off with a throw of his hatchet.

Even without its "head," the "killer tree" still gave Kevin a chill. It made his eyes focus more on the twisted limbs that reached out at him from the withered trunk of the dead tree. He quickly lowered his eyes to the heart that had been carved into it. That would be his target for today. Yesterday he got the "head." Today he would get the heart.

The "head" was still lying on the ground, right where it had fallen yesterday afternoon. There was something about it that still disturbed him. The chink in its gnarled "face," which made up the "mouth" of the thing, still reminded him of a taunting smirk. For some reason it gave him the willies. He kicked it with his foot until it began to roll. It tumbled awkwardly away from the tree until it was stopped by a rock. He then felt comfortable enough to turn his back on the tree and began to count off paces, like in a Western, where the gunfighters walked away from one another before turning to fire. As he paced, he drew the hatchet out from beneath his sweater. When he reached the prescribed count, he spun on his heels and hurled the hatchet off the tips of his fingers as expertly as he had the day before. This time it cartwheeled, end over end, and scored a perfect hit—right smack in the center of the carved heart. He wished now that Josh and Peter had decided to come along with him after all.

As he approached the tree to retrieve the hatchet, something out of the corner of his eye made him stop. He thought the "head" he had kicked off to the side of the tree had moved. Best to pay things like that no mind, he told himself. If you start thinking things like that can really happen, it could make you go funny in the head. He forced all his attention to gather before him like a focused beam on the hatchet as he struggled to remove it from the tree. It had gone in so deeply that it took some doing to get it out.

He had to admit to himsef that being there all alone made his heart pound faster than it should, like when he was running his laps. He carefully paced off the distance from the tree for a second time. He was sure there *was* something about the way the "head" appeared to be smirking at him from the ground. The thought of it made his hands shake, no matter how hard he tried to put it out of his mind. It was as though it had some strange power over him. The hand in which he carried the hatchet was shaking so badly that he wondered if he could hold on to it long enough to get his second shot off.

When he got to the spot where he had to turn and throw, he paused. If it had been a real gun duel he would have been shot in the back, right where he was feeling something like a trickle of electricity licking at him. He pushed it out of his mind and wound up with the hatchet in that same slow-motion curl, spinning on his heels to hurl it. But it never left his hand. The boy froze solid still. The "head" *had* moved! The stupid smirk it wore across its crooked "mouth" sneered at him more mockingly than before. His father had told him once how if you ran too fast and too hard for too long, you could sometimes see things that weren't really there. *Hyper*-something, it was called. He wondered if that were happening to him now. He remained where he was for a moment and thought about it.

When he was much younger he had been terribly scared of cats. He never knew why. Then one day he decided not to be afraid of them anymore. He went to a neighbor's farm, where he knew a big ol' tom lived, and found it in the barn. He chased it, and when he caught the cat he held it in his lap until the thing started to purr like a whole team of fiddles. He thought he would apply the same logic to overcome his feeling about the gnarled "head" of the "killer tree."

With the hatchet still in his hand, he slowly approached it, never once blinking his eyes. That, he figured, would keep it from looking as though it had moved again. He was right. By the time he was standing before it, with his feet spread wide to either side of it, it hadn't moved. He let his breath out slowly and raised the hatchet high above his head. Gonna split you good! he thought as he forcefully brought the blade down toward that mocking grin.

WHACK! WHACK! WHACK!

The sound of his hatchet going into the gnarl of wood rang out as though he were banging an old frying pan at the start of New Year. He then got down on his knees so he could have better leverage and control over his aim. He wanted to chop the darn thing to smithereens, once and for all. But it joggled back and forth so much from his frenzied blows that he decided he should stop for a moment and readjust the thing so he could better hack its mocking smirk to pieces.

He placed the hatchet next to his knees on the ground and was about to twist the "head" so that the curve of the thing's twisted "lips" ran in a straight line away from him. That way, when he brought the hatchet down on it, he stood a better chance of splitting the thing in two. But when he touched the "head," it seemed to move in his hands as if it were a living thing! He pushed himself away from it in such a hurry that he toppled over backward, heels over head.

When he scampered back upright, he immediately realized what it was. The head wasn't alive at all. He had been chopping at it so hard that it had begun to resemble someone—someone he knew quite well. He almost laughed. The "head" now reminded him of the town librarian, Emma Prescott. He picked up his hatchet and took one last mighty swing at the thing. It split down the middle, from "forehead" to "chin," in two even pieces. They spun like coins on a tabletop before they settled down and stopped. He studied them in amazement. One half still looked like the nice old town librarian he had known ever since he could remember. But the other half gave him the shivers. It looked just as mean and wicked as the devil himself. He reacted to it without thinking and got right back down on his knees, chopping the evil-looking half until there was nothing left but a pile of chips! Somehow, that made him feel better—*safer*—than he had in a very long time.

CHAPTER FIFTEEN

It was shortly after one in the afternoon when Adams called from Mosstown to find out if Arthur had checked in with any news of what might have been discovered with Billy Chadwick's hound. He had half expected that Arthur would be up at Mosstown with the dog by now. Since he wasn't, Adams figured that something had turned up.

Ben shook his head and said he hadn't heard a word from Arthur since the deputy had left to pick up the hound in Hannerville. That was over three hours ago.

"Did you check with the vet up there?" Adams asked.

Ben nodded his head up and down. "Yep," he answered. "Did that just as soon as I figured Arthur should have been checking in. He had already picked up the dog before I called. Figuring the distance there and back, we should have heard something from him over an hour ago." Ben paused. He knew what was going through Adams's mind. "I checked with the highway people, too," he offered before Adams had a chance to ask. "They've heard nothing about an accident or anything like that. Neither have any of the hospital people over that way."

That seemed to narrow down the possibilities of what might have happened to Arthur to the one thing that Adams didn't even want to think about. He knew Arthur was as conscientious a man as there ever could be. He had strong family ties and was known all through the valley as a good man. He didn't smoke, he didn't drink, and the last thing on earth he would ever think of doing was to take up with another woman. His only weakness was attention to detail. Sometimes he went way overboard with it. But he liked his job and was thrilled with the notion that he was soon going to become a state trooper. So he would have called in, no matter what.

"Ben, is there any way you can contact the school to find out if they've seen the cruiser about? He was supposed to stop over that way."

At the other end Adams could hear Ben clear his throat. "Jeff," his deputy began, "I was about to tell you. I've already checked that out, about an hour ago. One of the teachers happened to be looking out the window and saw him leaving the school parking lot in the cruiser. He was after the boy's dog."

Adams leaned back against the glass wall of the highway telephone booth he was calling from. The roar of traffic wiped across his mind like the roll and crash of waves on a stony beach. Maybe that's it, he thought. Arthur was out behind the school, trying to pick up a scent with the hound, and . . . and either the dog broke loose and headed for home, or it had picked up a trail.

"I suppose you checked with the boy's parents to see if the hound showed up at home?"

"Yes," Ben replied. "It's not there."

The thought that Arthur was out there somewhere,

hurt, made Adams wince. He tried to console himself with the notion that the cruiser's call radio was broken. It had been down before. But somehow that didn't set his mind at ease. Neither had any of the answers Ben had just given to his questions. Adams knew Ben was as thorough as they come. If there had been anything at all to dispel the dark thought that something bad had happened to Arthur, Ben would have told him right out, without Adams having to ask a bundle of questions. But there was one more question, and he had to ask it. He felt compelled to plainly discover if his deputy shared the same dark thought he had.

"Ben," Adams said, "there's something wrong, isn't there?" He could feel his deputy searching for an appropriate response in the time it took for him to answer.

"Jeff," he finally began, "it's just a feeling, you know. I can't go ahead and quite put my finger on it, but something's not right. Arthur would have checked in by now, no matter what. That's the way he is. He's never neglected to do the right thing since I've known him. I'd be out looking for him right now if it wasn't that someone has to be here in case Hatcher calls again."

"He's called?" Adams asked with a heavy touch of incredulity in his tone, enough to signify that it might be a good idea if they got off the topic of Arthur's not calling and change the subject for a while. "What did he want?"

"He said he heard something about a kid who got killed in some sort of an automobile accident up in Mosstown. Someone had told him that the kid was from around these parts. He wanted to know if we had any details."

"What did you tell him?"

"I told him we hadn't heard anything about any kid getting killed in any car accident, but if we did, I'd be the first to give him a call about it."

"Jesus, Ben! Why the heck did you want to go ahead and put your behind on the line like that? You know he's gonna put it together real soon. That slob can eat us alive if he has a mind to."

"He does have a mind to, Jeff. But he hasn't done it yet. Ain't going to do it, either. The man's an ambitious pig and a liar to boot. It's only a matter of time before people begin to see what he really is."

"You're right about that, Ben. But before they do, he can still have our butts on a plate anytime he wants. I don't really think he can do me much harm, but he sure as blazes can wipe you out. If he calls again, give it to him straight."

"Even about Arthur?"

That stopped Adams for a moment. "We don't know anything about Arthur right now, Ben. The only thing we do know is that state regulations mandate we report a missing or wrecked cruiser within a couple of hours of discovery. Don't hide that from him, or anything else he's likely to find out on his own. So far, only the cruiser's missing. Period. You don't have to tell him anything about Arthur unless he specifically asks. And that's an order, Ben. Save your backside."

When Adams replaced the receiver he felt a distinct pang of nausea in the pit of his stomach. It wasn't all due to the conversation he just had with Ben. It also had something to do with the fact that he hadn't slept a wink last night and, he now suddenly realized, hadn't had anything to eat since early yesterday afternoon. While the thought of food didn't really appeal to him, he knew by the pounding headache he had that he'd better get something into him real soon. Across the road from the phone booth he could see the pound where the window of Betty's Volkswagen was being replaced. There was a country hamburger stand beside it. But what he really wanted to have was a drink. The desire for alcohol really troubled him, troubled him almost as much as the anger and frustration he felt about beginning to lose his grip on an investigation that was leading him deeper and deeper into despair. He knew if he ever again touched another drop of alcohol, it would be the end. He had won that battle once, right after he left Vietnam. He didn't know if he had the strength to ever win it again.

They both had a glass of milk, and there was a heap of fragrant buttermilk cookies, fresh from the oven, on a plate between them atop the kitchen table. Emma Prescott smiled at the sheriff's children and told them that when they finished their after-school snack they could begin doing their homework at the wide writing table in the living room, in front of the window that faced Betty Lineham's house—where she would be if they needed her for anything.

Kevin and Kathy could only nod to indicate that they had understood what Miss Prescott said. Their mouths were already stuffed with the first buttermilk cookies.

"Mmmm . . ." Kathy said after she had taken a gulp of milk to wash the cookie down. "How many can we have?" she asked, catching her breath and wiping away the milk-mustache with a paper napkin.

Kevin shot a look at her. If his sister hadn't asked such a fool question, they'd be able to eat them all! Now the librarian was sure to place a limit on the number they could have.

"You can have what you want," Emma Prescott said with a motherly warmth in her voice. "Just you make sure that there's some left for your dad when he comes home."

That was one limit on the number of cookies that Kevin didn't mind at all. He knew his dad liked Miss Prescott's cookies as much as he and Kathy did.

"When is he coming home?" Kevin asked. "Did he tell you?"

Emma shrugged her shoulders. "He said he'd be home early enough to fix your dinners himself tonight."

Kathy said, "Yuk."

Kevin stuck his tongue out and placed his hands about his throat as though he were choking. "Canned macaroni and beans," he said.

Kathy said yuk again, and reached for another cookie.

Emma Prescott laughed at their mocking. "Well," she finally said, pulling on her coat so she wouldn't catch a chill as she walked across the dooryard to Betty Lineham's house, "I expect to be hearing from your dad soon. I'll just tell him that I went ahead and fixed a chicken casserole supper for Mrs. Lineham next door, one that's big enough for everyone once he gets home. I suspect he'll be too tired to do any cooking, anyhow."

The children's eyes shone brightly at the thought of a

hot casserole supper.

"So don't stuff yourselves all the way up with cookies," Emma Prescott said. "And be sure to save a little pile of them for your dad, and maybe one or two for your school lunch tomorrow too."

Kevin quickly calculated the diminishing number of cookies in the plate. He scratched his forehead with the fingers of both hands as though he were tickling his eyebrows. "That means we can only have another one or two cookies more," he said.

"You get your A in math today!" the librarian quipped. "Besides, if either of you eat much more than that, you'll have the dickens of an ache in your stomachs."

"You can have the rest of mine," Kathy said to her brother, extending to him a soggy half-chewed cookie she had just removed from between her lips—lips that now quickly broadened into one of her playful pearly-tooth grins. "It's not even mushy," she added.

Kevin just sneered at her. "You're so smart," he said, and let it go at that. He had such good feelings for his little sister that usually anything she said or did to him was okay. "You just wait," he said with a wink. "I'll get you for that."

Both Kathy and Emma smiled. Neither of them believed for one moment that he ever would.

"Why did Mommy die?" Kathy asked as she and Kevin were doing their homework by the window in the living room.

Kevin had been looking up "air" in Volume I of the old set of encyclopedias his father had picked up at last summer's Lion's Club auction. His science homework was to tell, in his own words, what "air" was. Darn, if it ain't all that simple, he thought once he got into it. On the next page "Alexander The Great" loomed up far more interestingly than "air." He was reading about the conqueror with such attention that he hadn't heard his sister's question.

"I asked you something, Kevin."

He looked up at Kathy with a far-off expression in his eyes. He was still at some oasis in the middle of the desert where Alexander had gone to speak to an oracle, and he hadn't heard the question. But that was the thing about dictionaries and encyclopedias. You start to look for one single thing, then you have to go on and on, just to find out what the darn thing is talking about. And hang it all if you don't know how to spell what you're looking for to begin with!

"I said, why did Mommy die?" Kathy repeated.

Kevin closed his pencil in the encyclopedia and squinted. He realized that she had probably never asked that question before, not even of their own father. Many times, when a thought came to her, she would go to Kevin with it first. Then, if something about the answer didn't satisfy her, she would ask her dad. But it wasn't the same. Kevin knew how to explain things to her in a way that she understood it better. Not only that, but she could ask him anything and he would never act as though she were too little to know about what she had asked.

"She was sick," Kevin answered simply. "She caught cancer and went to the hospital. I don't remember it too good."

Kathy appreciated that; she didn't remember it at all.

But her eyes had widened at the word *cancer*. "Did Mommy smoke?" she asked.

Kevin shook his head. "Don't know," he responded.

Kathy saw the way his eyes were wandering back to the encyclopedia. "Daddy smokes," she said. "We better make him stop!"

She had said it so plainly that Kevin focused all his attention on her again. For a moment it was as though she were the grown-up and he were the little one. "He's our dad. Can't make him do what he doesn't want to."

"Maybe somebody's got to tell him he doesn't want to. If Mommy was here, bet she'd tell him!"

Kevin just stared at her. The shade of the old lamp was tilted in such a way that her eyes were in shadow. The light curved down from the bridge of her nose and spilled over the lower part of her small round face in a wash of whiteness. When she lowered her head back to her notebook, to continue with the math sums she had been doing, the light moved further up along her face. Kevin saw that there were small beads of tears strung into her eyelashes. It wasn't all about their mom that she had been asking about. Kevin knew she had been thinking of her best friend Jennifer, too.

Kevin thought suddenly that no matter whatever happened, he would love his sister—and that he would never, *never* let anything bad happen to her.

He looked out the window in front of them and, through the darkness outside, focused on the illuminated window of Betty Lineham's house. Through the lace curtains that covered it, he could see that Emma Prescott was standing there, looking over at them. She turned her head in profile and spoke something to Jennifer's mother, who was sitting in a chair at Emma

Prescott's side. The librarian's profile reminded him of something. Maybe it was the way that the pattern of the lace curtains shadowed across her face, but her profile reminded Kevin of the gnarled "head" he had so frantically hacked to pieces that afternoon. Something made him think that he'd better get down to the cellar right after his homework and file out the nicks and dullness he had put into the hatchet blade by doing it. A boy could never tell when he might need a real sharp hatchet inside his belt.

They sat there looking at one another from opposite sides of the office. Adams could hardly form the words that stung his thoughts like a shower of hailstones. It was almost six o'clock and he had just returned to the office from Mosstown, empty-handed, without a single clue as to who might have been responsible for Jennifer's brutal death. He hadn't even had time yet to check in with Emma Prescott to find out how she was doing with his children and Betty Lineham. He was slumped into the chair at his desk, looking exhausted and pale. His eyes had shifted away from Ben's and were now fixed on Arthur's desk. The emptiness of it gave him a cold feeling. He didn't like what he was thinking.

Both men knew something had gone wrong. Both men feared the worst. The only thing they could do was hope that they were wrong. That, and wait for the radio phone from the cruiser to ring in.

"He's never done anything like this before, has he?" Ben asked, knowing full well what the answer was.

Adams simply shook his head and tried to sort out

his own thoughts. He looked at the old pendulum clock that was ticking on the wall. Sometimes it seemed so loud that he had a mind to reach up and stop it. "The last you heard was that he had picked up the hound in Hannerville, and after that, someone saw him leave the school parking lot with the cruiser; he was after the dog, which was headed in this direction along the highway, is that right?" Adams asked.

"That's about right," Ben answered.

Adams squinted. His eyes were red. *"About* right?" he pressed. "What do you mean?"

Ben shrugged his shoulders before beginning. "Les Knowel, over toward Bannion, called in and said he heard something that sounded like an automatic pistol being emptied up in the hills behind his cabin. He couldn't tell where it was coming from, though. It echoed so bad."

Adams responded without thinking it out too clearly, the way a man who had not slept in almost two days would. "Hunting season's coming up in another couple of weeks. Maybe someone's getting a jump on it."

"It was a pistol Les said he heard. Nobody I know hunts with an automatic handgun."

Adams rubbed his eyes. "Jesus," he said. "I must be more tired than I thought." When he stopped rubbing his eyes, Ben saw how red they really were. "Bannion's on the other side of Tweed Hill," Adams finally said. "It's also between Mount Tom and Hunger Rock, and a half-dozen other hills that close in the valley. Shooting from any one of them would be difficult to trace, even with one of those fancy sonic devices that the state has."

Ben agreed. "I'd have gotten somebody out there hours ago if I thought something would come of it. But that would be just like sending someone into the woods to find one particular acorn. Those shots that Les heard could have come from someone practicing target at the gravel pit just down the road."

"What time did Les call in?" Adams asked.

"A little after one this afternoon, right after you called in from Mosstown."

The only thing that was beginning to make more and more sense to Adams was that something had indeed happened to Arthur. What that might be caused a knot of frustration to twist so tightly in his mind that without thinking he slammed his fist down on the desk, rattling everything on it.

The noise brought Ben to his feet. His nerves were none too steady, either. When Adams saw him standing there, looking at him as he tried to avert his eyes from Arthur's desk, he stood up, too. "Let's get us a cup of coffee and finish talking in the other room," he said. He pointed in the direction of the single jail cell. It had two cots opposite one another. Sometimes, to get away from the front of the office for a private talk, he'd take either of his deputies in there. Somehow, sitting on one of the cots with his feet up and back to the wall took the pressure off the whole business of being a sheriff.

Ben picked up the coffee pot that had been keeping warm on the wood stove and carried it into the other room where Adams had preceded him with two clean cups from the kitchen. Both of them drank their coffee black.

Adams took a sip and set the cup on the small table

beside the cot on which he sat. "Anything new about the pepper?" he asked. Earlier that morning Ben had mentioned he was going to check with some wholesalers.

Ben shook his head. "Nothing," he said. "There's only one distributor for such quantities of pepper in these parts and that's over in East Hartfield. Their record keeper was out today. No one there knew anything that might be useful." He glanced at his watch and frowned. "Someone was supposed to get back to me," he said. "That was over three hours ago."

As Ben had been speaking Adams took out a fresh pack of Camels, his second for the day. He lit one up and offered the pack to Ben. The deputy took one and lit it with a lighter from his shirt pocket.

"I don't think that pepper thing is going to pay off, anyway," Ben said after easing two vaporous snakes of smoke from his flared nostrils. "And it's too crazy to tell you what I think about it."

Adams frowned. "What are you talking about?" he asked. "Nothing's too crazy to consider when you're dealing with a mad killer."

Ben took another drag on the Camel and began. "You know I like to read a lot," he said. "Well, I read this Mafia book once. It told how they sometimes disposed of dead bodies. The lime pit is a standard. Even bones go to powder after a month or two of that. Sometimes they even plow their victims into a field with an industrial tiller. Gets them in pieces so small that crows have a feast. What's left is just fertilizer, bits and pieces so small and rotten that nothing could ever be traced to an actual person. Then they sometimes get someone from a pet food canning plant that owes them a favor." He shook his head. "Can you imagine someone's body turning up in a case or two of canned doggie chow?" he concluded, taking a drag on the Camel again.

Watching him inhale so deeply, Adams thought, probably for the thousandth time, that he should stop smoking. He snuffed out his own Camel in a tin can on the small table between them. The smoke was beginning to taste bad to him, anyway.

"What does all that have to do with crushed red pepper?" he finally asked.

"I was just getting to that," Ben said. "They use it, a whole sackful at a time, to cover a corpse—just so hound dogs or other critters won't go digging it up out of a grave."

As tired and as frustrated as Adams was, he almost broke into a grin. "Ben," he said. "You don't mean to tell me that you think the Mafia has something to do with all this, do you?"

"No, not really. What I'm saying is if we ever find those missing children alive, that'll be fine. But what do you imagine they will say when asked where they've been?" He paused as though he had made a point. "The Mafia is also in the business of kidnapping and selling little children, you know."

"But not killing them, Ben. A dead child is not worth anything to anyone."

Ben thought about that for a moment. It was good to have his mind on something other than the disappearance of his fellow deputy. Adams felt it, too.

"You know something," Ben finally said; it was not a question. "What we could be dealing with is a person who knows a lot of mean things from television or reading."

"Like you?" Adams couldn't resist the tease.

Ben drew back, taking it good-naturedly. "No," he said. "Not like me. Like someone neither of us, or anybody else, would ever in a thousand years suspect."

"Doctor, lawyer, Indian . . ." Adams began.

". . . teacher, minister, saint!" Ben finished. He stamped out his cigarette on the sole of his shoe before dropping it into the can on the table. It hit bottom with a plink, as though to punctuate what he had just finished saying.

Adams liked Ben a lot. He thought he had some quirks, like him wanting to connect the missing children with some sort of Mafia thing. But the man was as good as he was willing to go out on a limb with some foolish notion. He was about to change the subject back to Arthur when the phone in the office rang. If it had been the cruiser's radio phone, he would have leaped for it. But a regular line call coming in at this hour could only mean that it was the state. And, as though to confirm his suspicion, Ben said, half beneath his breath, "I forgot to tell you, Jeff. Hatcher's secretary has been trying to reach you all day."

"I'll get this one," Adams said, pulling himself from the cot. "They're probably wondering where I've been." He turned to Ben before leaving the cell. "You didn't tell them I was up at Mosstown, did you?"

Ben made a sign with both hands moving in opposite directions across the tops of his knees as he remained seated. It looked like an umpire's signal that a player had slid safely into home plate. What it meant was that he had not told *anyone* where Adams had been all day.

This time it was Reid Hatcher himself on the phone.

"Where the hell've you been?" he asked as soon as Adams answered the phone. "My secretary's been trying to reach you all day."

"Working out in the field today," Adams responded. He offered no further details.

Hatcher went right to the heart of it. "Anything new on the cruiser yet?" he asked. "I saw the report that your deputy dictated to central records. What happened with it?"

Adams began a controlled sizzle. "You know, Reid, that's none of your business—not unless you're looking for something that's going to get you into my investigation. I don't have to report to you about anything right now, and I'm not going to. If you want to go over my head, you go right ahead and do it."

He listened for a response, but none came. All he heard was the quiet sound of Hatcher's receiver hanging up on him. There was something else, too, something that sounded to him like a soft chuckle just before the line went dead. He didn't like that. It made the back of his neck as hot as the flame he could see licking out of the crack in the corner of the wood stove's door.

"Ben," he said, turning to his deputy who was now standing beside him. "Do me a favor and put all the files—everything we've collected so far on the investigation—into a box for me. And, I know this is asking a lot, but I'd like you to stay here tonight in case anything turns up on Arthur."

Ben nodded. "I already called my wife on that," he said. "A neighbor's on his way here right now with my supper. So I'll be okay. I'll call you the minute something comes in."

"I'll probably be up all night too, working on the files. The phone's right beside me. Maybe there's something in those reports we missed. There has to be a clue somewhere."

By the time he called Emma Prescott at Betty Lineham's house and told her he was on his way home, Ben had the box of files collected. It consisted of a dozen or so thin folders, affidavits, and official reports. Somewhere in all of that there had to be some kind of an answer as to what was going on.

"I'll tell you one thing, Ben. If nothing comes of all this tonight, I may not wait for Hatcher and his boys to come storming in on their own. I'll probably ask them in myself. Things had been so quiet for a while. Then suddenly it's Billy Chadwick, Jennifer Lineham, and—and I don't like this new thing about Arthur . . . all one right after the other like that. It's got me scared. Things are happening too fast. I don't know if we have what it takes to go on with it by ourselves."

He was out the door before Ben could say a word. He didn't want to hear another thing tonight. Not from anyone. He clutched the box of files under his arm as though it were a life preserver that had been tossed to a drowning man. It felt like a straw, but he had to try.

CHAPTER SIXTEEN

When Adams pulled into the driveway next to his house he could see that Emma Prescott's pickup was parked across the way, next to Betty Lineham's front door. He assumed the librarian was still there but went first to his own house so he could greet his children. He knew they were inside because of all the lights that were on. The front door was locked. With the box of files in his arms he didn't feel like grappling for the keys in his pocket, so he simply walked around to the back porch where the kitchen door was always open. It too was locked. If it weren't for the fact that he was so tired he would have figured it out quicker. Instead, it took a moment for him to realize that when Emma had gone to Betty's, she had probably locked Kevin and Kathy inside while they were doing their homework. No one without a key could get in. He liked that.

He put the box of files down on the floor and searched his pockets for his keys. When he couldn't find them he knocked at the door. He could hear the children in the kitchen. From the sound of knives and forks against their plates, it seemed as if they were having a good go at the casserole supper Emma had told him about on the phone when he called her before leaving the office. His knock on the door had finally raised a silence inside.

"What's the password?" he heard Kevin ask from the other side of the door.

"It's your dad," Adams said, lifting the box of files back up into his arms. "O-o-o-o-pen ol' sesame!"

Kevin unlatched the door and swung it open. "That's not the password," he said. "But I knew who you were."

Once Adams placed the box of files on a chair that was just inside the door, he walked over to Kathy at the table and gave her a big hug. "What's all this about a password?" he asked.

Kathy quickly gulped down the food that was in her mouth so she could answer before her brother. "Miss Prescott doesn't have a key," she began. "So she told us a password she would say when she wanted to get back in." Then she took another spoonful of the chicken casserole that the librarian had prepared. "Miss Prescott said it was okay to start without you," she said, swallowing quickly. "There's even some yummy cookies in the tin on the counter."

"The rest of the casserole is in the oven on low," Kevin said once he had seated himself at the table again. "Miss Prescott said you should get to it before it all dries out."

"Well, I'll do just that," Adams said, getting up to remove his jacket before taking a clean plate from the cabinet above the stove. "What's the password she gave you, anyhow?" he asked, opening the oven. "Might be that I should know it."

"Hiccup!" Kathy replied, again before her brother could respond. She looked at him and smiled.

"Hiccup!" Adams said. "That's more like something you *do,* not say."

"When you *do* it, you *say* it," Kathy replied with a giggle.

Somehow that wiped all the frustration and weariness out of Adams's mind for a moment, and he couldn't help smiling. It was the first good feeling he had had in the last couple of days. "Come here," he said, sitting down beside her with his plate of food. "I want to eat those freckles off your nose. Bet they're just as sweet as a bunch of chocolate-covered ants."

Kevin pretended he was choking as he watched his father kiss the bridge of Kathy's nose. "Chocolate-covered ants!" he mocked. "Yucko."

Adams leaned back. It was all so good to be there with his children, teasing about like they were. He had never thought they'd have to be starting their suppers without him—and behind locked doors, too. When he was a boy, most people in the valley didn't even *have* locks on their doors. No one back then ever felt the need for them. But times were different now, and he was thankful that Emma Prescott had been wise enough to lock up when she wasn't around to watch them. She'd have made someone a real proud wife and mother, he thought. Too bad she never married and had children of her own. She sure knew how to care for them.

Emma Prescott didn't like the way she was feeling. The dishes were all washed and put away, and Betty Lineham was sitting in her favorite chair in the living room, staring ahead of her at nothing in particular, just like a zombie. But it was Emma Prescott who *felt* like a zombie. It was a feeling that was becoming more and more familiar to her. She felt like someone who was trapped inside her own head, as though the soul of some perfect stranger had somehow managed to sneak inside of her a long time ago and now it didn't know how to get out, no matter how desperately it attempted to do so.

The fears and doubts Emma Prescott felt about herself divided themselves equally in half. Then those uneasy thoughts divided themselves still further. Soon there was a whole chorus of jumbled words going through her mind like a furious chant. Some of the words rose more distinctly above the others: *kill . . . mother . . . demented bitch . . . die!* If it weren't for the fear she had of scaring the rest of the life out of Betty Lineham, Emma would have started to prance up and down. Sometimes that made the voices go away. But she didn't have to do that tonight. Just as soon as the doorbell rang and Adams let himself into the vestibule, Emma's thoughts quieted to a point where it was suddenly as though there had never been any words shouting themselves in her head at all. They vanished as if by magic.

"How are things?" Adams asked as he entered the living room where Betty and Emma were sitting.

"Just fine," Emma answered. "How was the casserole? Kathy and Kevin tell you about the cookies?"

Adams thanked her for making the supper and told her that the kids were real good about the cookies. They even managed to save a few for their school lunch tomorrow.

Betty stared at him as he spoke. She seemed a lot

worse than when he had driven her home from the hospital that morning. He suspected it had something to do with the fact that Jennifer's funeral was going to take place in the morning. He also felt that she had made a difficult decision not to see her daughter's body at the hospital morgue. She had wanted to remember her alive, "reading" a copy of *The Yearling* as they drove in the Volkswagen only the day before. Now that the sedatives that were first administered to her at the hospital were almost out of her system, the shock of it all was penetrating to the core of her soul like a bar of cold-rolled steel.

Adams examined her eyes for a moment as he sat himself down in an easy chair opposite her. There was hurt in them. He expected that. But there was something else, too, something that showed concern for things other than her own hurt.

"How is Kathy taking it?" she asked. "Has she asked you about Jennifer yet?"

The question almost stopped his breathing. He had always known her to be a strong person, but to be concerned for the feelings of her dead daughter's best friend, at a time like this, showed even more metal than he ever thought she had.

There was something about Betty's question to Adams that made Emma Prescott suddenly want to get out of there in a hurry. She didn't know what that might be, but it was as though there were something terribly urgent she ought to be doing. Every cell in her body began to vibrate. It felt as if she were coming apart. If she sat there another moment, she thought she would scream.

Before Adams had a chance to answer Betty's

question, Emma rose to her feet and excused herself. "Guess I should be going over to your place to tuck the children in," she said to Adams. "Maybe read them a story."

Adams looked at her. It was almost eleven o'clock. He had put the children to bed almost two hours ago. Emma knew what time they turned in during a school night. But he smiled at her. "Did that myself a while ago, Emma. Guess the time has gotten away from you."

Emma never wore a watch. She glanced at the wall clock beside the stone fireplace. "Goodness!" she said. "It certainly has." She shrugged her shoulders in a gesture that indicated she didn't know where the time went. "In that case," she finally said, "I'll go back home and read *myself* a story."

Even Betty smiled at that. "Emma," she said as the librarian walked to the vestibule where her coat was hung. "I don't know what I would have done without you today. Thank you for coming by and helping out. I appreciate it more than I can say."

Emma was touched. She walked back to Betty as she slipped her arms into the sleeves of her coat and kissed her on the cheek. "You never mind about that," she said to Betty. "Helping folks gives me pleasure. I'll be here any time you need me." She walked back to the vestibule and reached for the door. "Just you give me a call, anytime." Then she was gone.

Adams shook his head as he listened to the roar of the pickup's engine turning over. Through the window he could see her struggling to put it into gear. When she let the clutch out the pickup smoothly backed away from the house and onto the road. It then nosed its way down the hill toward the main highway. Emma lived less than a quarter of a mile away.

"So, how *is* Kathy taking it?" Betty asked once Adams refocused his attention on her.

He chewed the inside of his upper lip. He didn't want to tell her how his daughter had broken down and cried herself to sleep in his arms. His eyes wandered to the window beside her as he tried to think of something to say. Through the lace curtains he could see the lights on in his house, just the way he had left them. He had even remembered to take the keys with him so he could get back in.

Betty did not press for a response. His silence answered the question. And for a long while after that, there was more silence. Neither of them knew the words that might possibly lead them back to the comfort they usually felt in the presence of one another. It seemed there was a time now for something more than words, but neither of them could bring themselves to express it—not tonight.

He had before him a photograph of each child that had been reported missing from the valley over the past year. There were almost a dozen of them. They ranged in age from six to ten. There were almost as many boys as there were girls. Among them there were only two known dead. The others? Adams dreaded to think about it.

He looked at the photographs he had in his hands and shuffled through them. They were pictures that had either been removed from a family's photo album or had come from school photos. They were all the last pictures ever to be taken of each child. On the back of each photo Adams had written a few simple statistics: name, age, height, weight, color of eyes, unusual physical characteristics, and a description of the clothing they were wearing when last seen. He could hardly hold his eyes on the picture of Jennifer. It seemed to burn in his hand as hotly as his tired eyes.

He was worn out. He had been at the box of files ever since having returned from Betty Lineham's house. It was now almost 3 A.M., and he hadn't heard a word from Ben who was spending the night on one of the cots in the empty jail cell. They had spoken only an hour ago, and there was still no word as to what might have happened to Arthur. The deputy's wife was already beside herself with worry. Adams knew that Ben would be getting as little sleep as he would that night.

Betty Lineham's lights were out now. The part of the house that faced him went dark not too long after he returned to his own house. He wished he were with her now, holding her in his arms as she slept against him. From where he sat, he couldn't tell if the light in her upstairs bedroom was on or off. He hoped she had managed to find some rest.

He put the pictures of the children aside for a moment and removed a single sheet of paper from the box. It was a one-page report from the FBI's National Crime Information Center, a computerized system that can be used by local law enforcement agencies throughout the country to report cases of missing persons. It told him that a couple of years back the system received reports of over two hundred thousand cases of missing children! Although a vast majority of them had been located—it didn't tell whether dead or alive—it concluded that the system showed evidence of the existence of over twenty-eight thousand cases of children missing at any one particular time. It was a figure difficult for him to grasp. It was over three times that of the entire population of his state's capital.

Where the heck *are* those kids? he wondered. A clipping from *U.S. News and World Report* placed the long-term missing child population at a probable two hundred thousand. He thought of Ben's theory of a Mafia connection, and he shook his head. He just didn't know.

Adams didn't seem able to think clearly anymore. His eyes ached with tiredness. He had to close them for a few minutes, just so he could rest them. There were so many more reports that he wanted to go through tonight: interviews with the friends, relatives, teachers, and parents of each missing child, as well as copies of all the official records and reports that had been submitted to the state. If there was anything in that box of files that he had missed before, he was determined to dig it out tonight. But with two more days—going on three—without any sleep at all, his eyes were heavy. It wasn't long before the struggle to keep them open began to fail. If he could only sleep a few minutes, he told himself, like he used to do in the army, maybe . . . maybe . . .

CHAPTER SEVENTEEN

For the past several nights, ever since he had that bad dream about being turned into a doll, along with his sister and her best friend Jennifer, Kevin had been wearing his clothes to bed. He knew it was weird. But he couldn't help it. He felt he had to be ready for . . . *something.* He would have kept his sneakers on, too, but he thought that would have been too much, even for him. Instead, he placed them on a chair beside his bed, right where he could rest his hand on them as he fell asleep.

Maybe it was all his getting ready for that unknown *something* that caused it. He didn't know. But since he had begun to wear his clothes to bed, he once woke to find himself walking about his room in the middle of the night. The odd thing about it was that it didn't seem to frighten him. He merely pulled his sneakers back off, placed them on the chair beside the bed again, and got back under the covers, pulling them well up to his chin so that if his dad ever did come into the room he wouldn't know he still had all his clothes on beneath the bed covers.

Tonight, at the same moment that his father had

fallen asleep over the files in the living room, Kevin opened his eyes. He was still asleep but somehow managed—as he had during his one other sleepwalking experience—to slip into his sneakers without waking himself up. He had been dreaming of the "killer tree" and the "head" he had hacked into two separate pieces earlier that afternoon. This time it wasn't only one half of the gnarled "head" that resembled Emma Prescott. As the pieces whirled about in his dream they formed a whole, and it looked more and more like the town librarian than ever before.

He walked in a circle about his bedroom as though he could see perfectly in the darkness. Nothing got in his way. His eyes were opened and it appeared as though he were fully awake, except that his hands were out before him, palms faced outward in any direction he turned, as though they were sensing devices to guide him through the dark. As he approached the wall opposite his bed, his arms drew in until his elbows touched either side of his waist. Then he stopped, turned at a sharp right angle, and proceeded to the other wall, against which there was a dresser. Again his arms drew in and he turned. He continued in this fashion until he had gone about the room a half-dozen times, never once bumping into anything and never once making a sound.

He was at the center of the room now, at the spot where he had awakened the last time he walked in his sleep. But this time he didn't. He simply stood there, swaying slightly from side to side with his hands out before him. The expression on his face was completely blank. The pale light of the moon filtering in through the window washed across him a like a thin film of electric-blue. He looked like a ghost.

Then something registered itself across his face as though a deeply buried thought had suddenly risen to the surface of his consciousness. His eyes flickered and he began to walk toward the bed. Instead of getting back in, he reached one hand beneath the pillow and pulled out the hatchet he had sharpened and honed to a razor-sharp edge before going to bed. It glistened in a crack of moonlight as he rose with it in his hand. He turned and walked with it to the door. There, he hesitated for a moment until he worked his hand down the jamb and grasped the knob. It twisted easily and he was out into the hallway and on his way to the kitchen with a sureness of foot that appeared as though he were fully awake.

His father was sleeping over the pile of files at the table by the living room window and didn't see the boy pass from the darkened hallway to the kitchen, where the lights had been left on. When Kevin got there he went directly to the porch door and unlatched it. He was outside and into the chill of the night without a sound.

The breath escaping from his nostrils vaporized in the cold air as he slowly walked down the road toward the post office. It was after 3 A.M. He had never been out that late before, but it didn't matter. He was sleeping and the only thing that registered upon his unconscious thoughts was the dream he was having. He was after the killer!

Right after passing the post office, he had to cross an old steel and wooden bridge in order to get to the main highway. The river pounded against the boulders beneath him. So, too, did the loose creosote planks beneath his sneakers. They thumped against the steel frame of the bridge as he walked, making the same noise an automobile would, only much quieter. When he reached the highway he made a sharp turn and headed north along the shoulder of the road. It was only a short distance from there to the house where Emma Prescott lived.

She was not at home. The itch that Emma Prescott had inwardly felt earlier in the night while she was still at Betty Lineham's house, the sensation that something urgent had to be done, had later materialized into full bloom. She was now in her battered old pickup, winding her way up the abandoned logging trail to the isolated cabin at the end of it. A thick ground fog swirled about the beam of her headlights and obscured all but a few feet at a time in front of her. But she knew the path well. Emma had made this trip so many times before that she knew every rock and deadfall like the back of her own hand. Nothing could make her falter from the path, even the thickest downpour. The only thing that might possibly stop her would be snow. Maybe it was the threat of it that drove her on so vigorously tonight. Snow would kill any hope she ever had of completing her macabre doll collection—a collection that had to be completed before . . . before *what* she wondered as the twisted trail thickened with fog. Before she went *completely* mad? Before they came to take her away, like they did her mother?

At a turn in the path, just before a steep upgrade where she always had to downshift and apply more gas, she was forced to a sudden halt. Just ahead, in the tunnel of light that poured from the pickup's headlamps, she could see the police cruiser that Arthur Winston had abandoned there earlier that afternoon.

"What in blazes . . . ?" she wondered out loud. But her amazement subsided just as quickly as the whirring of her engine had when she came to a full stop, only inches from the rear bumper of the police car.

She stared at it through the windshield of her pickup as though it might have been a prank of some sort, a circus elephant that someone had tied to a tree beside the path, just to get a rise out of her. She cackled as though it were the funniest thing she had ever seen. It almost made her forget the burning mission that had compelled her to leave the library and drive up to the cabin that night.

"Go on!" she howled at the cruiser. "Scat! Can't you see a body's got to pass? Things to be done, don't ya know?"

The fog rose from the brook down at the bottom of the steep embankment beside the trail and rubbed against the cruiser like the fingers of a giant hand. To Emma it looked as though the cruiser had been turned into a living thing. She didn't like it. The only living thing that had been up that way in almost a century had been her. Only her and her dolls.

"Get going I said!" she screamed as she slipped the engine back into gear. "Or I'll ram you back into the bush!"

Her foot slipped off the clutch and the pickup lurched forward. It struck the cruiser and caused both its front wheels to leave the edge of the trail, just far enough to make it pivot off balance and send it crashing down the embankment. It didn't stop until it landed in the brook at the bottom. All Emma could see was that it had vanished from the trail before her very eyes. Magic! she thought.

"Let that be a lesson to ya!" she shouted into the swirling mist as she revved up her engine for the steep turn just ahead. "Nobody plays a prank on ol' Emma."

Even though she wore a grin after that, there was something deep inside of her that quietly whispered she had played a prank upon herself, had been playing pranks on herself ever since she was a little girl.

"QUIET!" she shrieked. "You don't know what you're talking about!" She looked to the side, where the voice appeared to be coming from. Seated next to her was her mother! Just as though she were still alive. Only it wasn't her mother. Even in Emma's ravaged state of mind she could see that. It was *herself*—just like the vision she had seen reflected back at her from the fogged-up mirror in the bathroom that morning. It was herself, but it was her mother, too. She shook her head. It didn't matter, she told herself. It never had.

I love you, dearest, the phantom said. *Too bad you're crazier than anything I ever used to be.*

Emma Prescott hurled her arm out at the mirage. It disappeared with a quiet chuckle when her tightened fist passed right through it and struck the empty seat beside her.

"Damn you!" she hissed, shaking her hand and blowing her foul breath on the knuckles—the knuckles of the same hand she had used to smash in the window of Betty Lineham's Volkswagen. It stung like blazes.

"I'm better than you, Mother!" she cried out into the emptiness of the pickup's cab. "Better than you ever were or could ever be! You had no imagination,

Mother! All you wanted to do was to keep those old wooden dolls of yours all to your very own self. You didn't know how to make them live . . . make them come alive through the blood of little children. Your body produced me, Mother. But my hands and my mind produce *my* children! You're an imposter! Do you hear me, Mother? You're a fraud! A demented old BITCH!"

One wheel of the pickup left the trail and the other was headed toward doing the very same thing when she regained control of the battered old vehicle and brought all four of its wheels back onto the narrow trail. "You'll do anything to stop me," she said in the tone of someone who had almost been defeated but had somehow miraculously triumphed. "Anything at all. Won't you?"

There was no response. The momentum to accomplish what she had come this far up into the hills for now whipped her into a frenzy. Nothing could stop her. In the beam of her headlights the cabin loomed up before her like the enchanted vision of her most cherished dream. She knew she had won. She was home, and there was important work to be done.

Kevin marched in place before the door of Emma Prescott's empty house. His body rocked gently from side to side as he lifted one foot after the other in a slow-motion gate, like that of a saddle-bred pony prancing in place. The breath poured from his nostrils in clouds of vapor. He did not feel the cold. In his hand he held the hatchet above his head, ready to strike the first person to emerge from the front door of the town library. He was still alseep, still dreaming of the spinning halves of the gnarled "head" of the "killer tree."

With wide, unblinking eyes he drank in what was before him and transformed everything into abstractions that became the core of his nightmare. The Doric columns that rose from the front steps of the library, supporting a canopy that resembled the rounded prow of a schooner, became the grappling arms of the "killer tree." The front door, with the low moon reflected in the center of its large glass pane, twisted and turned with each draft of wind and became the killer's icy-white heart. And above that, where a barn swallow had made her nest on the ledge of a cornice and had long ago abandoned it to the approaching winter, the moonlight dappled an eerie shadow that became the killer's head. If anything made the slightest move toward him, he would kill it, whatever it was. That's why he was there. That's why he had sharpened his hatchet.

Something suddenly flashed across his unconscious thoughts like a quick and hurried burst of something bright. It gave birth in his mind to a hazy reality, a realization of that unknown something he had been getting ready for ever since the nightmares began. The monster who had chased him and his sister through the woods lived in the house he was standing before. It was the library house in which Miss Prescott lived and worked. *She* was the one who caught little Jennifer and turned her into a doll. *She* was the mad killer.

Something jabbed into his unconscious thoughts like the point of a hot needle. It left a speck of something dark encoded there, something that might possibly trigger a memory after he woke up. "She has to be stopped" something whispered out of the darkness of his dream. "Stopped before she kills anyone else!" And with that, somehow, came the knowledge that he was the only one capable of doing it.

It was the most delightful surprise Emma Prescott had ever had. As she approached the abandoned old cabin at the end of the logging trail, in the beam of her headlights she saw that the front door had been opened. Her eyes widened in anticipation as she stopped the pickup and cautiously stepped from its cab with a flashlight in her hand. Something inside her head screamed for joy when she saw the body of deputy Arthur Winston just inside the door. The heavy broadaxe had caught him squarely in the middle of the forehead and the look of surprise was still to be read in his wide open eyes. She played the beam of her flashlight directly into them. They remained dilated.

Her heart was beating faster than she had ever known it to do. It was the first time she had ever killed an adult, and the feeling that ran through her blood was like a raging fire that had gone out of control. She would have liked very much to abandon herself to the glorious blaze of it, but there was other work to be done, other chores to be completed. As she yanked the axe from the dead deputy's head and dragged him down off the porch of the cabin and around to the back of it, she cursed his intrusion, for now the work would have to wait until she could dispose of him.

She left the deputy's body on the ground in the clearing of her private graveyard and went back to the cabin to fetch a shovel, a lantern, and a sack of pepper. When she returned, she began to dig furiously at the ground with a vigor that only a person in the clutches of an intense madness could muster. A night creature, hearing the first slice of her shovel cutting into the earth, let out a screech and scurried through the fallen leaves on the forest floor until the sound of it disappeared into the deeper darkness of the woods. Emma's spade didn't skip a beat. It sliced and poked and burrowed and emptied itself in a rhythm that was like music to her soul. When she thought the hole was finished, she dragged the deputy's body by the heels and slid him into it. She had been used to digging graves for small children and hadn't properly gauged the extent of the effort necessary to bury a full grown man. He sat in the hole as though it were a shallow pot. His arms and shoulders hung out the sides of it, and his knees and legs remained above the ground on the opposite side. "Damn!" she said half to herself. "Guess I'll have to do better than that!" She hauled him out, squatting with both feet planted firmly on either side of his shoulders and lifting him by the armpits. The strain of it would probably leave her muscles sore for days, but she was worked up to a fever and couldn't think things out as clearly as she usually did. There was a doll that needed to be finished before dawn, and she had the feeling that tomorrow was going to be the last day she'd ever have before the snows began to fall.

Emma dug faster. When she thought the hole was now large enough to bury a deer, she dug for another fifteen minutes at the sides of it, just to make sure. Then she climbed out and shoved the deputy in. He disappeared into the darkness of the pit as though the earth had swallowed him up. "Now that's a darn sight better!" she said, congratulating herself. "All you need now is a cozy cover." And she filled him in, pepper and all.

She was about to head back to the cabin when she came upon a sight that startled her. A grave that she knew had been freshly dug and covered had been opened. In the darkness the beam of her flashlight played across the other graves. No other one had been disturbed. She approached the open grave and saw what it was that had probably brought the deputy up to the cabin. Inside the dug-up grave of Billy Chadwick was the boy's hound dog. It had bled profusely across the body of the little boy before it had died. She frowned. So that's what Arthur was poking about these parts for, she thought. Well, I'll just bury it in, like it was before, she told herself. And that, too, she did with great speed. When it was finished she stood back for a moment and squatted to skim the ground of the small clearing with the beam of her flashlight. Everything, with the exception of the deputy's new grave and that of Billy Chadwick's, looked as it had before. Maybe one day, when all her work was finished, she thought she might then have time to erect little grave markers for the children who were buried there. But not tonight, she told herself. There was much yet to be done.

When she got back to the front of the cabin she left the shovel beside the door and went inside with the lantern. After resetting the booby trap on the front door, she lit the candles that were on top of all the doll boxes. The dance of candlelight penetrated the sheets of dusty glass that covered the front of each box and appeared to make the delicately carved features of the dolls come alive. The sight of it always made her feel better. They were her children—her very own.

She carried the lantern to the workbench in front of the window and placed it beside the doll she had driven up to the cabin to finish. It appeared to smile at her as she worked on its face with a thin paintbrush of color. For some curious reason, the doll's smile troubled her. It had never happened with any of the other dolls. She looked up for a moment at the darkened window before her. In it she saw the candlelit reflection of the dolls in their boxes. A chill shot across the back of her neck. It looked as though the dolls were actually twisting about beneath the sheets of glass that covered them. They wanted to get out, she thought. Now, why would they want to do a thing like that? she wondered. Didn't she love them better than anything else on earth?

She shrugged it off and turned her attention back to completing the doll of her next little victim. It continued to smile at her in a way that was almost mocking.

"Well, my little miss. We'll wipe that smirk off your lips right this minute." She dipped her thin brush in a dish of red paint that was beside the lantern and touched its needlelike point to each corner of the doll's lips. The "smirk" instantly vanished.

"Now, that's more like it," Emma Prescott said. "Don't you ever look at me like that again. I'm gonna be your mommy now. First thing tomorrow. You just wait and see."

In the wavering light of the lantern the doll appeared to lose more and more of its life as Emma continued to work on it. But to the demented woman it looked as wonderful as anything she had ever done—a perfect likeness of the child it was meant to represent. It was a girl doll, and it looked exactly like Kathy Adams.

A single flake of snow fell from the darkened sky like a star, landing on the tip of Kevin Adams's nose. It rested there briefly, in all its intricate glory, before dissolving. Without waking, his tongue licked out at the speck of coolness that then rolled to the corner of his lips. It was the only snow that fell. Not another flake of it would fall again that night.

It wasn't the snowflake that caused him to turn and leave the front of Emma Prescott's house. It was something else, something that quietly urged him to get back home. He had to be with his sister. All that seemed to matter was that she needed him, and he had to protect her.

It was almost 5 A.M., and the sky was still black by the time he reached home. He had slipped the hatchet handle into the loop of his belt and, with his hands out before him, walked in his sleep up the steps of the back porch without faltering. He entered the kitchen and latched the door so that it was locked. Then he walked to his sister's bedroom and stood before it for a moment before reaching for the door knob and twisting it.

Adams lifted his head from the reports he had fallen asleep on. He thought he heard something in the kitchen and went to investigate. Had he done so a moment sooner he would have bumped right into Kevin as the boy entered Kathy's bedroom. In the kitchen he tested the door latch and looked around.

Everything was just as he had left it, lights on and all. He looked at the clock and saw that it was just 5 A.M. He decided to make a pot of coffee before waking Ben with a call to the office.

When Kevin entered Kathy's bedroom he slowly walked about the room. He passed in front of the windows, made a turn by the bed, and remained at the foot of it. His body swayed back and forth as he stood there, softly lifting one foot after the other in the same slow-motion prance as when he had stood before Emma Prescott's house, only this time he did not withdraw his hatchet and hold it above his head.

He hadn't been there very long before a familiar noise from the kitchen caused him to wake up. For a moment he thought he was in his own room and that the same thing as had happened the other night, when he first walked in his sleep, had happened again. It was still dark and the familiar noise from the kitchen was quickly identified as his father fixing a pot of coffee in the old Silex. It was only when he was about to climb back into the bed he thought was his own that he realized his sister was in it. He wondered what on earth she was doing in his bed. It was with a start that he then understood he was not in his own room at all.

Kathy stirred but did not wake. Through the window, Kevin could see that the sky was just beginning to turn gray. In a little while his father would be calling them for breakfast. He went to the door and cautiously peeked out. The way was clear. He returned to his own room and got back into bed as noiselessly as he had left it less than two hours before. It was then that he felt the cold. He touched his hands to his cheeks and they were icy. So were his clothes, which he still had on beneath the covers. He touched the sneakers on the chair beside the bed and they were cold too, as though he had been wearing them outside. They even smelled of fresh earth, like when he worked in the garden with his father.

For the next several minutes, as he attempted to search through the darkness of his thoughts in an attempt to figure out what had happened, his body warmed. And with the flow of it came the memory of a dream. But it was only that—that he had had a dream—and that was all. No matter how hard he tried, he couldn't remember anything about it. That somehow caused him to feel a sickness in the pit of his stomach, as though he were falling out of a tree. His body jerked, and he almost came fully awake again. But the soft comfort of the warmth that had overtaken him urged him further and further back into the darkness of the dream he had been struggling so hard to remember. If he could just let himself go, he drowsily thought, maybe it would all come back to him. It seemed terribly important. He had to remember.

CHAPTER EIGHTEEN

It rained when everyone had expected snow. The funeral mass for Jennifer Lineham was over, and almost half of the townspeople were now gathered at the small hillside cemetery that overlooked the valley. A field of umbrellas dappled the site like a crop of black mushrooms in the heavy downpour. Since the plot in which the child was to be buried was at a corner of a cluster of grave sites, the minister had suggested that everyone remain in their automobiles. They could then form an open angle about the grave while he conducted a brief service, after which the small white casket would be lowered into the ground. But, as the minister had suspected, his congregation would have none of it. What was a good soaking to folks whose roots went all the way back to the early settlers of the valley—men, women, and children who toiled in every sort of weather imaginable?

An awning, just wide enough to cover the open grave and barely broad enough to shelter the minister and Betty Lineham, shed the rain from its edges in sheets. It reminded Adams of the vinyl casing that had surrounded Betty's Volkswagen in the factory parking lot at Mosstown. He stood to the side beneath his umbrella, with Kathy and Kevin huddled close beside him. School had been cancelled for the morning so that the children could attend the services. The yellow school bus was parked down at the gate of the cemetery, waiting to take the children back to school. Beside it was the larger bus that had been hired to transport the chorus of the upper school to the site. They had hurriedly rehearsed "Amazing Grace" all morning and were now taking their places behind the minister. They all wore the yellow rain slickers that a local merchant had donated to the school's marching band.

Kathy clung to her father's arm. It couldn't be discerned if the wetness on her face came from the tears that she was shedding or from the rain that splattered at her like arrows from a nearby tombstone. Adams looked down at her and pulled her closer to his side. When he turned to see how Kevin was, he saw that the boy was staring off in a direction that was to the side of the grave site. He followed the boy's line of vision to see what he was looking at, and saw that it was Emma Prescott. Adams couldn't imagine why Kevin had such an expression of troubled concern knotted in his brow. He thought it might have something to do with the boy's way of deflecting the grief he was feeling.

Adams turned his attention to Betty Lineham who sat alone in the only chair that was beneath the canopy. She had insisted on a quick burial. The only family she had left was a sick and aging mother who lived over seven hundred miles away in Pennsylvania. She hadn't yet spoken to her about what had happened. It would probably be several more weeks before she could bring herself to do so.

Adams bent his knees so that he could talk to Kathy without shouting. "Would you like to come with me and stand by Betty?" he asked.

For the first time since they had been there, Kathy's little face brightened. "Can we?" she replied.

Adams shook his head. "Yes," he said. "I think she would like it very much." He turned to Kevin and asked the same thing. "How about it?" he concluded.

Kevin's eyes came back to his father's as though the boy had just returned from long wandering thought. Adams felt a bit uneasy about it. Kevin had also acted strangely at breakfast. He wasn't his usual self these days. Maybe he was taking the death of little Jennifer harder than he thought. And there was still the matter of that dream Kevin had a few nights back. He hadn't had a real chance to speak to the boy about it yet.

"So how about it?" Adams repeated to Kevin. "Would you like to go over to where Betty is? Kathy wants to."

Kevin shook his head, seeming to have snapped out of whatever it was he had been thinking of. "Yes," he said. "It looks like she's all alone."

They slowly worked their way through the maze of umbrellas until they reached the canopy. People parted for them as though it had been the most natural thing in the world for the sheriff and his children to be passing. There was Arthur's wife, and standing beside her were the parents of the little girl whose body Arthur had discovered in Pomfrey. Their eyes made Adams feel awful; there were so many unanswered questions in them. And not too far from them stood the parents of little Billy Chadwick. Their lips were pressed together with such a firmness that Adams felt a lump swell in his throat. He nodded to all as they made way for him and his children to pass.

Ben, who had spent the night in the jail cell and had not heard a word from or about his missing co-deputy, was there too. His eyes scanned the gathering like radar. He had a strong feeling that whoever was responsible for the killings was there. He wondered who that could possibly be. Who could have kidnapped and killed two innocent little girls and be responsible for nine or ten other children missing? he asked himself.

As the chorus began to sing, Adams closed his umbrella and stepped beneath the canopy with his children. Betty's eyes did not move but she knew he was there, standing right beside her chair. Kathy went to stand on the other side of Jennifer's mother and rested her head against Betty's shoulder. That was when the tears began to fall from Betty Lineham's eyes. Up until that moment she had somehow managed to block the hurt she was feeling. But the gentle touch of Kathy's head against her shoulder brought her daughter momentarily back to life. She stared through her tears at the little white coffin that was suspended on tie ropes above the open grave, ready to be lowered into it.

Tears streamed freely from Betty's eyes as the chorus sang the words to "Amazing Grace." Their voices worked like a mystical balm into her soul. Something transfigured the singing. One note after another formed, vibrated, and sustained itself for a fleeting instant.

She felt the weight of Adams's hand go to her shoulder. Without hesitating she lifted her hand to his and clasped it tightly. The gestures spoke more eloquently than the words that neither of them could bring themselves to utter the night before, when they had sat in her living room.

"She's home now," Betty murmured very softly. "Just like the song." And she thought, *It's gone to somewhere we know nothing of—not until our own time comes.*

No one assembled about the grave had heard a word she said because of the rain that drummed so heavily on the canopy above her head. It didn't matter. Jennifer was no more but would one day be again, Betty thought. Perhaps she would be a note of music in a beautiful song, or a sudden burst of something warm and bright on a cold and wintery day. . . .

Something within Emma Prescott's head amused her. She was the only person there who, at the start of the chorus's singing, had closed her umbrella and stood there getting soaked to the skin. Somehow she was thankful it wasn't snowing—of that much she was aware. But why she felt so much inner joy was a complete mystery to her. She had to restrain herself from breaking into a childish giggle. It almost showed in her eyes.

Ben watched the librarian raise her face to the sky and have it washed slick with rain. People do peculiar things at tragic funerals like this one, he thought. He knew the librarian loved every child in the valley. She probably would have sacrificed herself in place of Jennifer had she only known how to do so, he thought.

When Emma lowered her eyes to the small white

coffin above the grave, she thought it could not have been any larger than one of those boxes that dolls come in when they're new. She pushed the umbrella open again, wondering what she could possibly have been thinking of when she closed it; the chill was running right into her bones. When she rose that morning, every joint in her body ached. She was getting that more and more these days, like she had been out doing a plowman's field work. But she knew it was only age catching up with her. That, and a bit of arthritis.

The snow that the radio had predicted would come by nightfall was also not making Emma feel any too good. She couldn't understand the why of that, either. Emma had always liked the first snow of the year. Why was she enjoying the fact that it had rained instead? Snow would have been so much better, she thought. So much prettier.

As soon as the chorus finished singing, the rain stopped and a hush fell over the gathering. It served well for the minister to step forward and offer his final remarks about the dead little girl. But nothing he said held more meaning for Betty Lineham than the thought she had had earlier—of her daughter revealing herself as a particle of something warm and bright in the midst of gloom. And no sooner had the minister completed his remarks that a shaft of sunlight suddenly fell through an opening in the darkened sky and filled the cemetery with a radiance that was dazzling. It lasted less than a minute, as long as it took for the tiny white casket to be lowered into the ground. Everyone felt the magic of it.

* * *

As the children piled back into the school bus, the sky lifted and it appeared as though it hadn't rained at all. The thick gray clouds that clung to the peaks of the surrounding hills seemed held in place by a peculiar updraft that rose from the floor of the valley and swept uphill into the sky. The sun came through like a promise of spring.

Adams looked down the sloping hill toward the school bus and watched as Kevin helped Kathy up the steep first step of it. In less than fifteen minutes they would be in their classrooms, studying their lessons.

The minister, who had arrived in the hired bus with the chorus, now returned with them. He would be let off where he was picked up, just outside the parish house, which was less than half a mile from the upper school in Woodville. It seemed that the only people who remained behind in the cemetery with Betty Lineham were Adams and his deputy Ben. They all walked quietly toward Adams's old Peugeot, Ben trailing slightly behind. For some curious reason all three of them had their eyes focused on Emma Prescott's old pickup. It wound its way along the highway and was headed in the direction of the library.

"I told Emma that you might be needing her for a while today," Adams said to Betty. "All I have to do is let her know."

Betty shook her head. "That's all right," she said. "I'll be fine. It's over now, and everything about me knows it." They walked a few more steps in silence before she spoke again. "I'm going to spend the day getting her things out of the house. The sooner I do that, the better. I'd offer to let you have all of her clothes, but I don't know how Kathy would take to that. It would probably upset her to be wearing anything of Jennifer's after what's happened."

Adams remained silent, once more in awe of the strength of the woman who walked beside him. "If there's anything I can help you with, anything at all, just let me know. I'll probably be at the office all day."

By the time they reached the car the sky had grown darker than it had been all morning. He wished Ben weren't there. He would have liked nothing better than to tell Betty what he was feeling for her. But that would have to wait, he thought. He knew he'd be seeing her later that night, after his children had gone to bed. Maybe he'd tell her then. Somehow, after seeing her face as the sun came through the clouds earlier, he knew she had the strength to hear what he had to say.

CHAPTER NINETEEN

Adams couldn't remember who said it, but in Vermont, if you didn't like the weather—so the saying went—all you had to do was wait twenty minutes and it would change. And it did just that. By the time he dropped Betty off at her house and drove the short distance with Ben to the office, the sky had gone as dark as pitch. Just as his Peugeot pulled into the driveway of the sheriff's office, a bolt of lightning, thick as a rod of sizzling steel, licked out of the sky and dropped to the ground not more than ten feet from where Adams had pulled into his parking spot.

"Judas Priest!" Ben said. "Did you see that?"

Adams nodded, obviously as shaken about it as Ben. "Felt it, too," he added.

They both got out of the car and raced for the entrance of the office. There were two lightning rods at either peak of the roof, and the closer they got to the building the better their chances would be of having a direct hit deflected by the rods. Once inside, another thunderous blast rattled the windows. The vibration of it shook the small frame structure with such force that, at first, it wasn't clear if it was the thunder that caused all the phones to start ringing at once or if a call was actually coming in. A beat or two later they knew. It was a call, and it seemed as though the phones had been on the ring long before they got inside. They looked at one another, knowing full well what it all meant. The state had finally put two and two together and realized that Jennifer Lineham lived within Adams's jurisdiction. By now they might even know something about Arthur being missing.

Although it was damp and cold in the office, Adams was sweating as he lifted the phone. As he suspected, it was Reid Hatcher.

"Ya know, Jeff, you should have told me that this Jennifer girl lived just next door to you. I was beginning to bring some heat down on the sheriff up in Mosstown when he told me about who she was. Why didn't you let me know that when I spoke to you yesterday?"

"Because it's none of your business," Adams replied evenly.

"Now you listen to me, Sheriff. I may not have the authority, *yet,* to compel you to be more responsive to my queries, but that time may be coming much sooner than you expect. And when it does, Adams, your ass is mine!"

The phone went dead. The moment Adams replaced the receiver the phone rang again. This time he motioned for Ben to pick it up at his own desk. He wanted to get some wood in the stove before the fire went out completely. He was beginning to feel the chill of the place. The rain had returned and there was a thickness to the sky that made it appear as though it might turn to snow.

Ben picked up the phone on the third ring. He liked the number. Had he missed it, he would have let it go to six, then nine. He liked any number that was divisible by three. He was married on the third day of the third month, had three children, a thirty-year mortgage and tomorrow, on the twelfth, he was going to be thirty-six years old. He was looking forward to a lucky day.

He listened at the phone without saying too much as Adams restoked the fire. When he hung up he told Adams that the call had been from Hatcher's secretary. She wanted to speak to Deputy Arthur Winston.

"So they figured that out, too," Adams said, sitting down heavily in the chair at his desk. "What in the name of all that's merciful are we going to do now?"

He didn't know. Neither did Ben.

Emma Prescott had that buzz going in her head again. She had trouble imagining what needed to be done. She looked at the cold rain falling outside the library window with an abstraction in her gaze. Her reflection came back to her in distorted rivulets that cascaded down the window in front of her. She had been sitting in her captain's chair in the library nook when the sky darkened and the rains returned.

Now, as icy droplets formed on the thin branches of the trees outside her window, she was once again tormented by the itch for something to do—something urgent, something that had to do with the possibility that the rain would surely turn to snow before the end of the day. Somehow, that made her feel as though the end of the world were at hand. She didn't know why.

Neither did she know why she hesitantly rose and left

the room, heading for the small closet at the back of the stairs that led up to her apartment. Somewhere, between the arch where the library ended and the hallway began, her steps grew less hesitant. By the time she reached the old Empire couch beyond the archway, she knew perfectly well what it was that needed to be done. All the doubt and confusion that had been buzzing about inside her head had suddenly unified into a single, direct line of thought.

As though she had done it a thousand times before, Emma Prescott reached into the crease formed by the armrest and seat of the old couch and removed a key. It fit into the palm of her hand as though it were one of the lines that a fortune-teller could read to predict destiny. The life line was short but thick and twisted, far beyond that which even a gifted palmist could decipher. The key rested gently across the line that curved about the base of the thumb, abruptly disappearing in a jagged twist before reaching the wrist. The key felt comfortable and warm as she closed her hand and held it tightly in her clenched fist.

At the low closet behind the stairs she stooped over and pushed the key into the lock. One quick twist to the right, then another full turn after that, and she heard the bolt retreat into the shank of the old device. The door was opened. She had to get down on her knees to reach what was inside at the back of it.

The first thing she removed from the closet was an empty pepper sack. It had been tossed inside as though deposited there in great haste. She folded the burlap thing neatly in half and let it rest on the floor to the side of her. Then she leaned forward and peered deeper into the back of the closet. She didn't need a light to know what she was looking for. She knew it would be there, right where she had left it earlier, just before dawn that day.

"Come here, my pretty. Come to your mamma," she said with a lightness to her voice that was filled with warmth. When she withdrew her hands from the inner darkness of the closet, out came the most recent doll she had just completed—that of Kathy Adams. She rocked it gently in the cradle of her arms as though it were a newly born infant. "Mamma's gonna make you very happy," she said in a cooing tone. "And real soon, too!"

She placed the doll down and swathed it with the burlap sack as though she were wrapping an infant before taking it out into the cold. Then she rose and locked the closet before returning the key to its place in the crease between the armrest and seat of the old couch. She stood there for a moment with the bundle in her arms, rocking herself back and forth with it. "Nobody ever loved you as much as I do," she said.

And for a fleeting instant it looked as though Emma Prescott was about to cry. But she didn't. Instead, she broke into a peal of hysterical laughter. "That's right," she said. "Isn't it, Mother? Nobody loves my children as much as I do.

Emma danced a slow waltz with the wrapped doll at her shoulder and patted its back as she danced herself over to the back door of the house. Just outside was parked her battered old yellow pickup.

She didn't feel the cold rain that immediately soaked through her clothing once she stepped outside. When she was like this nothing mattered. She could go through the very fires of hell. Things that had to be done, were done. There're no two ways about that, she told herself.

She opened the door to the pickup and pulled the front seat forward. Behind it was a space just big enough for the bundle. She rested it there and pushed the seat back in place. "There now," she said. "That should hold you until the time comes." And when she said that last thing, a wild abstraction, as dark and bewildering as a fury, seized her like the paws of a wild beast. It seemed to have come from the sky. She was momentarily rendered immobile as she stared up into it. In her mind, the falling rain that pelted her face had turned to snow. It floated down at her like patches of embroidered lace that disappeared and turned to icy kisses as they struck her distorted face. It felt like the touch of something that had long been dead.

Emma Prescott screamed. No one heard her. If they had, they would have sworn that some wounded animal was being torn apart by a pack of angry dogs.

Adams pressed the tips of his thumbs together while the rest of his fingers remained locked together like a cradle in his lap. Arthur's wife had just called from Pomfrey, wanting to know if anyone had reported anything about her missing husband. He had to tell her no. Then he added a lie that probably wasn't going to be a lie much longer: He told her that the state was going to send a specialist in to help out—real soon.

"What do you suppose could have happened to him, Ben? He's the first adult that's missing since these cases started. Do you think he was on to something?"

Ben squinted through the window at the icy rain that

was hammering the panes. The thunder had stopped and it looked as though it was getting ready to snow. "Don't know," he finally responded. "If he was on to something, he would have called in; that was his way." He swallowed a knot of dryness that was bothering his throat. "I would look for some kind of an accident or something like that, one that took place on some back road, otherwise we'd have something on it by now. He was following Billy Chadwick's hound. I think it must have caught the scent of something and lit up some old trail into the woods. Arthur probably gunned the cruiser along after it in a hurry—you know how he loves to speed up on curves—and . . ." He couldn't finish. There were too many possible endings to contend with. Besides, his guts told him that his co-worker had ended up in a mess that was perhaps more horrible than he could imagine. After all, by now everyone knew they were dealing with a demented killer who would stop at nothing—not even killing a police officer.

"What do you think the dog caught the scent of?" Adams persisted. It was the only way to keep his mind from spilling over into the dark cavern of depression that appeared ready to engulf him if he didn't keep thinking. "Do you think it had something to do with the Chadwick boy? It was his hound, but after all that pepper caught in its snout, it might have been after anything—a rabbit, deer, or even a bobcat for all that matter."

"Okay," Ben said. "Let's assume that it was after the boy's scent. That would mean that whoever kidnapped him brought him up into the hills that surround these parts. Right nearby. And that would mean that the killer might live up in the hills along an old trail or something like that." He let his mind wander for a moment, then shook his head. "Too many old logging roads up in those hills. Most of them so grown over and disused you couldn't pass through with an army tank." He thought a bit more. "Besides, the only person here 'bout that lives up there anymore is old Les Knowel, over toward Bannion."

Adams looked up. "Didn't he call in yesterday, saying he heard shots coming from—" Then he remembered: Hearing a shot from where Les lived didn't mean very much. It could have come from anywhere, including the recluse's own backyard. Besides, ever since Les's wife died, some folks said the old buzzard was sometimes known to take a swig or two, even during the daylight hours.

Ben had jerked his head toward the window and was about to say something when the phone rang. He held one finger up in the air, meaning that he would get right back to what he was going to say just as soon as he answered the phone.

It was the bookkeeper calling in from the wholesale spice distributor in East Hartfield. She had been out the day before when Ben called to ask about any unusual purchases of large amounts of crushed red pepper. As he listened to the line his eyes widened. "How long ago was that?" he asked. "Did anyone see who it was?"

Adams picked up the extension to listen in. At first his eyes had expressed the same spark of interest that Ben's had. Then, as the bookkeeper went on, he lowered the phone back to its cradle. He had thought the call had something to do with Arthur, or with the peculiar sound he thought he had heard a moment before the phone rang.

When Ben hung up, he asked Adams if it would be all right for him to get on over to East Hartfield to see what was going on at the distributor's plant. It seemed that during the past year, over one dozen fifty-pound sacks of red pepper had disappeared from their loading dock. It was the only spice ever reported to have been missing like that. The bookkeeper thought it odd that there had been so much reordering of it. She had gone to the records when she heard about Ben's call to find out what was going on. The only thing she could figure was that the sacks had vanished before they ever went into inventory, which meant they had to have disappeared from the loading dock before they even entered the plant. She was going to ask around to see if anyone out there knew anything more about it.

"Sounds like she'd make a good detective," Adams said. "And it's a good idea to get on over there and check that out firsthand." He thought for a moment. The rain was slowing down and a uniform grayness had spread across the sky. "Did you hear something outside a short while back?" he asked. "Something that sounded like the howl of a wounded animal of some kind?"

Ben nodded his head. "That's what I was going to tell you about when the phone rang. Sounded peculiar to me."

Adams looked out the window. If anything had happened close by, the phone would be ringing about it real soon.

"Take my Peugeot," he finally said to Ben. "Pass along the local roads with it for a while before heading toward the interstate for East Hartfield. Maybe someone seeing my car will flag you for what it was that might have happened. It's probably nothing. Sounds carry funny in the rain. Could have been—could have been anything," he concluded. Somehow, his mind was refusing to deal with any more intangibles. It wanted hard, cold facts. Like the ones that Ben might possibly uncover at the plant in East Hartfield.

Ben wasn't used to driving a standard shift automobile. Although he knew how, he hadn't been behind the wheel of one since high school, when his older brother had let him borrow his old Ford a couple of times. Aside from that, all his driving experience had been with cars that had automatic transmissions, so it was no great wonder that Adams's Peugeot went jogging out of the driveway of the sheriff's office like a jackrabbit caught in a snare.

Adams had watched it all from the window and couldn't imagine what was going on. On top of everything else, he thought, it now appeared his deputy was on the verge of wrecking his car. He was about to call Ben back in on the police line when he saw the car begin to smooth out and head down the highway in the normal flow of traffic. Hope he doesn't get a ticket on the interstate, Adams thought. He was somewhat amused to suddenly realize that Ben hadn't told him about not being able to drive a standard shift car. That's Ben, he thought. No turning back on doing anything he's asked to. Had Adams said to go on over to the airfield in Rutland and charter a small Cessna, Ben would probably do that, too, learning to fly the darn thing at the same time!

Ben wasn't so sure. He had managed to get the car into third gear and it still sounded as though the engine were holding back. He wondered if the thing had an overdrive. There was some sort of a worn-out diagram on the knob of the gearshift that required him to take his eyes off the road for a moment to examine it. He took a deep breath, anticipated the sound of gears grinding to pieces, and pushed in the clutch. When he took the gear stick down to neutral and pressed it away from him and down, just like he thought the diagram indicated, it worked. Letting up the clutch made the old Peugeot coast along as smoothly as though Adams himself were driving. He smiled.

By the time he went up and down the local roads for a while, he had mastered the thing, learning how to downshift and everything else. He was thinking that one day he might even get himself a standard shift car. They were supposed to be very good on back roads and hills.

The roads were abandoned. Everyone was at work or at home, keeping out of the rain. He didn't see anyone attempting to signal him about something they might have heard. Neither did he see anything out of the ordinary. He and Adams must have been imagining things. He decided to head straight for the wholesale plant in East Hartfield.

By the library, Ben carefully downshifted to make the turn onto the road that led to the interstate. All went smoothly as the car glided around the curve that Arthur loved to take at such great speed. He was once again clutching it to get it back into overdrive when he glanced out over his left shoulder and saw something that caught his curiosity. Emma Prescott was standing out in her dooryard, clutching something in her arms. Whatever it was, it appeared she had just removed it from the clothesline just beyond her pickup. What was odd about the sight was that she looked as though she had been standing there a long time. She didn't have an umbrella and wasn't wearing a coat or jacket, either. Ben was about to stop the car and find out if anything was wrong, but as soon as he lifted his foot from the accelerator, the Peugeot again began to buck like a jackrabbit. He had forgotten to downshift.

The joggling of the car on the road that ran by her house caused Emma Prescott to look up. When she saw the sheriff's car, she opened into a broad smile and waved. Then she hurriedly ran back into the house, still clutching the object she had just removed from the line. To Ben it appeared she was attempting to conceal it from him. It looked soggy and brown, like an old rug or something.

Probably doesn't want people to know she left her wash out in rain, Ben thought. He smiled. The car was back up to speed and running smoothly along the road that led to the interstate. The next big thing he had to figure out was how to get the windshield wipers to go on. He hoped he could manage it.

CHAPTER TWENTY

By 5:30 that evening, Betty Lineham had disposed of almost every trace of Jennifer's existence. Everything that had belonged to her daughter—clothing, toys, games, books—was now packed in large plastic gardening bags in the cellar, waiting for the church to come and pick them up for the thrift shop. The only thing Betty kept upstairs in a bureau drawer, where she could get to it anytime she wanted, was a small flat box of photos and mementos of her daughter. That, she intended to keep as long as she lived. It contained the first baby tooth that the "tooth fairy" had taken from beneath Jennifer's pillow in the middle of the night and replaced with a shiny new dime. The tiny milk tooth was wrapped in a small silk cloth that came from the dress her grandmother had made for Jennifer to be christened in. There was even a snip of the child's hair, which had been cut when it was still pure blond, and some samples of Jennifer's first attempts to draw and write. There was also a photograph of the girl sitting on her grandmother's knee in Pennsylvania, taken right after the divorce, and the one picture that Jennifer had looked at a thousand times in her short lifetime—the one of her father, a man she had known very little about.

Betty Lineham knew it would be a long time before she could bring herself to open that box again. But she would keep it there, in that bureau drawer in her bedroom, forever if she had to, waiting for the day when the urge would move her to look into it again. She didn't know how long that would be.

Something about having gotten all that done—and sitting there in the living room by the window with a cup of warm tea on the table beside her—made her feel more peaceful. Having had Jennifer buried right away and clearing the house of any trace of her was the only way she could continue to function without falling apart. And when she prayed that the killer would be caught swiftly, it was not for the sake of punishing the beast, but to keep other children from becoming victims.

The rain had stopped and snow now flurried in the light that spilled out from the house into the early darkness. Across the dooryard, she could see Kevin and Kathy doing their homework at a table by the living room window. From time to time she saw Adams go over and sit beside one of them for a moment or two. He'd put his arm over their shoulders and say something close to their ears as he looked at the open notebooks on the table.

Emma Prescott had been over there earlier. She had picked the children up after school and started dinner going. From the way that Adams was walking back and forth to the kitchen, Betty knew it would soon be ready. Emma was nice enough to stop by to see if Betty needed anything. She stayed only a minute before heading back to the library to get some of her own work done. Her pickup almost skidded on the slippery leaves as she left, nearly going into the side of Betty's Volkswagen. It was now parked in the driveway at the side of her house. Someone from the sheriff's office in Mosstown had delivered it to her house that afternoon.

Just before it had grown so dark, Betty noticed that Adams had arrived home on foot. She wondered if his car had broken down or if it was being used by Ben. By now, most folks in the valley knew about Arthur and the missing police cruiser. They were talking about organizing a search party to get up into the hills before the snow began to blanket the trails.

Adams went over to Betty's house after dinner. He had called first to see if she cared to have some of the homemade beef soup that Emma had prepared. There were warm biscuits, too. Betty thought a bowl of soup would be just fine, probably more than she could manage.

Adams sat in the living room with her now, watching as she had the soup. He had brought it over in a pot so he could warm it for her once he got there. She ate slowly, as though she were engrossed in some faraway thought. She gently blew on each spoonful before placing it in her mouth.

"What happened to your car?" she finally asked, patting her lips with a napkin. She looked at him and placed the spoon in the plate beneath the half-eaten bowl of soup. "I saw that you had to get home on foot tonight."

Adams looked down at the floor for a moment. "Ben's using the Peugeot," he said after looking back up at her. "He called in before I left the office and told me he got a flat with it over toward East Hartfield. No spare." He knew Betty would want to know what Ben was doing over in East Hartfield but didn't expand any further on a topic that was sure to provoke memories she had best stay away from for a while. "I told him he might as well get me the set of snow tires I'd been needing. From the looks of things outside it won't be too long now before I have to have them."

He sure felt the need to spill out the whole jumbled mess that had been percolating through his guts for the past few days, but nothing would come. Yet, simply being there with her helped to ease his thoughts. He knew he should have made a call to the state before he left the office, telling them that they had better send in some help before anything else happened. The responsibility he now faced of attempting to go it alone was getting to him. If the killer weren't nailed before tomorrow, that would be the end of any hope he ever had of holding on to his job.

When he couldn't think of anything to say, he turned the conversation around to her. "If you don't mind my asking," he said, "how did you spend the day?"

When Betty told him about clearing Jennifer's things out of her room and bagging everything up in the cellar—ready for the church thrift shop—he couldn't imagine where the presence of mind to carry out such a dreadful chore had come from.

"It's just my way, Jeff," she said, as though having

read his thoughts. "Life has to go on, and it's the only way I can deal with what's happened. If I waited another day or two, I know I'd have her things around for another hundred years, as though she had only left for a little while and was going to come right back home. She's not going to, you know." She sat back for a moment and pulled a comforter from the floor beside her so that she could spread it across her legs.

He made a gesture of getting up and helping her with it, but she held her hand up. It seemed there were tears about to come into her eyes and the distraction of having to do something for herself was what she needed. "It's best you found her right away like you did," she said. "I feel sorry for the ones whose children are still missing. You know, probably as well as they do, that all those kids are killed. It would be better for their folks to know for certain that they're really gone. False hope can give you more grief than anything after a while." Then she told him about how, at the time of her divorce, she had imagined her husband had died. She then went into a short period of "mourning" over it and did her best to forget. After a while it was as though he had never existed. That's when the pain stopped. It was the only way. "He was as mean as some of those broncs he busted" was the only thing she then offered by way of describing his character. Yet, he had often heard Jennifer talking to Kathy about the man. He was a great rodeo man, she would tell his daughter. Won all sorts of prizes, too. But she would always go silent whenever Kathy asked for more information about where he was. She didn't know. It was clear to Adams that Betty had never bad-mouthed the child's father to her little girl. He respected her a lot for that and thought she was a full woman, hard and gentle at the same time.

Adams stared at her for a long time, remembering how she had held on to his hand when he placed it on her shoulder at the funeral that afternoon.

"Betty," he said. "Let me hold you."

Betty's eyes showed only the slightest trace of wonder, not hesitation. A soft sound emerged from her throat as she stood and went into his arms. It was a simple embrace and they did not kiss, but it promised everything. And for the brief time they held on to one another in the dense silence of that empty, empty house, they felt whole again.

An uneasy thought suddenly bolted through the under-roots of Adams's consciousness as he stood there with her. It made his stomach feel as though he had taken an unexpected fall into an uncovered mine shaft. He thought that if he didn't catch the person who murdered Betty's daughter—and soon—she might begin to lose respect for him.

He relaxed his arms about her and was about to say something when, through the window behind her, he saw Kevin race from the front door of his house and head across the yard toward Betty's. Adams went to the window and pulled the curtain aside. By the time he got there Kevin was at the door. At the window Adams saw that Kathy was still doing her homework at the table by the living room window. He quickly went to the door and let Kevin in. Betty was right beside him.

"What's wrong?" he asked his son. Even Betty was alarmed and had followed Adams to the vestibule.

"There's a call from the lieutenant governor's office at the capital," Kevin blurted out. "He's still on the line."

"Who's that?" Adams asked. He expected it would be Reid Hatcher.

"It was Jerry Malone," Kevin responded. He was still slightly out of breath.

Adams relaxed. It showed in his eyes. "You know Jerry Malone's a good friend of mine," he told the boy. "We were in the army together. Sometimes he calls just to talk." Adams began to pull his jacket on.

"I don't think so," the boy said. "I've spoken to him before, too. This time it sounds like there's something real important on his mind."

The relaxed expression disappeared from Adams's eyes. "You run back and tell him I'm on my way." He had intended to first return to the living room and tell Betty what his hasty departure was all about, but when he turned he found that she was standing a few feet behind him. He didn't have to say a word. She had heard it all. Betty's eyes showed the trouble she felt for him.

Adams gritted his teeth and took in a swallow of air before lifting the receiver from the kitchen counter where Kevin had left it. He had sent the boy back to the living room where he had been doing homework with his sister before the call came in.

"Hi, Jerry. Sorry it took me so long to get here. I was across the dooryard with a neighbor. What's up?"

"Jeff, Reid Hatcher is up here sounding like a rooster

that's backed into a piece of rotating farm equipment. In a couple of weeks, he's going to have his seat in the state senate, and in a couple of years he's either going to be the governor of this state or he's going to be a United States senator. Now, that makes him a man of sizeable power to contend with. I'll tell you straight, Jeff. I don't know where you got the balls to stand up to him!"

Adams felt like laughing and taking the whole matter in like some sort of old army prank that he and Malone sometimes played on their senior officers while they were in the service. But he couldn't. Things were different now. Jerry Malone, the obvious choice for the state's next lieutenant governor, felt politically threatened by the arrogant slob who had everyone believing he could solve any crisis that came along.

"It's *my* head, Jerry. Don't tie yourself to me. That's the best way to sink two boats."

"Why are you doing this to yourself?" Malone asked. "The man is kicking up such a storm here that he's making *you* look like some sort of criminal, intent on a cover-up."

Adams didn't respond. He felt a slight tinge of truth in the accusation. All he wanted to do was to solve the case himself. He was beginning to see how wrong that was. By going it alone and not asking for the state to help out, he had probably caused the death and disappearance of Jennifer Lineham and Billy Chadwick. To say nothing of his own missing deputy, Arthur. His heart sank.

"Okay, Jerry. Send him in. But I'll tell you one thing. Hatcher's not going to find out who the killer is, either. He's going to log it in as solved—don't ask me how—

but it's not going to be so."

"Jeff, that's not why I called. The lieutenant governor has been in the hospital for the past week and I'm taking his place until he gets out. Through the governor himself I managed to buy you a small piece of time. The governor knows what Hatcher is, but he doesn't want to take him on just now. So I arranged a meeting, for later tonight. You, me, and Hatcher." He paused for a moment and waited for a reaction from Adams. None came. "If you can't make it," Malone continued, "then that's it. Hatcher will be in your office by morning. I will not be able to help you." Again he listened. Again there was no reaction. But he knew Adams was listening and weighing every word. He continued with the assumption that Adams was going to agree to the meeting. "But I'll tell you one thing, Jeff. I have to report back to the governor on the meeting—probably tonight if we can get it all done before midnight. And I'll have to give it to him straight. If I come away from the meeting with the feeling that Hatcher can get the killer caught before you can, then I'll have to give that information straight to the governor." He couldn't bear the silence at the other end of the telephone any longer. "Do you follow what I've been saying, Jeff?"

"Every word," Adams responded. "What time do you have the meeting scheduled for?"

At the other end of the line Adams could feel the relief that surged through Jerry Malone's thoughts. He knew he had a friend there and also knew that Jerry had gone out on a shaky limb for him. Adams didn't want to let him down. If it had been Hatcher calling with the announcement that a meeting had been set up, Adams would have told him to do something vulgar to himself. The thought that he might be able to do that in person, later that night, was almost incentive enough for him to make the long drive.

"The time is up to you, Jeff. The snow here has stopped, but I understand that it's just beginning down where you are. We had eleven inches today, on top of the six that was here from a couple of days ago. So, you tell me when you can make it, and I'll set it up."

Adams thought. It was a three-hour drive, with the snow he figured close to four. He'd have to check in at the office to see if Ben had gotten back yet with the Peugeot. If he hadn't—and that thought troubled him as much as Arthur's disappearance—he'd have to borrow Betty's Volkswagen. Then there was Emma to call. She could stay with the kids until he got back. He didn't want to ask Betty for that, since she looked as though she hadn't had any sleep since she got out of the hospital. He would ask her only if Emma couldn't make it.

Adams looked at the kitchen clock. "How does nine, nine-thirty sound?" he asked.

"I'll take care of it, Jeff. I'll also book you a room at the Motor Inn on State Street."

"I don't want to spend the night, Jerry. I can't." He was thinking of getting his kids off to school in the morning.

"I think you may have to, Jeff. Because after the meeting with Hatcher, I've scheduled you to meet with Dr. York. He's our chief police psychologist."

Adams actually took the phone away from his ear

for a moment and looked at it in his hand. "What?" he asked after placing the receiver back against his ear. He could sense the puzzlement in Jerry Malone's voice when he began to speak again.

"What do you mean, Jeff? I—" Then he understood. "Jesus, Jeff. You don't think I was calling in a shrink to examine *you,* do you? It's not that at all." He hastily continued before Adams had a chance to respond. "It's just that he may be able to help you develop a psychological profile of the killer. He does that sort of thing. And the reason I want you to get to him first is that I just found out that Hatcher is going to meet with him first thing in the morning—for the very same thing. So don't you mention anything about Dr. York to him at all."

Adams chuckled. "You had me going there for a while, Jerry. Thought you felt I needed to have my head worked on."

"Your head's okay, Jeff. It's your heart that's always been a bit soft."

Adams appreciated that. It almost made him feel like wanting to be back in the army with his buddy again. He didn't think there was another living person who knew him as well as Jerry Malone.

It wasn't long before Adams returned to Betty's house. Without going into specifics, he told her about having to get up to the capital that night. Ben, who had just returned to the office from East Hartfield—and having had a new set of snow tires installed—was on his way over with the Peugeot and would be there any moment. He was going to stay with the kids until Emma Prescott arrived.

"I didn't want to ask you to care for Kathy and Kevin," he told her. "Not after all you've been through the last couple of days."

A fleeting glimpse of hurt had gone through her eyes when he mentioned having called on Emma Prescott to take care of his children instead of her.

"Not tonight," he added. "But after this, I'll always call on you first."

She took a deep breath. It was almost a sigh. "I'd just as soon get a full night's rest, anyway," she said, hoping her words would relieve his concern for her. "It's been a while since I've been able to."

They stood in the vestibule, awkwardly, their bodies close to one another. The memory of that healing embrace, only a short while ago, was still with them. What happened next occurred so unexpectedly—and so naturally—that it surprised both of them. They kissed. It was not a kiss of passion. It was more like the beginning of something they felt should have happened a long time ago.

They were still in each other's arms when the familiar sound of the Peugeot's engine went by and came to a stop outside of Adams's house.

"I have to go," he said, gently loosening himself from Betty's arms. "I need to find out some things from Ben before leaving."

Betty smiled, faintly, the way she always did. But for the first time Adams realized how radiant it could be if she ever let it go all the way. "Drive carefully," she said. "The snow's supposed to get a whole lot worse before long."

He left her knowing that whatever happened at the capital, he'd have her to come back to. And that was the best feeling he'd had in years.

"A big waste of a trip," Ben said at the door of the Peugeot just as soon as Adams got there from Betty's house. "The bookkeeper at the wholesale plant put me in touch with the loading dock manager. She thought he might know something. Today was his day off and when I called his house his wife said he'd be back in an hour or so. That's when I got the flat and called you about having that new set of snow tires put on, which didn't take much time at all. When I finally got to the loading dock man, all he could tell me was that the pepper had been disappearing over a period of about a year now, one or two sacks at a time. And get this. He said he thought some demented old *woman* was responsible . . . said he thought he saw an old lady acting strangely in the area of the loading dock—saw her twice. He thought nothing of it until the sacks started to count short. That's when he started looking out for her but hasn't seen her since. They've lost about fifteen sacks by now."

Adams had a feeling he knew what that number meant. He didn't have to respond. Ben knew it too. But what he never figured on was the possibility that the killer might be a woman.

"That makes it about one sack for each kid that has been reported missing over the past year," Ben added, reflecting Adams's own thoughts about the number of missing sacks. "That's why I took so long up there. I went back to the wholesaler and spoke to everyone. But I couldn't get any further that that." He looked at the snow that was beginning to accumulate on the roof of the car. "The last thing I would suspect would be for a woman to have been doing all this," he said quietly. "What do you think about it, Jeff?"

Adams shook his head. He didn't know. "I hope I'll have some answers by the time I get back from the capital," he said. "They have me set up to meet with a police psychologist who might be able to put together a psychological profile of whoever it is. Let's hope he can."

Adams thought of something as he stepped into the Peugeot. "How are you going to get back to the office when Emma gets here?" he asked. He had already asked Ben to spend one more night on the cot in the cell, just in case anything turned up about Arthur.

"My wife's on her way down here right now with my supper. She's going to sit with me at the office for a while until her sister comes to pick her up; then they'll drive back in my sister-in-law's car. That way I'll have my own car here in case I need it." He shrugged. "It's not too bad on the cot," he said with the smile of a man who was telling a lie. "Last night I pulled the space heater in with me and it was just fine."

Adams watched Ben walk toward the front door of his house. Kevin, who had been watching from the window, opened it up to let him in. He was like an uncle to the kids; so was Arthur.

As Adams got out onto the highway, Emma Prescott's old pickup joggled past him on its way to his house. The librarian had rolled down her window, despite the snow, to wave and let him know that everything would be all right. He felt relieved that there was someone like her he could count on in an emergency. Almost everyone else in town knew they could count on her, too.

CHAPTER TWENTY-ONE

Just before Adams had called Emma Prescott to ask if she could stay with his children for the night, she had been in her upstairs reading parlor looking for a certain book on magic. She remembered reading it many years ago and being impressed by the seriousness of the author's intent to impart the knowledge of ancient magic to the reader. She didn't think much of it at the time, but now, since she felt that Kevin had some latent power that might possibly be awakened, she was looking again for the ritual she remembered reading. It told the reader how to raise a hidden power to the surface, where it can become useful. If the boy did indeed possess such a power, which she was convinced he had, then the ritual might bring it out so that he could help his father catch the insane killer who was terrorizing the valley.

When her mind focused on the concept of an insane killer, it sent a chill through her. She, herself, had been thinking of seeing a psychiatrist because of all the weird things that appeared to be happening with her mind. That and the fact that her own mother and grandfather had gone insane at about the same age she was now gave her the feeling that there was something about her that had better be looked into. Whatever it was, she knew it couldn't be serious because it didn't appear to be getting in the way of her ability to function. She was doing her usual job at the library, getting more and more satisfaction from reading stories at the school—the children appeared to love her more and more too—and she was able to care for those folks in the town who needed her, like Betty Lineham, Sheriff Adams, and his two children. She came to the conclusion that the whole source of her temporary states of confusion might have something to do with one of those chemical imbalances she knew women her age are sometimes subjected to. Maybe it had something to do with the change of life thing, which for her had come later than is usual. It'll all pass, she told herself. No need to see a psychiatrist when some vitamins might be all I need.

Then she thought of the burlap sack that had been out on the clothesline that morning in the rain, when Ben Jenson had passed by in Adams's old Peugeot. Why had she ripped the thing from the line and tried to hide it from him, and how on earth did it get there, anyway? She had no memory of having put it there. The only thing she could remember was that it came from the tailgate of her pickup, several days ago. Maybe it flew off a passing truck and got itself caught there, she thought. But washing it out and hanging it on the line in her yard was a complete mystery to her. Maybe she simply wanted to wash it out and use it to store kindling or something. She didn't know. Neither did she know why she had made such an effort to conceal it from the sheriff's deputy as he passed by. She shrugged the whole thing off. Chemical imbalances, she thought. She made a note to herself that the next time she was downstairs in the main library she would look to see if there were a good book on nutrition. She hadn't been eating any too well these days.

She found the occult book she had been looking for. It was a small work on ancient Egyptian magic that had been written over a hundred years ago by a Victorian lady who appeared to have travelled in Egypt before the turn of the century. The slim volume was bound in Moroccan leather and its title hand-stamped in gold: *Ancient Egyptian Magic, As Described And Practiced From Earliest Times To The Present.* The book's hinges were loose, and its spine showed the faint line of a crack. She opened it carefully, found the ritual, and slipped a bookmark into its place. She then left it on the small oak table where she had been reading it and went to the kitchen. When she returned, it was with a ziplock baggie, into which she slid the book.

It was while she was sliding her fingers across the lock of the baggie that Adams had called and asked if she could come over and spend the night with his children.

Magic! she thought as she replaced the receiver. It seemed to be working already. There she was, thinking of how she was going to work the spell on the boy without making a fuss over it, and the opportunity for doing so came to her right over the telephone. It seemed to be an omen.

With the book in her coat pocket she stepped out the back door of the house and froze. She had no idea that it was beginning to snow so heavily. Instead of feeling good about it—she always loved waking up to the first snow of the season and seeing the trees outside her window hung with a soft, glittery whiteness—it seemed to strike a chord of terror deep within her. She didn't interpret the feeling correctly. She thought it had something to do with the dangers of driving on the roads before the town crew got out to sand them.

She checked her tires in the peculiar yellow glow of the outside bug light by the door. The tires looked good, lots of tread on the front ones, and the snows in the rear were practically new. She'd have no trouble with the roads for the short distance she had to drive to reach Adams's house.

As she left the driveway in front of the library and made the turn that headed for the sheriff's house, she wondered how she was going to get Kevin to go along with the little game she was beginning to devise in her mind. She knew that Kathy would play anything. The child had no better sense. But the boy, well, she didn't quite know if he would go for some foolish old game about ancient magic she was thinking up. He had a strong will, just like his mother, she thought. The woman had been so obstinate about dying that she didn't even admit it to herself, let alone tell anyone else about it. Why, Emma thought, it wouldn't surprise me if that boy just up and did any darn thing he had a mind to one day.

It was just as Adams was making the turn to get onto the main highway that Emma had spotted him and rolled her window down. She didn't like the feel of all the snow that flew in and whipped across her face, but she wanted to wave to him, making him feel comfortable in the thought that she would soon be with his children and that there was nothing on earth for him to be concerned about. By the time he gets back home, she thought, Kevin might even be able to tell his father who the killer is.

She liked that. The thought almost brought a smile to her lips as she rolled the window back up and slowly made her way up the hill to the sheriff's house. She knew that Kevin and Kathy would be eagerly waiting there for her—both of them with cheek-pinching grins on their well-scrubbed little faces.

PART THREE

CHAPTER TWENTY-TWO

The road unfolded before him like a black river that stretched all the way to the horizon—a horizon that kept receding into the velvet darkness beyond the beam of his headlights. Adams's four-cylinder Peugeot needed a tune-up and it slowed down while climbing some of the steeper hills. The farther north he drove, the thinner the snowfall became. It finally stopped when he was within sixty miles of the capital.

Huge snow drifts on the shoulders of the highway gleamed blue in the moonlight. The trees were hung with it, too. And when the winds picked up, the icy gusts caused his car to swerve. Whenever he came upon a stretch of road that wasn't shielded by tall trees or by cut-through rock walls on either side of the highway, he had to hold the steering wheel steady so he wouldn't end up in a drift. There were patches of ice, too. It didn't leave much room in his mind for the meeting with Hatcher.

He was tired, too, and shuddered to think of the field day that Hatcher was going to have with him. The words he was going to offer in defense of his not being removed from the case spilled into the matrix of his thoughts like tiny crystals of ice; they quickly dissolved before having had a chance to work themselves into solid arguments. All he knew was that he had better come up with something good. What that was going to be, he had difficulty imagining.

The bowl of a valley to his left was filled with fog. He could see how it rose to the edge of the highway and licked out over it with wispy tentaclelike fingers. They seemed to be reaching out to drag him through the guard rail and over the edge into the swirl of milky soup. He shook his head. God! he thought. He was falling asleep, too.

He hardly knew how he made it there. Montpelier was alseep. The only aspect of the town that seemed alive was the golden dome of the capitol building. The full moon played upon it as if it were an ancient temple in some forgotten land. The whiteness of the hills that surrounded it made it all seem as though it were a dream. He shook his head and made a left in front of the Stockyard Restaurant, heading toward State Street. The illuminated clock in the tower of the courthouse indicated that he had made the drive in just under four hours.

It was almost ten o'clock as he pulled to the curb in front of the state office building and parked. There were no other cars on the street, and not a single light was on in the capitol building opposite him. He walked briskly from the Peugeot to the door of the state office building where Jerry Malone had his office. It was locked, but on it was taped an envelope with his name. "9:30. Hungry as hell. Meet us at the Justin Morgan

Tavern." It was only a couple of streets from where he stood. The thought of having something to eat repulsed him, but a hot cup of coffee seemed inviting after the long drive. He decided to leave the car where it was and walk to the tavern. The cold air, scented with the fragrance of snow and wood burning in fireplaces, might be the very thing he needed to snap out of the impending gloom he felt.

When he entered the Justin Morgan Room of the tavern, he couldn't believe the number of people that were packed into it. The streets he had walked through to get there had been entirely deserted. He didn't think there was a soul around. Yet, just as soon as he opened the door, the chatter of loud conversation jumped at him like the roar of a lion. There had been some drinking going on and tongues were loose. He had been in the army and had heard all sorts of bad language, but what was coming from the mouth of a man at the bar was running like black silage gone to rot. He turned. It was Reid Hatcher. He wore an expensive suit that Adams could never afford to own. The attorney was about to lift a thick corned beef sandwich to his mouth.

Adams couldn't help himself. "You going to eat with the same mouth that just said all that?" he asked, smiling at Hatcher.

The man's face froze, so too did the expressions on the faces of some of the men who stood about him. Adams suspected they were his newspaper cronies. As Hatcher stood there, silently glaring at Adams, Jerry Malone stepped out of the men's room and looked back and forth at both of them. "What's going on?" he asked. "Looks like a shoot-out at OK Corral."

His words seemed to break the chill. Shoulders

loosened, and Hatcher placed his sandwich back in the plate on the bar without having taken a bite of it. "What's the matter with some colorful talk?" he asked, reaching out to shake Adams's hand. "We're all men here, aren't we?"

Adams didn't feel like shaking Hatcher's hand; neither did he feel like responding to his stupid questions. The man is an absolute ass, he thought, and he shoved both his hands into his pockets to avoid having to shake the lawyer's outstretched hand.

Hatcher lowered his hand slowly. "Well, well now," he said. "I suppose you have the case all solved," he said with a broad smirk across his lips.

One of the reporters took out a pad. Adams saw it. He studied the man's eyes. He was waiting for Adams to say something, anything. Adams knew that whatever he said was sure to be used against him. He meant to remain silent, but something made him begin to speak. It was so spontaneous—and so alien to his thoughts—that it even startled him when he said it. It was as though the words had come from someone else. "There's a strong lead," he said. "And it looks as though the killer will be apprehended within the next twenty-four hours."

Pads and pencils were out and the reporters scribbled in haste. A couple of them headed for the men's room, where there was a telephone, but were stopped by the sudden outburst that came from Hatcher.

"You're a goddamn liar!" he snapped at Adams. "You no more know anything about what's going on than the man in the moon!" He turned to the reporters. "You heard that fellas? You can print every word I just said." He drew in his breath and, with his thumb and pointing finger spaced two inches apart, ran his hand through the air as though he were composing the morning's headlines. "Sheriff from Tweed Valley is called a liar. Reid Hatcher of the attorney general's office demands an end to the series of brutal child-killings. Accuses local sheriff of a cover-up." He looked directly into Adam's eyes when he finished. It challenged him for a response.

Adams smiled. "You're supposed to be a smart lawyer," he finally said to Hatcher. "Why would you want to go and libel yourself like that?"

The coolness of the question brought a bulging knot of anger that swelled in Hatcher's throat. "You son of a bitch!" he blurted out. "You're poking around down there with a mad child-killer on the loose, and you're lecturing *me* about libel!"

If Adams didn't have his hands in his pockets, he would have hit him. In the instant it took his reflexes to jerk them out, he managed to calm himself. The man's drunk, he suddenly realized. There were Scotch glasses all over the bar, two of them next to the plate with Hatcher's corned beef sandwich.

Jerry Malone looked down at his shoes and squirmed. It had been Hatcher's idea to leave the note on the door of the state office building and go to the tavern for something to eat. Malone hadn't expected to meet up with Hatcher's cronies there. He felt as though he had led his old army pal into a trap. "Why don't we go over to a table and finish our—er—dinner," he said to Hatcher. "We can talk there more privately."

Hatcher now seemed to turn his anger on Malone. "I'm not afraid to speak on the record," he snapped. He then pointed to Adams. "It's this man here who's involved in covering up one of the most horrendous crimes this state has ever witnessed, not me!"

Adams's hands were trembling. He knew that from where he stood he could take one quick step forward and bring Hatcher down with a blow that would break his nose. But Hatcher's words had stung him harder than any physical damage he might inflict upon him.

It caused Adams's mind to go numb for a moment and he became oblivious to the events before him. He found himself wondering why he had said that thing about the killer being caught within the next twenty-four hours. He didn't have the slightest idea where such a notion had come from. It was sure to make headlines by morning. Why had he gone out on such a limb? It was then that a cool thought touched his mind. Well, he thought, if *he* had gone out on a limb, Hatcher had gone out on one too—even further. If the killer were caught, as he had so unwittingly said, Hatcher's political future in the state would come to a screeching halt—especially if his cronies printed up what he had just said about a cover-up. But what made him think the killer was going to be caught that soon? He didn't know. He could only remember that as a child, when he sometimes blurted out unknown events with such certainty, those events sometimes came about. His father even thought he might have had a special gift for such things.

Hatcher made a move to leave the tavern. Adams's sudden silence had pitched him into a sea of calm, as though he had scored a major victory over the small-town sheriff. He stopped at the door and turned. There was a smile on his face. His cronies gathered on either side of him. "Read the morning papers," he said to Adams while being helped on with his coat. "It might help to teach you something about how lawyers libel themselves." A gale of laughter erupted from the reporters as they stepped out into the cold with the senatorial hopeful.

"Jesus, Jeff! Why in the hell did you go and pull a thing like that? Do you really have a lead in the case?" Jerry Malone looked into his friend's blank stare for a response. None came. He shifted uneasily on his feet. "What am I going to tell the governor when he sees the morning paper?" he asked. Again there was no response. "Okay, okay, we'll talk about it later," he said hastily. Some of the people remaining at the bar leaned closer to find out what was going on. "Right now we'd better get back to my office. Dr. York should be there soon."

As they walked through the cold back to Malone's office, Adams loosened up. "I don't know what happened back there, Jerry. It was like I knew . . . like I *know* the killer is going to be caught soon. But why I would say such a thing is beyond me."

They walked a few moments in silence. The snow crunched beneath their shoes, making the same sound as packed cornstarch.

"You know, Jeff, when we were in the service, you once said something like you just did back at the tavern. Do you remember?"

Adams shook his head. "No," he answered simply.

"Well, in Saigon, when we were after that crazy soldier who was killing all the call girls, you said that he was going to be caught that same night. This guy had already done in over twenty women with a garrote. We didn't have the slightest clue as to what we were going to do. That night, while we were passing through the red-light district, you pulled the Jeep over to the side and stared into a dark alley beside a brothel. You said somebody was back there. We were just about to go into the alley when out came the killer. He still had the bloodied strangle cord in his hand."

Adams remembered. "I don't know what that was," he said. "But I sure hope it's going to be something like that again. It's the same kind of feeling that made me say what I did tonight. I sure hope it comes true."

"Maybe that's what made you a good military cop, Jeff. You always had hunches in those days . . . good ones, too."

They walked on in silence for another moment. "That's going to be my report to the governor," Malone finally said. "If you don't get the killer in the next twenty-four hours, like you said—and that's likely to be in all the state papers by morning—I'll have to recommend that Hatcher replaces you."

For some curious reason Adams didn't feel the gloom he had been feeling earlier. Relief now shuttled through his thoughts as though a burden had just been lifted. But it quickly settled back down on him with Malone's next question. "Anything new on your missing deputy?" he asked. "Hatcher thinks that's the trump card he's going to sting you with."

"I think he's gone, Jerry. I think he got himself too close to something and was taken by surprise. If he were still alive, we'd have heard from him by now, even if he had to crawl out of the woods on his hands and knees."

When they arrived outside of the state office

building, Dr. York, the police psychologist, was waiting for them. He had arrived a few minutes earlier and was standing outside of the locked door, watching the play of moonlight on the golden dome of the capitol just across the street.

Malone excused himself for being late, even though he wasn't, and introduced the two men as he unlocked the door. Dr. York's first name was William, but he insisted on being called Bill. There was something about that that Adams liked.

They had to walk to Malone's office on the second floor because the elevators were closed down for the night. Once inside the office Adams realized he hadn't been up there in over a year. It was the same simple and sparse office it had always been, just like the man himself. There were a few pictures on the walls, books neatly stacked in oak cases, and a thick hand-braided New England rug on the highly polished wood floor. The two windows behind the desk looked out on State Street and the capitol building. It was warm, too. The thermostat had been left up because of the late night meeting.

Adams studied the psychologist as he quickly removed his down jacket and hung it on the rack beside the door. He was young, clean shaven, slim, and didn't wear a suit. Jeans and an oiled-wool sweater made him look much younger than he probably was. Without speaking, he went directly to a pile of folders that Malone had assembled on his desk.

Malone answered the question that was in Adams's eyes. "Bill was up here earlier, looking into the files of the missing children." He pointed to the folders that the doctor now carried with him to a tufted leather chair, where he then sat with them on his knees and fingered the tabs. Bill York looked up and seemed a bit embarrassed to find both men staring at him. "Gosh, I'm sorry," he said. "Am I rushing things?"

Malone smiled. "Not at all, Bill. We'll be ready for you just as soon as we get out coats off." Malone was careful not to sit behind his desk for the meeting. Out front, on the matching tufted leather sofa beside Adams, was a better place for him at such an informal gathering. "Would anyone like something to drink?" he asked before sitting down. Both men shook their heads no. Malone slid himself onto the couch beside Adams. "So," he said. "What do you make of the whole thing?" he asked the doctor.

"I don't make anything of it," York replied. "The only thing I feel sure about, from having gone over the cases in these folders, is that the probability of the killer being a schizophrenic personality is very high."

"How do you come to that?" Adams asked, pulling out a freshly opened pack of Camels and offering one to the doctor. He knew Malone never smoked. Neither did the psychologist. He returned the pack to his shirt pocket without lighting up himself.

"So far you have only two known deaths. Both children brutally killed, the last one almost completely eviscerated. There are another nine or ten children missing too." He paused. "It adds up, to me, that the killer is someone who lives and works in the valley, a respected member of the community. Someone with at least two distinct personalities, otherwise you'd know who it was because of the obviously aberrant behavior. If all you were only dealing with was a mad killer, the deaths and abductions would be happening all over the state, probably in neighboring states too." He lifted the pile of folders from his lap and placed them on the table before Adams and Malone. "There are no such reports or documentation on anything like that having occurred, *except* within the confines of Tweed Valley; which is what leads me to suspect that the killer comes from there, is known by everyone, and is probably respected by everyone—even you."

Adams felt the back of his scalp crawl. "So," he began evenly. "Who—or what—am I supposed to be looking for?"

The young doctor shook his head. "I don't know," he said. "The only thing I can offer is a sketch of what this schizophrenic personality might be. You can then try to match it against anyone in the valley."

Adams leaned forward. "Go ahead," he said. Malone uncrossed his knees and leaned forward too.

"Unrelieved stress can sometimes build up in the unconscious mind and cause it to lead to a psychological state known as dissociation—a separation of an individual's mind or personality. This splitting of the personality is called schizophrenia, and it can be temporary or permanent. Sometimes a person can live with it his or her whole life through and it won't develop into anything further than a temporary form of amnesia. In others, two or more separate personalities may occupy the same mind, each with its own distinct characteristics and memories. When something like that happens, a person can commit some very horrendous acts—acts which usually represent the repressed frustrations or desires of childhood—and then go back to his or her normal self with no conscious memory of ever having committed them."

Adams leaned back again. This time he removed a Camel from his pocket and lit it. So this is a psychological profile, he thought. He had never heard one before and was having trouble assimilating the information and trying to match it up against anyone he knew. How was he supposed to do that? he wondered. Nobody can possibly know all that about another person!

Dr. York shrugged good-naturedly. "Guess that wasn't very helpful," he said. "Looks as though you're more confused now than you were before I began to talk."

Adams tried to smile. "Wish you can give me something more to hold on to," he said. "Can you?"

"The only thing further I can offer," the young doctor began, "is that with a schizophrenic killer, it could be anyone . . . the butcher, the minister, a kindly old school teacher. On the conscious level, one part of the split personality doesn't know what the other is doing. On the *un*conscious level, however, it sometimes happens that the good, or normal, personality wishes to trip-up the bad, causing it to do something foolish which will lead the police to the killer. If that happens, it's good. If it doesn't, sooner or later, you can expect the evil personality to take over, *totally*. That's when it's too late. The individual then snaps and goes on a rampage. From what I know of the cases so far, I would say that that has not yet happened."

Adams snuffed out his cigarette in the ashtray on the low table before him. "I need a better picture than that, Bill," he said, looking up. "I've never been up against anything like this before."

The young doctor nodded. "Okay," he said, pulling

his breath in between his teeth before going on. "The bottom line is this: If you haven't already done so, you should begin to look for someone gentle, a caring person—a school teacher or someone like that. *And,* if you find that a history of insanity has existed in the family of the suspect, don't wait. Move in fast!"

Adams slowly pushed himself back into the cushions of the couch. His eyes glazed, as though he had suddenly been confronted with a revelation—a revelation that sent particles of electricity charging through every cell and nerve ending of his body. There was only one person in all of Tweed Valley that matched the description Dr. York had just drawn up. As crazy as it sounded, it was Emma Prescott—and she was, at that very moment, at home with his own two children.

CHAPTER TWENTY-THREE

Earlier that night, after Ben had left the librarian at Adams's house, Kathy sat close to Emma on the living room couch. The little girl was almost ready for bed. She had taken a bath and brushed her teeth, and now Emma Prescott was running a brush through her silky hair.

"When you grow up, you're going to have the prettiest, longest blond hair that anyone has ever seen," the librarian said.

Kathy hunched her shoulders as if to indicate it didn't matter, but Emma could tell that the child was pleased with the comment. "Thank you," the girl said softly.

Kevin, who sat across from them in an armchair, where he was reading something from an encyclopedia, looked up at Emma and asked, "What's an oracle?" The one thing good about having the town librarian over to sit for you was that you could ask her almost anything and she would know the answer. It saved a lot of time looking things up.

The hairbrush in Emma's hand slowed and missed the beat of its steady rhythm through Kathy's hair.

"Ouch," the girl said.

Emma Prescott looked down at her. "I'm sorry," she said. "I guess I wasn't paying attention, trying to think of your brother's question."

Kathy pulled Willie, her stuffed giraffe, closer to her side. "That's okay," she said. "What's an *oricoal* anyway?"

Kevin laughed. *"Oracle,"* he said, correcting his little sister. "Not *oricoal."*

As Emma continued to brush Kathy's hair, she answered the boy's question. "In ancient times," she began, "it was the way the gods spoke to their people. It told them what to do and predicted events that were supposed to happen—things like that." She couldn't imagine what had prompted the boy to ask such a question. Was he already able to *see* that she intended to introduce him to the Egyptian ritual later that evening? "What makes you ask such a question as that?" she asked, this time making sure not to get the brush caught in Kathy's hair again.

"Something about Alexander the Great," Kevin said, pointing to the encyclopedia in his lap. "He went into the desert, to some oasis, to speak to an oracle. It was supposed to tell him something."

"I know what an oasis is," Kathy said brightly. "It's a place in the desert where they have water. I saw it on the pack of cigarettes that Daddy smokes." She swung around to face the librarian so quickly that she almost got her hair tangled up in the brush. "Does smoking give you cancer?" she asked. Her eyes searched the librarian's for an answer she plainly did not want to hear.

Emma placed the brush down beside her on the

couch and took the child's small face in her hands. "It's not good for you," she said. "It can give you cancer. That's what it says right on the package." The librarian looked over to Kevin with an expression on her face that indicated she'd have more to say about oracles just as soon as she answered any other questions that Kathy might have about smoking. It seemed important to the child.

The boy nodded. He agreed. Besides, he wanted to hear it, too. Some of his friends at school were already experimenting with tobacco.

Kathy took a deep breath. "Did my mommy smoke?" she asked. "I asked Kevin and he doesn't remember."

Emma swallowed against the lump of dryness in her throat. "Yes," she said softly. And that's all she said. A silence then filled the room for many moments.

Kathy finally looked over to Kevin. Her small sharp chin looked as though it were made of iron. She poked the air with her pointing finger, as if to punctuate what she was about to say, and then said it. "That's it! Daddy is going to stop smoking. And we're going to *make* him do it!"

At that moment, Kevin loved his little sister more than he ever imagined he could. "And you're not going to smoke when you grow up either," he said, pointing his finger right back at her.

"And you too!" Kathy quickly retorted. "So that's settled," she said, scooping Willie back up into her arms. She leaned forward again, clutching the stuffed giraffe tightly.

Emma stroked her hair with her hands before she began to brush it again. Although neither child knew exactly how they were going to get their father to quit smoking, they somehow felt that it was going to happen—it was just as simple as that.

"Well," Emma said with a touch of breathlessness in her voice. "I guess I'd better not begin to smoke either!"

The children laughed. The librarian was one of the nicest, kindest women they had ever known. Smart, too. *She* would never smoke.

Something in Emma's eyes changed. It was imperceptible to either the boy or his sister. She had just glanced out the window and saw that the snow was beginning to build up. She got that itchy feeling inside her for a moment. "So what else about this oracle?" she asked Kevin as she began to glide the brush through Kathy's hair again. The girl yawned. It was a sure sign she would soon fall asleep, right there in Emma's arms if she would let her. "Was that when Alexander was in Egypt?" she asked Kevin.

The boy's chest inflated. It wasn't every day he got a chance to offer information to a grown-up like Miss Prescott—even if he didn't know what some of the words meant. "Yes," he answered eagerly. He pointed to the opened encyclopedia on his lap. "It even says here that he got lost in the desert going to the oasis. Then two large blackbirds flew out of nowhere and showed him the way." Kevin shook his head. "Do you believe that?" he asked the librarian.

"Sometimes, back in those days, things happened that we don't have any answers for today." Emma didn't go any further. The words had been measured out as carefully as a skilled angler baiting a hook.

Kathy was now leaning further and further back into Emma with each stroke of the hairbrush. The librarian stopped and wrapped both her arms about the girl.

"My, my," Emma said, looking down at the girl. "I can see someone's *real* tired." She cuddled Kathy tightly and whispered something close to her ear. The girl shook her head with a sleepy smile and lifted herself from the couch. She then scooped up her pet giraffe and ambled to her room where Emma had just promised to follow and tuck her in with a story. She couldn't help smiling at the sleepy child as she left the room, nightdress raised slightly off the floor in one hand and Willie dangling by a leg from her other hand.

Emma then got up herself. She looked at the boy as though she had just remembered something. "I guess I really *don't* know about oracles and blackbirds," she said. "Guess that's something people just hear nowadays . . . then get themselves to believe it until someone like you comes along and asks an intelligent question." She paused for a moment as though she were considering whether or not to tell him something more, but then decided not to. "No," she half said to herself, turning to leave the room. "He's too young yet for anything like that." The ploy worked immediately.

"What?" Kevin asked. "Who's too young for what?"

Emma turned. She feigned a startled expression on her face, as though she hadn't intended for the boy to have heard what she just mumbled half beneath her breath. "Oh, my," she said, raising one hand to her cheek. "I guess I'd better tell you before you make something bigger of it than it really is."

"What is it, Miss Prescott? Is it something about Alexander the Great? About oracles?"

Emma smiled. The boy had taken the bait and swallowed the hook. "It's not about either, but in a way

I suppose it's about both. I brought a book along with me tonight, one that I was intending to read after you and your sister had gone to bed. It's about ancient magic. Maybe you'd like to have a look at it while I go and tuck Kathy in."

It was as though the boy rose several feet above the armchair without moving an inch. "Yes!" he responded. "Does it tell you anything about oracles? Like the one that spoke to Alexander?"

Emma shook her head. "Not directly," she answered. "But it tells a lot about ancient magic. How to do rituals, cast spells, and things like that." She walked to the front door, where her coat was hung, and slid her hand into the pocket of it without removing it from the rack. She quickly pulled out the book. It was still in the ziplock baggie she had placed it in earlier.

"It's a real old book," she said as she walked back to the boy and removed it from the baggie. "Do you think you can handle it gently while I go in and get Kathy to sleep?"

Kevin took the slender book into his hands as though it were an object to be revered. As for the librarian, she had merely plopped it into his outstretched hands before leaving the room. It looked so old and fragile that he could hardly believe she would trust him with such a precious-looking thing—especially with her not even staying around to see if he would handle it properly. She sure knows how to make a boy feel all grown up, he thought, gazing down at it in his hands. He read the title. *Ancient Egyptian Magic, As Described By . . .* His lips moved with each word, the way they sometimes did when he thought something was important and wanted to remember it.

The title was a long one. He couldn't wait to find out what was inside. The book seemed to open naturally in his hands, to the place where Emma had left the bookmark. He began to read, silently shaping each word with his lips. *Ritual for the awakening of the hidden power of the mind.*

By the time Emma got to Kathy's room, the little girl was fast asleep. She looked so clean and fresh, as though she had just been born. The covers that were pulled up to her shoulders lifted and fell with her breathing. There was a rhythm to it that was very peaceful, very assuring. Emma smiled and walked to the windows to see if they had been double locked as Adams had taught Kathy to do. They were. What a frightful thing to have to teach one's own children to do, she thought. But there was no choice. With all that's been going on in the valley, she thought, it's no wonder most parents were at their wit's end to know what to do. If Kevin could only be made to *see,* she told herself, he might be able to tell his father who the child-killer was.

Emma leaned over Kathy's bed and touched her lips to the child's forehead. "Sleep tight," she whispered. And as she drew away, Kathy murmured a word in her sleep. "Mommy," she said softly, as though it hurt to say the word. There was a touch of dampness in the corners of her closed eyes too. Seeing it there, and having heard that one word the child had just murmured, placed a bead of moisture in each corner of Emma's eyes too.

We have to get that killer! she thought, leaving the room. The sooner we do, the better off everyone in the valley will be. In her mind, the *we* meant she and Kevin.

She headed straight for the living room where she had left the boy.

Kevin looked up at her with a knotted brow as soon as she entered the room. "I don't understand any of this," he said. "What's it supposed to do?"

Emma took a seat on the couch opposite him and faked as much puzzlement as he had just expressed. "I don't really know," she said. "Maybe you'd better let me have a look at what you mean."

Kevin rose from the armchair and went to sit beside her on the sofa. "It's all this about rituals and spells," he said once he had settled into place. "What are they supposed to do?"

Emma carefully took the book from his hands and studied the page at which it was opened. It was the page of the ritual for the awakening of hidden powers. The bookmark was still in it. After a few moments she said, "I guess I don't know what this is all about either." She allowed a beat or two to pass, then asked, "Should I read you some of it after you get into bed?"

Kevin hadn't been read to in bed in a long time. Besides, how could he sleep with his clothes on if the librarian read to him there? "I don't think so, Miss Prescott. Can't we do it here?"

Emma thought quickly. She wanted him to be in bed because it was better to recite the ritual while he was in a relaxed state of mind. "You don't think you're too grown up already to have ol' Miss Prescott read to you in *bed,* do you?"

Kevin didn't know what to say. The librarian had phrased the question in such a way that it sounded as though she'd be offended if he refused her offer. He didn't want to do that. "Okay," he finally said. "Just give me a chance to get ready and I'll call you in when I am."

Emma smiled. "My, my," she said. "You *are* growing up fast."

Kevin's ears tingled with redness at the praise. He quickly left the room and "prepared" himself for bed. He went first to the bathroom where he brushed his teeth loudly, so that the librarian would hear, and then went to his room where he allowed himself enough time for the pretense of having undressed and gotten into his pajamas. Just before he climbed into bed he switched off the overhead light and popped his head out the door to let the librarian know he was ready. He then scooted over to the bed before she got there and pulled the covers up to his chin so she couldn't tell that he still had all his clothes on.

The only light in the room came from a dim lamp on the night table beside his bed. Beside it was a chair, the chair on which he had for the past several nights kept his sneakers—in case he needed to get at them in a hurry. He knew the librarian would be sitting on it when she read to him so he placed the sneakers beneath his pillow, right on top of the hatchet he had been keeping there. The lump they made didn't bother him at all; as a matter of fact, there was something reassuring about it.

Emma came quietly into the room and checked to see if the boy had locked his windows, just as she had checked when she had gone to Kathy's room earlier. The locking devices that Adams had installed on all the downstairs windows were of the same kind. By turning a key, a dead bolt ran into a stop hole that was drilled into the side of the window jamb, preventing it from being raised. There were several stop holes in the jamb so that the window could be left opened in warmer weather and locked into place, three inches top and bottom. Kevin's windows, just as his sister's, were shut tightly against the outside cold and locked. The key hung from a hook that was beyond anyone's reach should the window have been left opened from either the top or bottom. Emma checked to see if the key was on its hook. It was, just as the one in his sister's room was.

"Well, now," Emma said as she sat in the chair beside Kevin's bed. "Let's see what we have here." She opened the old book and scanned the page for a moment before looking over to the boy. He was already beginning to breathe deeply and she could tell that sleep was not too far behind. The small lamp beside his bed offered her barely enough light with which to read. She tilted the shade toward her so that she could see better.

"Are you ready to hear what it says about ancient magic?" she finally asked.

The boy nodded. "It's not going to be scary, is it?" he asked, suddenly realizing that it might be.

Emma shook her head. "Now would I do a thing like that, just before you're about to fall asleep, too?"

Kevin smiled at her. "No," he said. "I just asked because I don't want to have any bad dreams." And with that came flooding back a montage of images created in his mind about the "killer tree" and having hacked its "head" into two separate pieces—and the one piece that resembled the librarian herself. He could feel the small hairs on the back of his arms stand up as he looked at her in the shaded light that spilled across her face from the lamp. The shadows made all the wrinkles and creases in her face resemble the wood grain of the old gnarled "head." He quickly turned his head away and closed his eyes as the librarian began to read.

"Arise O Light. Ascend to thy height. Cast thy blaze upon this child. That he may See. Thou who art within, lift thy shadow. That this child of Light may See. Reveal to him thy power. That he may See."

Without opening his eyes, Kevin asked, "What's that?"

"It's a ritual," Emma said. "If someone has an undeveloped gift to see things before they happen, or to know about things before they hear them, this ritual is supposed to bring all that good magic to the surface where it can be more useful—so that the person can be helpful to other people who don't possess the same power to see."

"Why does it say, *this child?* Is it a child's ritual?"

Emma drew her breath in slightly, not wanting to betray the pleasure that the boy's response had given her. "Usually the power to see things that are not known comes to small children. By the time we grow older, such an ability goes back to where it came from—especially if no one is around to recognize it and help the child develop it." She paused for a moment before going on. "This ritual is supposed to come from the days of the ancient Egyptians. Their priests used it on those who showed signs of being gifted with such hidden powers."

Kevin wanted to open his eyes and ask some more questions, but they were so heavy with sleep that he couldn't. He couldn't even be sure he wasn't dreaming at that very moment. His eyelids fluttered without opening. He could hear Miss Prescott continue reading as though her voice were coming from very far away. As she read, his mind drifted further and further out into a vast sea of darkness—a sea in which all the dreams he had been having lately blended with the smooth flow of the librarian's words.

"Arise O Light. Ascend to thy height. Cast thy blaze upon this child. That he may See. Thou who art within, lift thy shadow. That this child of Light may See. Reveal to him thy power. That he may See."

Emma Prescott repeated the spell until her throat went dry, until long after Kevin had fallen asleep. She quietly closed the book and placed it on the night table beside him. From the heavy rhythm of his breathing there was no doubt in her mind as to the depth with which he slept. She rose from the chair and drew her hands across him until they were poised in the air just above his shoulders. She counted to three, held her breath, then shouted "Boo!"

Kevin's eyes shot open. She held him down by the shoulders. "Who's the killer?" she asked. "Who's responsible?"

The boys eyes dulled. There was no life to them. They quickly closed, but before he fell off to sleep again, he murmured a response. "You are," he said, as though the voice whispered from another being deep within him. "You," he repeated.

There was a heavy silence in the room as Emma straightened herself up. A smile darted across her lips. So much for magic! she thought. *Me,* the killer! It was almost enough to make her laugh. The boy had simply fallen asleep.

She carried the book out into the living room and

replaced it in the ziplock baggie. So much for all that, she thought, still smiling to herself. She was tired herself and decided to sit down in the armchair and close her eyes for a minute before going to the kitchen to finish washing the dinner dishes that Adams had left in his haste to leave for the capital.

She must have dozed. When she opened her eyes again it was way past midnight. Goodness! she thought, pulling herself out of the comfortable chair. I could have stayed here the rest of the night! She thought of leaving the dishes for morning, but the idea of piling breakfast dishes on top of dinner plates did not sit well with her. It was easier to get a fresh start in the morning if everything was cleared off from the night before. It was the way she liked to live. Life was so much less complicated that way.

At the kitchen sink Emma looked out the window in front of her and saw that Betty Lineham's house was completely dark. Good, she thought. She hadn't expected that Betty would be getting a full night's rest for some time to come. She felt happy that it appeared she was on the way to one.

There was something else out there in the blackness before her—something that affected her in a totally unexpected way. It was snow. It fluttered down from the sky and into the spill of light from the kitchen window as though someone had opened a feather pillow above the roof. The icy chill it brought to the base of her spine was almost as painful as if someone had touched her there with the point of a dentist's pick. She squared her shoulders and turned around. She could have sworn someone had been standing there. But no, there was no one there. It was just a feeling she had.

But whatever it was that had caused Emma Prescott to spin about, it now moved into her as though she had been standing there naked, drenched in quickly evaporating alcohol. In her head a familiar voice rang out. Only this time, there was something different about it. It didn't belong to anyone else; it was her own.

Now scat you prig and do your rightful thing! it screamed inside of her. *No time to waste. I got ya good! For now and for the rest of time!*

Something inside of her unraveled. Long, loose ends of complex circuitry shorted out and flared in the darkness of her ravaged mind—a mind that was rapidly slipping into an abyss, never to return. Her body wrenched and twisted about the kitchen. Plates crashed to the floor and chairs toppled. She landed against the wall as though someone had hurled her there. The voice continued to scream inside her head.

Mother always said you'd end up like this. Like her. Burn her dolls just because she wouldn't let you play with them! That killed her, don't ya know? But don't feel badly. She was as crazy as a bat. Like you. Like me. Like US.

Emma tried to block it out by clapping her hands tightly to her ears. It didn't work.

I got ya good! it shouted. *Not like all the other times before. You played my tune too many times. You've grown to like it. Can't do without it. Just like me. Just like you. Just like* US. *We're one now, Emma. You and me are* US. *No use to try and get us caught with magic words from ancient times. The boy's asleep. We'll get him, too. You'll see. We're in it together now. You hear me? The boy's asleep and he can't see. The girl goes first, then follows he! Ha! Ha! Miss Prig, you're dead! You are now* ME!

Emma lifted herself from the floor where she had fallen. It had felt as though a mighty hand had held her down while the words ran through every cell and fiber of her mind—transposing it, altering its complex circuitry until she became united with the killer within. She knew it now. The boy was right. She was the killer!

Why then did she not feel the dread of it?

Emma rose from the kitchen floor forever changed, as though some curious baptism had taken place inside of her. She felt united with the evil thing and she didn't care. She was jubilant. The joy of having gone completely mad! Her mother and grandfather had it. And now she had it too. She let a chilling howl escape her lips as she recognized how stupid it had been for her to have held it back all these many long years.

Must get it done, she told herself. No time to waste.

She left the kitchen and was headed toward the children's bedrooms when she stopped like an animal in her tracks. Her eyes screwed themselves up until only the whites showed. She thought she heard a noise. She listened carefully. There it was again. She turned. It was the doorbell.

Now who on earth could that be? she wondered. And at a time like this.

It was exactly 1 A.M.

CHAPTER TWENTY-FOUR

Adams didn't bother with the hotel room that had been reserved for him at the capital that night. Right after his meeting with Malone and Dr. York, he climbed into the Peugeot he had left right outside the state office building and headed directly home.

Emma Prescott! he thought as he drove to the nearest filling station to get some gas and make a telephone call—a call he didn't want to make from Malone's office in the presence of his friend and the police psychologist. The idea that Emma might be the dreaded child-killer was too bizarre. Yet, there *had* been madness in her family. It had always sounded like a rumor to him, but when he was younger, he remembered having heard it told around—with some conviction—that her mother had to be put away because of it.

He saw an all-night filling station just before entering the interstate. He pulled in and, while the car was being filled, went inside to the telephone and dialed the number of his office. Emma had spent so many nights and afternoons with his children that he could hardly believe he was about to ask his deputy to take a drive over to his house, just to see if everything looked okay. He didn't want Ben to go in and stir things up. If Emma was the killer—and that was a big *if* in his mind—it might be best just to ease her out of the house by having Ben tell her he had called and was on the way home, and that Ben would stay with the kids until he arrived.

There was no answer. Adams let the phone ring about ten times. It was almost 12:30 A.M. Where the hell could he be? He considered calling Betty, but her mind was in such a fragile state of recovery that there was no telling what a call in the middle of the night might do to her. Besides, what could he ask her to do? Go over to his house to see if everything was okay? Get herself dressed in the dead of night and drive over to his office to see if Ben was there? It would be too crazy to ask of her unless he was willing to go into an explanation. And what could *that* possibly be? That Emma Prescott, one of the most highly respected and good-natured members of the community, was possibly the crazed child-killer that has been terrorizing the valley? That the kindhearted town librarian might possibly have been responsible for the murder of her own daughter, Jennifer?

He knew how absurd it would all sound. Emma couldn't hurt a fly. Yet, the words of the young psychologist crawled in his mind like a nest of uneasy hornets: *Look for someone gentle, a caring person—a school teacher or someone like that . . . If you find that a history of insanity has existed in the family, don't wait. Move in fast!*

Despite the cold, there were beads of perspiration on Adams's forehead as he went back out into the cold for his car. He could call Emma, he thought. But what would that do? If she were the killer, that would only make matters worse. The best thing to do was either get home as quickly as he could or try Ben again before leaving the station. Maybe he had dialed the wrong number.

Adams paid the attendant and returned to the telephone inside. As he counted the rings at the other end of the line, he suddenly realized what the trouble might be. If Ben had taken the small space heater back into the cell with him, as he said he had the night before, and the heavy door that separated the jail from the office accidentally closed in a draft, there was a good chance that Ben wouldn't be able to hear the telephone. And at that time, Ben was probably sound asleep. Shit! he thought.

After twenty rings there was still no answer. He replaced the receiver and stepped outside into the cold again. He was surprised to see that the service attendant had pulled the car right up to the door for him.

"Snow's pretty bad if you're headed south," the attendant said, wiping his hand on a rag.

Adams looked down toward the interstate. There were few cars on the road. "Do you know if the road's been sanded yet?" he asked, indicating to the attendant that he was indeed headed south.

"Trucks probably won't be down that way for another hour or so. Why don't you go and get yourself some coffee at the Stockyard Restaurant. It's just walking distance back up the road you came from. They're open all night."

Adams shook his head and thanked him for the

suggestion, but he couldn't. He was in a hurry.

"I'll tell you something else," the attendant pressed as he watched Adams hastily climb in behind the wheel of the old Peugeot. "You've got a sticky valve. Engine's missing badly. I could put in a new set of spark plugs if you like. It might fire the engine with more power and blow it free. That sometimes happens. I don't know if I'd trust getting up some of those steep grades you have ahead, what with the snow and all."

Adams almost wavered. But with old cars like his, one had to consider that sometimes the simplest jobs led to major repairs. A nut might snap, and with a foreign car, parts weren't easily replaced. He didn't want to risk being laid up without a car altogether.

The farther south he drove, the steeper the hills became. He realized he should have taken the attendant up on the matter of the new plugs. The Peugeot came close to stalling out on some of the longer climbs. Due to the sticky valve, the car would sometimes have to rely on only three cylinders, instead of four, when going up hills. It would then slow up badly while gas fumes, from having to depress the accelerator all the way to the floor, filled the car. Adams rolled the window down and let the cold air hit his face. It felt good and would help to keep him awake. And then the snow started.

The road before him grew whiter and more slippery with snow. The moon was lower now and occasionally dipped behind a stand of tall trees beside the road. Their naked branches would then cast long shadows on the highway. They looked like twisted tentacles reaching out at him. If he could find another all-night filling station he'd stop and get some new plugs. The attendant up near the capital, now about forty miles away, was right. He needed more power if he was going to get back home before dawn. The snow was beginning to slow him up too. And for some reason the windshield wipers weren't working too good either. He suddenly remembered Ben using it to go over to the spice wholesaler in East Hartfield that afternoon. He made up his mind never to lend his car to Ben again. The deputy wasn't used to it. Maybe that's why it was running so bad. It hadn't been earlier.

He rounded a curve, and when he saw the steep hill that loomed up before him in the beam of his headlights, he swallowed his breath and jammed the accelerator all the way to the floor. The car picked up speed and for a while he thought it would make it, but he hit an ice patch that was covered over with fresh snow and did a figure eight. Without stopping, he came out of it and headed for the hill again. The snow rooster-tailed on both sides of the car as though it were a ship plowing through a raging surf. There were no other cars on the road and he thought that if he got it headed just right he could make it all the way to the top. He was almost there when the old Peugeot shuddered . . . and then quietly died.

It was 1 A.M. The precise moment that Emma Prescott had welcomed Ben into Adam's living room.

CHAPTER TWENTY-FIVE

It had been 12:30 A.M. when something caused Ben to leave the cot in the jail cell and wander out into the main office. He didn't know what it was. Then he looked at the calendar on his desk. It was the twelfth, his birthday! If he had been at home, he could expect his three children to come rushing in at dawn—two on foot, the nine-month-old carried in his wife's arms—and they would all, in their fashion, sing "Happy Birthday" to him. After that he could expect to have a very special breakfast prepared for him. In spite of the fact that he was going to be at the office when they all woke up, he smiled. He was a lucky man, he had told himself. He was now thirty-six, married six years, and had three wonderful children—and all the numbers were divisible by three. He knew for sure he was going to have some kind of a special day.

He was on his way back to the cot in the jail cell when the report he had been working on before turning in caught his attention. It was lying next to the calendar on his desk. Something about the report had made him sit down with it again. It told of his trip to the spice wholesaler in East Hartfield and of the interviews he had had with the bookkeeper and the manager of the loading dock. It was something about the manager's statement that only now seemed to form a peculiar picture in his mind. Maybe it was the long trip to the plant—over a hundred and fifty miles there and back—and having spent all that time getting a flat fixed and the new set of snow tires installed, but there was suddenly something about the manager's statement that piqued his curiosity. The manager said he thought a demented old woman had been responsible for stealing all those sacks of pepper. He wondered why it now made him think of Emma Prescott.

Ben slowly sat down at his desk and squinted at the report as though it had suddenly leaped into flames before his eyes. *Demented old woman? Burlap sack?*

He remembered driving by the library on his way to the spice plant earlier that afternoon. Emma Prescott had been standing out in the rain clutching something she had just pulled from her clothesline. To a stranger who didn't know her, wouldn't she look like a demented old woman, standing out there like that? And the thing she had just pulled from the clothesline . . . Wouldn't it seem that she was trying to conceal it? Couldn't it have been a burlap sack—like the ones that the manager had shown him at the plant? It now seemed to him that it was.

Ben's eyes had widened. It was many moments before they softened again. Everyone has a burlap sack in these parts. They come in useful for all sorts of things. He had a couple of them down in the cellar himself. Having one didn't prove anything. Even if you happen to be standing out in the rain with one? Trying to conceal what you're holding from a deputy sheriff who happens to be driving by?

Ben found himself down in the hole of doubt just as quicky as he imagined he had dug himself up out of it. He knew at once what Adams would say about such unfounded speculations. The sheriff would tell him that he read too many books and that he was overexercising his imagination.

Ben rubbed his chin and stared off into space. The thing about such bizarre murders is, it could be anyone, he thought. Anyone at all. Especially if they are thought of as the least likely person to ever commit such a crime. And the town librarian was over at the sheriff's house right then. With his own two children.

Ben wasted no time leaving the office. He was down the road and on his way to the sheriff's house when the telephone calls came in from Adams at the filling station near the capital—the calls that Adams had thought his deputy didn't hear because he was sleeping.

Ben parked his car down near the post office and walked up the hill to Adams's house. He didn't want to disturb the neighbors with the sound of his car's engine groaning to get up the hill on a slippery road. His breath was frosty as he approached the house. There were lights on. They came from the kitchen, the living room, and the children's bedrooms that were around to the side of the house. He'd check those first.

The snow was up to the tops of his boots as he quietly made his way to the windows of the children's rooms. Kathy was sleeping peacefully with her giraffe tucked in beside her. And Kevin, in the next room, was sleeping too. The dim light beside his bed revealed a deep and steady rhythm to the boy's breathing.

He felt relieved—and a bit embarrassed for having

made so much of so little—but he still wanted to know what Emma was doing with the lights on in the living room.

It was ten minutes before 1 A.M.

Ben cautiously walked back to the front of the house and peeked in through the living room window. Emma was sleeping soundly in the comfortable old armchair. It appeared she had fallen asleep while reading a book. Something he often did himself. He suddenly felt quite foolish for having dreamed up all those horrible thoughts about Emma being a psychotic child-killer. Maybe Adams was right after all. His imagination did work overtime. Maybe he did read too much.

He was about to return to his car down the hill when Emma woke up. Ben ducked out of the spill of light from the window and held perfectly still. The last thing he wanted now was to frighten the poor librarian out of her wits.

After a few moments Emma's shadow crossed the window and fell on the snow outside. Ben watched it move across the elongated patch of light and disappear as she headed out of the room. Then he heard the water being turned on in the kitchen. From the sound of it, it seemed she was finishing the dinner dishes. He reasoned she had fallen asleep earlier and was just now getting to them. Sometimes, his own wife did the very same thing. He moved away from the house as quietly as he could and, once out onto the road, started a slow jog down the hill to his car.

Ben was almost to the post office when he thought he heard something. He stopped and listened. In fresh-fallen snow, sounds traveled differently. You could be stalking a deer through woods in heavy snow, thinking it was just in front of you, when it was really a quarter of a mile *behind* you. Only this was not the sound of an animal, or was it? He heard it again. This time he was sure it came from the direction of the sheriff's house. It sounded as though someone had just hurt themselves. He thought it might be Emma.

As he raced back up the hill through the snow he heard the unmistakable sound of a dish shattering against the floor. Furniture was being pushed around too. A chilling howl then pierced the snow-still night. He drew his gun and ran the rest of the way at full speed. There was no use going back for the car. It would take too long.

By the time he reached the front door of the house everything was quiet again. Approaching the house, he noticed Emma's shadow cross the long patch of light that fell from the living room window onto the snow-covered ground. He pressed his thumb to the doorbell.

It was exactly 1 A.M.

Inside, Emma spun about. She couldn't imagine who it might be. She had been headed in the direction of the children's rooms and quickly turned away to answer the doorbell.

"Goodness!" she said, opening the door and seeing Ben standing there all out of breath. Her eyes caught the tail end of the swift movement with which the deputy holstered his gun when she opened the door. "Is there something wrong?" she asked.

Ben looked past her into the house. All seemed normal. He didn't know what to say. "I was just passing by," he finally offered. "Saw the lights on and thought I'd stop in to see if everything was okay."

Emma ushered him into the house with a welcoming

gesture, taking a quick look outside before closing the door. He had not arrived by car. There were no tire tracks in the fresh snow—only his footprints approaching the house from the road. She didn't say anything about how he got there, or about how he happened to be passing by at a time like that.

"Everything's fine here," she said. "The lights are on because I fell asleep in the armchair after the children went to bed. I was just fixing to turn them off and do the same when you rang the doorbell."

"I heard something that sounded like a dish breaking, or something like that."

Emma laughed. "My word," she said. "Guess sound travels all over the place in fresh snow. I dropped a glass in the kitchen a few minutes ago, when I was finishing up the dinner plates." He appeared to believe what she had said. "Can I fix you some coffee?" she asked.

Ben shook his head. "Thank you, no," he said. "I should be getting back."

Emma looked at him without saying a word. Maybe it was her silence that did it, but he suddenly decided he should stay for a few minutes after all. It was not like the librarian to let him go so easily—even if it was the middle of the night.

"You know," he said with a smile. "I'll take you up on that offer for a cup of coffee after all. That ol' electric pot we have back at the office hasn't been working too good lately."

"Well, you just have yourself a seat, Ben. I'll go fetch you some."

When Emma went to the kitchen, she did something that she had never done before: She closed the door behind her. Before starting the coffee in the Silex, she went to the sink and turned the water on full force. The noise of it would help mask the sound of her picking up the broken dishes from the floor. She also had to right the toppled chairs. Back at the counter where the Silex was, there was also a counter-top knife rack. The blades of the long carving knives were pushed into the slots of the thick butcher-block rack right up to their jet-black wooden handles. Something about them made her eyes go narrow.

Ben didn't know if she had deliberately closed the kitchen door behind her, or if it had closed accidentally. It didn't matter. It was a good thing for him that it had. It gave him the opportunity to now quietly walk past the door on his way to the children's rooms just down the hall, opposite the kitchen. He wanted to see if everything was still as normal as it had appeared when he looked in from outside their windows—before he heard what he thought was the sound of dishes shattering.

One at a time, Ben opened their doors and popped his head into the children's rooms. They were sleeping as peacefully as when he had looked in on them from outside, not more than fifteen minutes before. He hurried back to the living room and took a seat in the armchair before Emma returned. He didn't know why he was feeling the way he did. There was absolutely nothing wrong with what was going on. It was him and his overactive imagination. He was manufacturing the whole thing in his mind. He shook his head when he thought of the fun the sheriff would have with him if he ever told him about this night. He knew how crazy it would all sound to him.

Ben was just about to go to the kitchen to see if Emma could use some help with the coffee, when the book in the ziplock bag, lying on the table beside him, caught his attention. He picked it up and squinted at the title through the plastic. Ancient Egyptian magic? he thought. What on earth is she reading a thing like this for? The book looked old and valuable.

He had removed it from the bag and was looking through it as Emma came out of the kitchen with a tray in her hands. On it was a pot of coffee, two cups with saucers, and a plate of cookies. She instantly noticed the water marks made by Ben's boots on the wooden floor of the hallway leading to the children's rooms. With the kitchen door closed, the deputy hadn't noticed them because the light had been cut off.

The cups rattled on the tray as Emma walked over to where Ben sat. Nothing about her eyes had changed from the moment she first saw him with the book in his hands. Without missing a beat, she told him it had belonged to Lewis B. Olcott. "He had a lot of different books," she continued. "My great-uncle was an avid reader. A great man." She smiled, knowing that Ben liked to read a lot too. "Thought I'd have a look at it sometime when I had the chance, but I fell right asleep in the chair before I ever got it out of the baggie. See anything in it that's good?" she asked, setting the tray down on the table beside him. "I've always had an interest in ancient Egypt; most people do. But *magic?* Well, I don't know about all that!" she concluded as though it were a lot of nonsense.

Ben carefully placed the book back on the table next to the tray. "I don't understand things like that either," he said. "Hocus-pocus stuff has always baffled me.

Seems such things are better suited for the insane."

The corner of one of Emma's eyes twitched at the remark. He didn't miss it. It set the whole thing tumbling in his mind again: the burlap sack she had tried to conceal while standing out in the rain that afternoon; the loading dock manager's comment about a demented old woman stealing fifty-pound sacks of crushed red pepper. He thought Emma was as physically fit as any man her age and could easily have lifted such sacks without difficulty. She was probably even capable of hurling a small child twenty feet up into a tree too.

"You know anything about the Mafia?" Ben asked in as casual and as distracted a way as he could manage.

Emma looked at him and frowned. "Gracious, no," she said, pouring some coffee into his cup. "Should I?"

"I borrowed a book from your library about it once," Ben responded, again with as little effort in his voice as he could muster. "I thought by some chance you might have read it." He concluded by locking his eyes onto hers as tightly as a clamp.

Emma shook her head. "Should I have?" she asked. There was a faint touch of something on her lips that he couldn't be sure of. It was as though she were in the presence of a precocious child.

"Not really," Ben said. "But if you ever come across it, there's an interesting chapter on how they get rid of their dead victims."

Emma's cup rattled in her saucer when she reached for it to pour her own coffee. It steadied quickly. "Why on earth do you think I would find something like that . . . interesting?" Her tone was now as rock-steady as the cup and saucer in her hand. "Do you take milk?"

she asked brightly, nodding to the deputy's cup of coffee on the table beside him.

The subject was changed. Ben felt she had considered what he said about the Mafia was small talk, intended to fill up time. He shook his head. "Thank you, no," he finally responded. "Haven't used milk in my coffee since I was a boy." And he smiled that broad, boyish smile of his.

Emma rose from the chair and placed her cup on the tray beside Ben's. "Then you'll excuse me for a moment while I go into the kitchen to fetch some for myself? Don't know what I was thinking of to have come out without it."

Ben made a motion to rise. "Let me get it for you," he said.

Emma motioned him back into the armchair with a gesture of her hand. "Don't be silly," she said. "I'm already up and halfway there."

He had an urge to follow her but settled himself back down. He didn't want to make a complete fool of himself. What was she going to do in there, anyway? Conceal a carving knife beneath her sweater? The idea almost made him laugh.

"What's so amusing?" she asked, returning from the kitchen with a creamer of milk in one hand and a cloth napking beneath it to catch the spill. "Did I do or say something funny?"

"No, Emma. It's nothing like that. It's just that—" he couldn't finish.

"Just that . . . what, Ben?" she pressed, pouring some milk into her cup of coffee. When she finished, she picked up a spoon and carried it back to her chair with the cup of coffee. In the absence of a response from the deputy, she said, "Seems there's something troubling you, Ben. Anything wrong?" she asked, stirring her coffee.

Ben took a deep breath and risked it. One way to clear the air was to gamble it all and go out on a limb. After all, today was his lucky birthday.

"I was just wondering if you'd really like to know why I came over here tonight," he finally said.

The coffee stuck in Emma's throat, but she managed to swallow without choking. "You mean, it wasn't because you just happened to be passing by and heard a noise?" she asked.

"No, Emma. That wasn't it at all." He leaned back in the armchair and reached for his coffee, allowing her enough time to do something that he might be able to read some significance into.

"Well, to tell you the truth, Ben, I never did believe you were wandering about in the middle of the night during a snowfall, listening for odd sounds. Besides, you arrived here on foot. Saw your footprints in the snow where tire tracks from your car ought to have been, had you been driving like you said. But, I'm not one to raise questions of a police officer who comes panting up to someone's door in the middle of the night—and him with just having had his gun out, too. Sometimes, even the most trusted citizens get to going off the deep end about things—things they imagine up, mostly. Gets them a little . . . crazy, if you know what I mean?"

Ben couldn't believe what he was hearing. The librarian's words were very perceptive. But nothing she said indicated that she might possibly be a crazed child-killer. He was almost ashamed for having thought it all up in the first place. *Cowed,* is how he felt. It showed in his eyes.

"You've been working awfully hard on these cases of the missing children," Emma continued. Her tone appeared to be gathering momentum. "So has Jeff, and Arthur, too. I think you, being the most imaginative of the lot, have conjured up the notion that I must somehow be the one to look more closely at. You're tired and exhausted, Ben. Grasping at straws. You read too many books, too—police stories and things like that. If I'm the killer you have imagined me to be, what's my motive? That I love children more than anything else in the world?" She paused as though she were out of breath. She was angry, too. "You know you can't get a decent conviction in a court of law without first establishing the motive for a crime."

Ben's fingers trembled. It was as though Emma had read every thought in his mind. If she ever mentioned to Adams what had happened there that night, he wondered if he'd still have a job. It surely seemed as though he had unduly upset the innocent woman.

"I'm sorry, Emma. I guess—I guess you're right. I do have an overactive imagination. It's just—"

He caught the sudden movement of Emma's hands going to the top of her sweater. She was twisting it about her throat as though she were freezing cold. The knuckles of her hands were chalk-white. He leaned forward. "Is there something wrong?" he asked.

Her eyes told him there was indeed something wrong—something terribly wrong. She was focused on him as though he had suddenly become another person. A stranger. He rose from the armchair and touched one of her cheeks with his hand. It was like a block of ice.

"Emma?" he called to her quietly. "Can you hear me?"

When he received no response, he took her by the shoulders and gently shook them. "Emma? What's wrong?"

Her eyes rolled up into her head until they were all white. He dropped his hands and took a step back. "If this is some kind of joke, I—"

Her lips curled back and exposed her teeth. They looked like glistening fangs. He almost swallowed his Adam's apple. "I'm going to call the hospital," he said. "You need a doctor."

In an instant he was dialing the emergency number on the desk phone by the window. And in the same instant she was right behind him, pulling a long kitchen knife out from beneath her sweater. He turned. With both hands on the jet-black handle of the carving knife, Emma swiftly lunged its sharp blade down into the soft flesh between his neck and shoulder. He tried to say something, but the only sound to emerge from his lips was a gurgling noise that reminded the demented old woman of a child blowing soap bubbles through an old-fashioned pipe.

She laughed as the deputy fell to his knees with the knife still protruding from the side of his neck. It had gone in up to the hilt and was now pulsating to the same rhythm as the blood that pumped out of him. It splattered the wall, the desk, and the curtains, making a large crimson pool on the rug.

Emma carefully reached down and removed the telephone from his hand. It came easily from his tight grip because of the slippery blood. The moment she replaced the receiver in its cradle on the desk, it rang—while it was still in her blood-stained hand.

It was 1:30 A.M.

CHAPTER TWENTY-SIX

When the Peugeot died on that steep hill, Adams had placed it in neutral and coasted backward until he felt the car picking up speed. When he thought it was going fast enough, he engaged the clutch and shifted into reverse. He then let his foot back up off the clutch pedal, and the old Peugeot bounced and started. He was delighted. Although he knew that such a thing was possible, he had never before had the need to try it.

But the slight elation he felt was quickly dispelled when it kept stalling out everytime he tried to climb the hill. There was no way he could do it. He cursed himself for not having had the sense to have purchased a new set of spark plugs from the attendant back near the capital. He could now have put them in himself. It would only take a few minutes to do so.

He backed the Peugeot off the road onto the shoulder. It didn't matter. He could have left it right where it was, in the middle of the highway. There wasn't another car in sight, in any direction. He looked back in the direction of the capital, some fifty miles to the north of him. He cursed again.

The snow was not as heavy where he was, but he

could tell by scanning the sky to the south that it would be picking up real soon. The chill howling through the trees beside the road reminded him of his youth, when he had to rise each day before dawn to help his father with chores. He'd have given anything at that moment to be that little boy again. There wouldn't be the slightest hesitation out of him about having to do all that needed to be done on a farm.

He was about to get back in the car when a gust of wind parted the trees beyond the shoulder of the road. He saw something through the snow-ladened branches that he thought was a light. His mouth dropped open. It looked as though it might be a filling station.

Adams got back in the car. If he backed it all the way to the last exit he had passed, he might be able to drive toward the light. From where he stood, it looked to be about three miles by road, or a mile or so by the way a crow flies. He'd drive. It was a lot faster. But when he turned the key and pressed the starter button, the engine refused to turn over. Shit! he thought, slamming both his hands against the steering wheel. He should never have turned the ignition off after backing the car off the road.

He got out again and started to push it back onto the highway. Once he got it rolling down the hill, he jumped in behind the wheel and tried to start it like he did before. But once the engine turned over, it refused to keep going. It stalled after a few seconds, time after time. He left it back on the shoulder after that. He would walk.

The one advantage about walking, he told himself as he stepped over the metal railing of the highway and headed directly toward the light, is that you don't have to keep to the road.

After dragging his feet through boot-top-high drifts for a half hour or so, he was less than halfway there. He had estimated the distance all wrong. He was on the point of fatigue. It wasn't that the snow was all that deep, nor that he was worn out from all the sleep he had missed the last couple of days; it had to do with the effort of keeping himself upright. Every so often he would slip on a smooth rock that was hidden beneath a cover of fresh snow. And several times he actually fell. The worst part was that each time he fell he wanted to stay there and go to sleep. His breath was beginning to come short, too. It caught in the air before him like an angry ghost. Don't let yourself get pissed, he told himself. He knew how many people simply died in the snow, sometimes within a few yards of their own dooryard, just because their minds got to wandering all over the place until they just sat down and stayed there. It was an easy way to die. You simply fell asleep and that was it. It put you into the deepfreeze of eternity.

He pulled his gloves off, reaching down with both hands and scooping up a heaping pile of snow. He rubbed it briskly into his face until he could feel the blood rushing back to his cheeks. With it came warmth. That's better, he told himself. He'd be able to make it now.

He was almost to where the source of light should have been, but somehow he lost it. He was beginning to think he had become disoriented when he suddenly came out from behind a small stand of pines and saw it again. It was indeed a filling station!

He raced the rest of the way there, thinking all the while about a telephone—and a hot cup of coffee. But when he reached the station, it was closed. "Jesus!" he shouted down at the ground as he doubled over with his hands on his thighs. He was out of breath and his legs cramped from the run. Why in hell keep all the lights on when you're closed, he thought. When he was able to stand upright again, he walked to the door of the small filling station and read a sign that was taped to the inside of a glass panel in the door. *Closed,* it said. *If you need anything call.* The brief message was followed by the telephone number and the name of the proprietor. The only telephone around, probably for miles, was inside the station!

Nice, Adams thought. He was about to smash the door in when something made him try the handle first. It was open.

The first thing Adams did when he entered the station was to call the owner. The man's wife answered on the second ring. She had been sleeping. She listened to what Adams had to say, then said, "Well, I'll be! The door was open? And you're a sheriff from . . . where did you say that was?"

As he repeated the information he could hear the woman trying to wake her husband from what appeared to be a sound sleep. Finally the man got himself to a point where he was able to speak coherently on the phone. Adams had to go over everything he had already told the man's wife.

"Well, I'll tell you what you'll have to do, Sheriff. I don't handle any foreign car parts, so I don't know what you might need. But if— What's that? You know the number of the plugs? Well, that makes it easy. I have some of those. I can be over in about five minutes with the wrecker and get you off that hill in no time."

While Adams waited he called Ben. He let the phone ring over fifty times. God! he thought as he replaced the receiver. Either he's sleeping like a bear or . . .

He didn't want to think any further than that. He went outside and took a swallow of cold air to clear his thoughts. Then he went back in and dialed the number of his house.

That was when the phone rang in Emma Prescott's bloody hand. It was 1:30 A.M., and she picked up on the third ring.

"Hello." It sounded as though she had been sleeping.

"Emma?"

"Well, Jeff! It's you. Everything all right?"

"Tell you the truth, Emma, I'm worried. I've been trying to reach Ben at the office for about an hour now, and there's no answer. Did he say anything about not going back there after you got to my house?"

"No, Jeff. He didn't." She paused for a moment. "You want me to take a run over there now and see if I can wake him up?" she asked.

It was the perfect response. Adams could feel his shoulders relax. There was nothing wrong with Emma. He felt stupid to have thought otherwise.

"No, Emma. You don't have to," he said. "I'll be home before long and can do it myself."

"Before long?" she asked.

"Yes," he said. "The meeting ended sooner than I expected. Instead of taking a hotel, I thought I'd just come right on home."

"How soon?" she asked. "Where are you calling from?"

Although her question sounded innocent enough, her tone raised some doubts in his mind.

"I should be there within the hour," he lied. At best, he couldn't make it much before dawn. "How are the kids?"

Emma squinted down at the deputy on the floor. He was laid out flat on his back with his legs tucked beneath him, just as he had fallen only moments before. It was as though he knew who was on the other end of the line. His hands moved in jerks, like he either wanted to reach up and strangle her or take the knife out of his neck.

"What's that noise, Emma?"

"What noise, Jeff? I don't hear anything."

"Sounds like—like something bubbled."

"Oh, that. That's me. I just took the phone away from my mouth to clear my throat. You woke me from a deep sleep."

He relaxed. "How were the kids tonight? Are they okay?"

Emma walked away from where Ben was lying on the floor—as far away as the phone cord would reach. "They're just fine, Jeff. Tucked in and tuckered out. I read to them before they went to bed."

Just then the owner of the filling station arrived. "I have to go now," Adams said. "You get back to sleep now. I'll be as quiet as a mouse when I get in, and you can fix us all a good breakfast in the morning."

"My pleasure, Jeff." There was a pause. "Are you sure you don't want me to take a run over to the office and see if I can wake Ben up?"

"Thank you, no, Emma. I'm sure everything's all right. It's just that the door to the outer office probably closed while he was asleep. He just can't hear the phone through it."

"Probably so," Emma responded.

After replacing the receiver she stood there for many moments, staring down at the squirming deputy at her feet. Then she laughed. The sound of it carried out into the snowy night and disappeared.

CHAPTER TWENTY-SEVEN

She had no time to lose. She was also confused. The recent joining of both parts of her personality into one left her feeling as though she were a totally different person.

Emma Prescott stepped over the deputy and raced from the house. She hadn't bothered pulling a coat on over her sweater because she was coming right back. She only wanted to get something from her yellow pickup that was parked beside the house. Out in the cold she studied her bloody hands in the light that spilled from the living room window. She stooped down and wiped them in the snow, leaving long crimson gashes in it before she opened the door of her pickup.

Behind the front seat, right where she had left it earlier that afternoon, was the burlap bundle. She quickly removed it and unwrapped the doll that was inside. She cradled it in her arms as though it were a living child—her child. It was the doll of little Kathy Adams. She turned for the house and hurried back.

The door had blown shut when she left the house and now she couldn't get back in! She looked up into the snow-filled sky and held back an anguished cry. Something inside her head urged her to hurry. Her fingers tightened about the doll's throat. She knew the porch door was locked too. And so was every window she could reach downstairs. She brought the doll up before her face and studied its eyes, as though they might possibly hold the answer to her unexpected dilemma. Her eyes suddenly widened and she left the front of the house and hurried around to the side, past the living room, to where the children's windows were.

Vapor streamed from her flared nostrils like some sort of mystical beast as she stood outside Kathy's bedroom. Inside she could see that the child was sound asleep. She'd have to wake her, try and get her to unlock the window. It wouldn't do to smash it in. She wouldn't be able to reach the key. It was inside, hanging from its hook beside the window jamb—way beyond anyone's reach.

The dim light pouring out at her from the child's room made her skin look yellow. Every crease, every wrinkle, and every expression in her wicked eyes were exaggerated by the deep shadows that clung to the sinister crevices of her contorted face. She ran her tongue out over her pale lips and lifted her hand to the child's window. *Tap-tap . . . Tap!*

Kathy remained asleep. She hadn't stirred an inch.

Again Emma tapped on the window with her bony knuckles. "Ka-a-a-th-e-e-e," she called softly. "Come see what I have for you."

The child remained as unaware of the librarian's presence outside her window as she had before. Emma pulled her lips back. She'd have to hammer louder, running the risk of possibly waking Betty in the house next door. This time she knocked on the wooden sill outside the window. It gave out a deeper, more hollow sound than the thin hammering noise on the glass.

And still the child did not stir.

Emma thought for a moment. She couldn't ring the doorbell because it would wake the boy too. She didn't want that, not just yet. His turn would come. She wanted to save him for last. Like a fine dessert, he would be extra special. After him, her collection would be complete—at least for this season! But how was she now going to get the little girl?

She didn't have to stand there thinking about it for long. Inside, Kathy turned in her sleep and reached for her stuffed giraffe. It started to slip off the bed. She raised her head and tried to catch it. She even opened her eyes as it landed on the floor.

Emma quickly rattled the window with her knuckles. This time, the girl turned and looked. Her eyes were still half closed with sleep. When Emma then stood the doll on the windowsill and tapped the glass with its small wooden hands, the girl appeared to come more fully awake.

Kathy thought it was a dream—a dream in which she herself was standing outside on the windowsill, tapping her hands on the glass to get in. She almost giggled.

"That's right," Emma said softly. "Everything's all right. Hiccup! Hiccup! See, I know the password. Just come to the window and let us in."

Kathy didn't hear a word of it. All she saw, with ever-widening eyes, was the doll that looked exactly like her. The longer she watched, the more she realized she wasn't dreaming. But what was going on? she wondered. Why was the librarian standing outside?

And what a beautiful doll she had!

The girl rose from her bed at the beckoning gestures of the librarian and walked across the room to the window. Emma made a twisting motion with her hand, as if she were holding an invisible key in it. Then she pointed to the locks on either side of the window.

Kathy squinted. She was still having some trouble deciding whether or not this was all some kind of a dream.

"Why?" she asked, rubbing one of her eyes with the ball of her hand.

Emma inwardly exploded. *Why! I'll tell you why! You just do as you're told, little Miss Snip, or I'll—* But what came out was something quiet different. It flowed from her lips as smooth as maple syrup.

"I went outside to get this doll I made for you. The door closed behind me and now I'm locked out." The librarian shrugged. The gesture indicated it could happen to anyone.

Kathy studied the doll that had now been lowered into the librarian's cradled arms. The child wondered again if she were dreaming. The doll looked just like her, and it was even dressed in some of her own clothes too. But if it was a dream, why didn't the librarian just float through the window? She didn't think about it too long. Dreams just weren't that way.

"I'll go and let you in the door," Kathy finally said.

The librarian shook her head vigorously. "No," she said. "You don't have to do all *that.*" If the child left the room to open the door, she'd see the deputy in all that blood on the living room floor. "Just unlock the window and I'll climb in. It's easy. I'll even read you a story so you can get back to sleep again."

Kathy's eyes opened wide. A story in the middle of the night, and the doll too! She knew for sure it had to be a dream after all.

Kathy took the key from its hook and opened the first lock, then the other. She didn't have to do anything else. Emma dropped the doll and quickly lifted the window with one hand; with the other she reached in and pulled the child out into the cold. Before Kathy had a chance to scream, the librarian smothered her small mouth with the palm of her hand. Kathy struggled fiercely. It was a silent battle filled with muffled gasps and stifled cries—until she bit Emma's hand. The demented woman then dropped her, just as quickly as she had dropped the doll. The snow-covered ground cushioned the child's fall.

"You snip!" Emma shouted at the girl. "I'll show you!"

But Kathy was up and running. She headed straight for Betty Lineham's house.

Emma lunged at her as though she were a trapeze artist hurtling through the air. Her outstretched hands caught one of Kathy's feet, and the child toppled into the snow. Emma hurriedly gathered her up and once again smothered her mouth with her hand. Kathy kicked and tore at her all the way back to the pickup. The old woman had never encountered such a fight-back creature before. She had trouble holding onto her. The girl's arms and legs never stopped their running motion as she was being carried.

"Hold down!" Emma said. "No need now for all of that!"

Kathy twisted like a snake and was suddenly out of the librarian's grasp again. "Help!" she screamed as she fled through the snow toward Betty's front door. "Help me!"

Emma swore and chased the little girl who now ran a broken-field maneuver in a desperate attempt to escape the ever-gaining arms of the crazed woman. Her brother had taught her how to run zigzag like that, but he had never taught her anything about an insane killer who had a set mind to catch you. There was nothing she could do about that. By the time she caught her breath enough to scream for help again, Emma was at her. This time the child crumpled up like a disjointed rag doll. Hot tears streamed down her cheeks between Emma's strong fingers as she was carried to the pickup. Her nightgown was tattered and soaked through with icy snow. She was shivering with fear and cold.

Emma opened the door of the pickup with one hand and, with the same hand, reached beneath the front seat of the cab and removed a wide roll of heavy tape. She then tore a swatch of it off by holding one end in her teeth and giving a sharp jerk to the roll in her hand. She pasted it across the child's mouth. All was suddenly silent, except for the constant squirming and kicking of the little girl. Emma quickly took care of that, too, with a length of clothesline that was on the front seat. When the child's hands and feet were tied securely, Emma slid her over to the passenger side of the cab. She then left her there alone while she went to fetch the doll she had dropped in the snow. On her way back, she paused for a moment to look into Kevin's room. The boy was sleeping as soundly as when he had first fallen asleep. You're coming too, she thought. But not just yet. Got my hands full right now. Besides, you're special. Gotta plan you out so that you'll be the prize of my whole collection.

Emma was smiling by the time she returned to the pickup with the doll. She dusted the snow from it and pushed it over to sit right beside Kathy. "There, now," she said. "Now you'll have some company."

Her words had been smooth, but there was a blaze in the librarian's eyes that told the child it was useless to try and struggle anymore. The ropes were beginning to cut into her wrists and ankles. She looked at the doll beside her and suddenly convulsed in a fit of muffled crying.

Emma scowled at the girl as she climbed into the cab beside her. "If you know what's best for you, young lady, you'd quit all that blubbering right now. There's nothing you can do about anything. So just you sit back with your doll friend beside you and take the ride. We're going someplace special tonight. Someplace you've never been before."

With Jennifer? Kathy wondered in terror.

"That's exactly right," Emma said, as though she had read the child's mind. "*Exactly* right!"

And with that, Kathy let out one of the most mournful cries she had ever uttered in all of her six and a half years of life. It remained inside of her, unable to escape the swatch of tape that sealed her lips. She almost gagged. Mucus flowed from her quivering nostrils.

As the pickup rolled away, a light came on in the upstairs bedroom of Betty Lineham's house. It fell across the truck for a single moment as it skidded out of the driveway and into the snowy night. Its tracks would soon fill up and disappear in the freshly falling snow.

CHAPTER TWENTY-EIGHT

The wrecker's lights blinked a warning of caution, intended for the safety of passing vehicles. But there were none. And from the way the snow was dumping out of the sky, it looked as though it would soon develop into a full-scale blizzard.

They stood there in all that, on the hill where Adams had left his car. The wind howled mournfully through the trees beside the road. The station owner didn't seem to mind. He steadily replaced one spark plug after the other until there was only one more to go.

Adams was chilled to the bone. The drive from the filling station hadn't eased that chill either, even though the wrecker's heater had been turned up quite high. He stamped his feet and tried to get the blood moving again. He made a mental promise to keep a pair of old snowshoes in the trunk of his car, just in case he ever got into another jam like this one. It was stupid of him to have miscalculated the distance he had to walk from where the car had stalled to the filling station. He could have died out there in all that snow! And from the way he was feeling just then, that didn't seem to bother him much. The only thing that kept him going was the thought of his children. Betty Lineham was in it too. But even before her, came Ben. How could his deputy have slept through all that telephone ringing?

"Well," the filling station owner said as he pulled his head out from beneath the hood of the old Peugeot. "It looks as though everything's back in place. Want to get in and start her up?"

Adams climbed in behind the wheel and turned the key. Before pressing the starter button, he pumped the gas pedal twice and pulled out the manual choke. Okay, baby, he said to himself. Do it! It fired perfectly on the first attempt and remained going. There was a bright smile on his face as he stepped out of the car.

"Maybe you want to follow me back and get yourself a cup of coffee at my place," the station owner said, wiping his hands on a tattered cloth.

Adams thanked the man and told him he didn't have the time. And now that the car appeared to be its old self again, he was sure he would soon be home to fix some for himself.

The man looked up at all the snow that was falling and shook his head. "I wouldn't count on that for a sure thing," he said. "Maybe you'd better try to find a place and stay for the night. Plow trucks probably won't be out for another hour or two. By then there could be a foot of snow on the road."

Adams couldn't afford to waste any more time. The gloom he felt earlier was returning rapidly. Jesus, he thought. If Ben had only answered the phone.

He told the station owner that he couldn't express how much he appreciated his having come out in the middle of the night during a snow like this, and paid

him. He couldn't believe how little the man asked for.
"Are you sure that's all?" he asked.

The man looked at him, puzzled. "I already charged you half again what it would normally be—for me having to open the station and all. How much would they have charged you down where you come from?"

Adams really didn't know. He had been working on his own car ever since he bought it fifteen years ago, used. "I'll tell you one thing," he said to the station owner. "I'll be back in a few days to have my valves reset, if you don't mind doing them for me. One of them is stuck."

"Is that a fact?" the man said, bending his head closer to the engine block. "I don't hear it."

Adams listened too. "Looks as though the power from a new set of plugs blew it free. I heard such a thing is possible. Is it?"

The man shook his head. "Maybe," he said. "The only thing I can tell you is that it's running good now."

They parted then. Adams lowered the hood of his car as the wrecker went back down the hill toward home.

From a dead stop on a steep hill, the Peugeot had no trouble climbing it, even through the snow. He silently thanked Ben for having had the new set of snow tires installed. Without them, he'd have one more problem to contend with.

At the crest of the long hill he had just climbed, Adams had to stop. What he saw down the steep slope ahead puzzled him. It looked as though the road had run out. The longer he studied it, the clearer it finally became. A wave of snow had crossed the road about a half a mile down the hill. If it weren't for that, he might have coasted down with enough speed to keep him going for another mile or so without ever having to touch the gas peddle. He scratched his chin. Either he could turn around and go back in the direction he had just come from, and find himself a place to stay for the night, or . . .

He pressed the accelerator right down to the floor and started down the hill at full speed. He didn't want to think about anything. He was too tired. All he knew was that he had to get home *now*, not in the morning. Ahead, in the swimming beam of his headlights, the wall of snow grew larger and larger. There was no way he could stop. If he touched the brake pedal at that speed, he was sure to go spinning off the road and through the guard rail. He had made the decision at the top of the hill to shoot down and plow right through. Now he was going to do it. It was just like being in the army again, chasing after murderers, thieves, and pimps. It felt so good.

His heart was pounding heavily and his breath began to fog the windshield. Good! he thought. He didn't want to see this, anyway. He closed his eyes when he was a foot away from the drift and braced himself against the steering wheel to keep it steady. He prayed it would be as soft as powder. When it hit, he opened his eyes again.

Whiteness exploded all about him. He grappled with the steering wheel in an attempt to hold the car on the road. The Peugeot swerved and went sideways, on what he felt were only two wheels. He stretched his body to the other side in the hope he might be able to balance it. After what seemed an eternity, the car thumped level once more and rolled steadily ahead. Breathing rapidly, he lifted his eyes to the rearview mirror. "Ya-hoooo!" he screamed. He couldn't help it. "Yaaaa!"

Ahead of him it looked as though the snow was stopping. Another good omen. It almost helped dispel the uneasy thoughts he had of Emma Prescott, but they quickly flooded back, leaving his mind with little room for anything else. He couldn't shake the thought of there having been insanity in her family. If he had only spoken to the police psychologist before.

Adams still had his foot all the way down on the accelerator. As he sped toward home, his fatigued mind tried to conjure up the image of his children sleeping peacefully in their own beds—and Emma on the hide-a-bed in the living room.

With any luck, he told himself, he'd be home sometime just before dawn.

CHAPTER TWENTY-NINE

The new Emma Prescott hated snow. It interfered with her plans. She would have liked nothing better than to have been able to reach the abandoned cabin up on Tweed Hill without having to go through the treacherously dangerous maneuvers she now performed on the old logging trail. The battered pickup spun and rocked, climbed and skidded, groaned and shuddered. If it weren't for the fact that she knew every twist and turn of it like the back of her own hands, she would have gone sailing off the narrow trail a dozen times. To focus herself she spoke to the child beside her without taking her eyes off the road.

"At some point we may have to get out and walk the rest of the way," she said. "You'd like that, wouldn't you? Then you'd have a chance to try and run away again." She cackled. Her breath was foul. It fogged the windshield.

Kathy had squeezed herself as far away from the mad woman as she possibly could. Tied hand and foot, she had inched herself, with each bouncing motion of the cab, across the seat and was now wedged against the door. Between her and the crazed librarian sat the doll. Just for the fun of it, Emma had plastered a swatch of tape across its mouth, too, just as she had with the little girl.

Kathy's eyes were blazed with the terror of what was happening to her. The thin nightdress she wore was torn and soaked. She hardly noticed the cold that had already turned her bare feet blue. All she could think of was the word she had heard whispered about the schoolyard by some of the older children: *eviscerated.* It was what had happened to her best friend, Jennifer. Although she didn't know what it meant, she knew it had to be something more terrible than death itself.

"Thinking about your little friend, aren't ya?" Emma asked, still not taking her eyes off the twisted, snow-covered trail.

Not a single sound escaped from beneath the tape that pinched the child's lips together.

"I know you are," Emma said. "You can't fool me."

Kathy turned her head so that Emma couldn't see her eyes. She stared out the side window at the trees with their snow-heavy branches. Because she was small, she could also look up and see the sky. The snow was stopping. She studied the moon skirting along, in and out of the rapidly shifting clouds, and thought longingly of her father. Would he come searching for her with his police lantern? It looked just like the bright disk in the sky.

Emma saw the moon too. For her it meant something quite different. It made her lose herself for a moment. She took it as a sign that everything was going to work out for her, as though by magic. If you really want snow to stop falling, she thought, then it stops! That's all there is to it!

She took her eyes off the trail for a moment and looked at Kathy. There was a crooked smile on the old woman's lips. She was about to say something when the pickup suddenly hit a slippery stone and began to fishtail. Emma shot her eyes back to the narrow trail and screamed an obscenity. It was one the girl had heard only once before, when her father dropped a log on his foot. She looked at Emma through the corner of her eye and saw that she was twisting the steering wheel from side to side with such looseness that it appeared to be broken. Kathy held her breath. The thought of an accident comforted her in an unexpected way. Maybe, if they hit a tree, the old librarian would die! The girl began to pray for such a thing to happen. It was the only way she might ever see her father and brother again.

The seat suddenly vanished from beneath the child and she felt herself go sailing all over the inside of the cab. She couldn't brace herself against anything because her hands and feet were bound. The pickup skidded badly and toppled over the edge of the steep embankment alongside the road. The small trees, which had struggled for a foothold on the rocky slope, were pushed aside like toothpicks as the pickup plowed a wide swatch through them. Smoke rose from jagged rocks that were scraped clean of snow and moss. The pickup finally came to a stop after it had rolled over onto its roof and landed in the brook. Its wheels spun in the air until they slowly stopped.

Inside, Kathy and Emma were piled up on one another in a heap. They had been knocked unconscious. Entwined with their seemingly disjointed bodies was that of the doll's. They all formed an eerie bundle of meshed arms and legs on the roof of the overturned cab. Icy water from the brook gushed in through the blown-out windows.

Kathy opened her eyes and lifted her head from the water that collected in the inverted dome of the pick-up's roof. She was dizzy and felt like being sick. The librarian was lying on top of her; her distorted face looked frozen with agony. Kathy thought she was dead and wanted to scream, but couldn't because of the tape. Her hands and feet were still tied, too. One of Emma's arms was pinned beneath the girl at her waist. It didn't move as she frantically tried to worm herself free of the scary tangle of arms and legs that held her in place. The water inside the cab remained at a constant level as it gushed in through the window on Kathy's side and out the other window where the steering wheel was all bent and twisted.

Through a haze of blurred thoughts and dizziness Kathy thought of getting out of there—as fast as she could. If she could only manage to wiggle herself free, she thought, all she then had to do was crawl out the window, cut herself loose on one of the shards of glass that were scattered all over, and head for home.

Her head spun with nausea. The tape across her mouth puckered in and out with the strain of having to breathe only through her nostrils. If she could only get more air! Maybe she wouldn't have to throw up!

Her eyes suddenly met with those of the doll as she attempted to slip herself free of the tangled mess she was in. It was still dark, but the moonlight on the snow-covered ground threw off enough brightness so that she could see everything clearly. There was something about the doll's eyes that startled her more than when she had first come to and found herself face to face with Emma Prescott. She jerked away from it with such force that the back of her head slammed against the pickup. She was almost out the window when that thump she took on the head made her see blackness again. She twisted forward in one last lunge and collapsed. Half of her was still entangled with Emma and the doll, while the upper part of her landed outside—facedown in the ice-cold water of the brook.

Emma had survived, but could hardly move. She gingerly lifted her head and looked about. The water that quickly flowed into and out of the overturned pickup was not deep enough to worry about. The only concern she had was for the shooting pain that surged through her left shoulder. It felt as though it might have been dislocated. The coldness of the water helped to extinguish the fire Emma felt within her shoulder, and she allowed herself to fall back into it for a moment. Her eyes were about to close when she suddenly opened them wide and pulled herself up. Damn the pain! she thought. Where's the girl!?

When Emma finally saw the child, she winced. "Don't you go and die on me now," she said. "I've brought you too far up here for anything like that!"

As though in response, tiny bubbles rose from the water about Kathy's partially submerged head. The coldness of the brook had kept her from passing out after she landed in it. But she was on the brink of drowning. If it weren't for the fact that her hands were bound behind her back and her feet tied together at the ankles, the child could have lifted her head completely out of the water and made her escape. All she could now do was arch her back and neck; that freed her face from the water for a brief intake of air before she collapsed again, exhausted, headfirst back into the rapidly flowing brook.

Emma struggled out of the overturned pickup as quickly as she could. When she stood upright, she knew she had indeed dislocated her shoulder. She was stooped over with pain when she reached for the back of what was left of the child's nightdress. She lifted Kathy up like a half-drowned kitten and examined her face in the cold moonlight. The child's eyes reflected back at her as white as the luminous disk in the sky.

"There now, my little pretty. Let me set you down and get that tape off your mouth, so you can breathe. Besides, there's no need for it anymore."

Emma rested the child on the upturned pickup. She had only one arm to work with but it wasn't that difficult to remove the tape. The water had helped to soften it.

Kathy's eyes came back as Emma pressed her foul mouth against the girl's lips and rhythmically blew her breath into the child's lungs. When she became aware enough to realize what was happening, she squirmed and tried to scream.

"Go ahead," Emma said, standing back from her. "There's no one up here for miles and miles. Only ghosts. And they don't hear nothing anyway."

Kathy opened her mouth but nothing came out. She tried again. Nothing.

"What's the matter? Cat's got your tongue?"

Emma's cackle ran about in the darkness and blended with the babble of the icy brook as Kathy rolled her head to the side so she could throw up.

"There, there," Emma said, rubbing the child's back.

"Get it all out. Do you a world of good."

Kathy was pale and shivering after that. There wasn't a scrap of anything dry anywhere. Emma looked up the embankment on the other side of the brook. She realized if she could make it up there with the girl, it would lead right to the cabin. Faster and easier than trying to climb back up to the trail from which the pickup had tumbled and walk from there.

The child was too weak to resist Emma tying her onto her back with a thick rope she pulled from the inside of the pickup. She tied the doll up there, too, right next to the little girl—both on their backs, facing the sky through the branches of the trees as the woman scrambled and fought to pull herself up the embankment on the other side of the brook. Their shadow crossing the snow looked like some extinct forest creature of enormous size. Even though her shoulder stung with fire, Emma managed to ignore much of it. It didn't matter that she could only use her right arm; that was all she needed to grasp the base of the small trees and pull herself along. Every time she did so, a shower of snow would fall on Kathy's upturned face; the doll's too.

Emma seemed to be working herself up to a pitch. Her breath billowed from her mouth and nostrils and hung in the freezing cold before vanishing. There was a rhythm to it, repeating itself over and over again. At times she would slide backward for as much as she struggled forward. But she never let up until she reached the top.

Still crouched over with Kathy and the doll securely on her back, and her hands almost touching the snow-covered ground, she let out a shout of glee when she saw the back of the cabin through the trees.

"This is fun!" she cried, suddenly bolting toward the clearing. "I'm coming home to you, Mamma. Can you hear me? You too, Grandpa! Home at last!"

All Kathy could see as she faced the sky was the moon racing through the naked branches of the trees. She closed her eyes and tried to imagine it was her father's police lantern, searching for her.

The tears that spilled from her eyes froze on the child's ice-cold face.

CHAPTER THIRTY

Kevin's eyes opened slowly. Outside his window the sky was showing signs of turning to dawn. He thought he heard a noise at his bedroom door. He listened. The house was as quiet as it always was at that hour. When he closed his eyes again he realized he had been dreaming. He had no memory of what it was about. It must have been the dream that woke him up, he thought.

Something made him slip his hands beneath the pillow for his hatchet. His fingers touched something that had an entirely different feel. He half lifted himself from the bed and twisted about to find out what it was. His sneakers? As he examined them through eyes that were still heavy with packets of sleep, he hazily remembered having placed them there himself, so that Miss Prescott could sit in the chair beside his bed to read. He recalled all that magic stuff she had tried to get him interested in.

Fully clothed from the night before, he sat up in bed and slipped his sneakers on. Then, since the house was so quiet and it was still dark enough outside for him to catch a few more winks before he really had to get up, he allowed his head to glide smoothly back down to the pillow. He was beginning to recall last night's dream, and if he could think about it for a moment or two, right now, he might be able to remember what it was all about. It seemed important that he should. Before closing his eyes he lifted the edge of his sweat shirt and slipped the hatchet into the loop of his belt.

The dream was very much like the one he had the night before little Jennifer Lineham was killed.

There is this house . . . no, a cabin. Lots of dolls. There is one that looked just like Jennifer! He wanders toward it, thinking it is alive. It is cold to touch and doesn't move. The other dolls look like children he knows. There's Billy Chadwick, and . . .

Kevin's eyes moved rapidly beneath their lids as he dozed. He saw a doll that looked just like his little sister. He was about to reach out for it when something in the cabin swooped out of the darkness of the rafters and raced toward him like an angry hawk. He tried to avoid it, but in doing so he saw what appeared to be a very special doll. It was not in a shabby wooden box like the rest. This one was in a tall glass box with corner strips of polished brass holding it together. A thick circle of flickering candles cast their glow upon its familiar face. It was him! Coming face to face with the lifeless replica of himself riveted him to the spot, allowing the thing that rushed at him from the rafters to claw itself into the back of his skull!

Kevin's body stiffened and he bolted upright in bed. His clothes were blazing hot, as though he were on fire.

"KATHY!" he screamed.

His eyes darted about the bedroom as though he were in an unfamiliar place. He sees fire and smoke. He sees his sister bound to a wooden chair. And he sees Emma Prescott going toward her with a knife raised in both hands above her head.

"KATHY!" he cried out again.

And, as though responding to his shouts, something heavy bumped against his bedroom door.

His sister's name caught in his throat as he was about to call it out again.

"Dad? Is that you?"

There was only silence from the other side of the door.

"Miss Prescott?" he tried.

Still no answer.

"Kathy?"

He cautiously went to the door and placed his ear against it. Nothing. Then he stepped aside and quickly flung it open, wide. What he saw spun him back into the room in a fit of terror.

It was Ben. The deputy stumbled into the room and collapsed at the boy's feet. The carving knife that Emma Prescott had planted into the soft flesh between his neck and shoulder blade was still there. His shirt was caked with blood. From the way his hand was working, fingers opening and closing—and his eyes—it appeared to the boy that the deputy was desperate to tell him something very important.

Kevin gingerly approached Ben on the floor. His father had once told him about never removing a knife from a wound because you'd probably cause more serious damage drawing it out. He didn't touch it.

"What is it, Ben? Who did this?"

Ben's eyes lost their focus for a moment. When they came back, the side of his lips were so close that the boy couldn't understand what he was saying. It sounded as though he had said, "Happy birthday."

The boy squinted. "What?"

But Ben went quiet after that. A deep gush of air escaped his lungs and his eyes went large and unfocused again. The boy stared down at the deputy's body for a moment. It was perfectly still. Not a single breath trickled from his lips or nostrils. Kevin knew he was dead. He suddenly rose and bolted past him and headed straight for his sister's room.

"KATHY!" he cried, crashing through her door. Her bed was empty. A window was open and the curtains billowed into the icy room. "KATHY!" he shouted again.

Something made him spin about. There was a sound of something rushing toward him.

"Kevin!" someone called. "Where are you?"

It was his father. Kevin rushed out and threw himself into his arms. "Ben's in my room, *dead!*" he sobbed. "And Kathy's gone too!"

Adams, who had been fighting sleep for the past seventy miles, was suddenly snapped into alertness. He knew the boy was right. He had seen the blood on the living room floor, and that the hide-a-bed hadn't been slept in. And now there was the emptiness of his daughter's room. His heart fell as he recalled the police psychologist's words: *Look for someone gentle, a caring person.*

"EMMA!" Adams screamed. "Can you hear me?" His voice echoed back through the emptiness of the house.

"You wait right here," he told the boy. "Don't move until I come back."

Kevin had wanted to say more but his father left too quickly.

It took Adams less than thirty seconds to go through the entire house, leaving his son's room for last. Emma wasn't there, either, only Ben. Adams knelt beside him and, even though he knew Ben was dead, felt for a pulse. There was none. He swiftly rose to his feet and went back to the boy.

"What happened?" he asked. "Do you know?"

Kevin's body was trembling inside of his loose sweat shirt. "I know what those dreams are now," he said quietly. "I know what they've been trying to tell me. It's Miss Prescott. She's the killer. I know it."

Adams squinted at the boy. Okay, he thought. Go with it. He recalled his own experiences of knowing things when he was a boy. "Tell me everything you know," he said carefully. "Where has she taken Kathy?"

Kevin went pale. His eyelids closed down and became two tiny slits of white. He seemed to be in some sort of a trance. Adams was about to shake him by the shoulders when the boy began to speak. His voice was dreamlike, coming from far back in his throat, as though speaking each word required a great effort.

There's a log house . . . a cabin . . . there's a porch . . . not far back of it, down a steep hill, there's a fishing brook . . . nothing else's around the cabin 'cept for an old fallen-down barn . . ."

A storm raged through Adam's insides. He struggled to control himself. That cabin he described! It had immediately awakened a distant shadow of something that Adams knew from a very long time ago, when *he* was a boy and used to go wandering all up and down the surrounding hills of the valley, looking for all the secret places where he would hunt and fish when he grew up.

Adams gently placed his hands on Kevin's shoulders. He swallowed the tense knot that formed in his throat and cautiously asked, "That barn, Kevin, what kind of a roof does it have? Can you *see* it?" He leaned back and stared at the boy as he haltingly began to speak.

"I . . . see it," Kevin slowly responded. ". . . used to be . . . all slate . . . all fallen in now . . . slate's . . . . . . landed on . . . crushed . . . two old hay wagons a long time ago . . ."

Adams sucked his breath in. He knew the place! The old Turner cabin, up over on the far side of Tweed Hill. No one had farmed up there since before he was born. The place was even deserted in his own father's time. It was the perfect place for a maniac killer, and Emma would have known about it, too. She was always going off by herself into the woods. Maybe that's why her pickup was all battered up the way it was. Tweed Hill, he thought. Didn't Ben mention that Les Knowel heard shots coming from up that way—the same day as Arthur went missing? Adams slowly rose to his feet, bitterly cursing himself for his failure to think of that sooner.

Kevin was still in some sort of a trance. Adams took his son by the shoulders and shook him.

"Kevin!" he called. "Wake up."

The boy's eyes fluttered open. They were filled with confusion.

"Do you remember anything you just said?" Adams asked.

Kevin shook his head. "About what?" he asked in

return. "About Ben?"

"No. About the cabin, about—"

It was obvious to Adams that the boy had no memory of the words he had just spoken. Kevin had looked at him blankly when he mentioned a cabin.

"That's okay," Adams said. "I want you to go over to—"

His words were cut short by the sound of something crashing to the floor in the living room. It was quickly followed by a shrill scream.

"What's that?" Kevin raced behind his father to the living room. They soon found out.

Betty Lineham was standing there, staring down at the floor where Ben had been. She had knocked over a lamp when she saw the huge blood stain.

She looked up at Adams and Kevin as they came around the corner of the hallway that led to the living room. Her eyes were frantic.

"What's happened?" she asked. "I heard a commotion and came over. What's this?" She pointed to the caked puddle of blood by the desk.

Her eyes searched theirs for a clue—anything that would give a hint of what had happened. But they remained silent.

"Where's Kathy," she finally asked. "Emma's pickup isn't outside, either."

Kevin looked up at his father. Adams didn't know how to tell her. Then, as the silence sat, there suddenly seemed no need to tell her at all. She knew.

"Oh God!" she said. "How could we have been so stupid?" Her voice sounded like a gentle creature breathing its last. "Tell me I'm wrong," she said. "*Please* tell me I'm wrong!"

Once again, the silence told her everything—everything except the blood. Her eyes fell upon the stain by the desk.

"Ben's," Adams said quietly. He didn't have to say anything more.

Betty covered her face with her hands but did not cry. "I thought I heard something in the middle of the night," she said. "I turned the light on for a while, but it was so quiet after that that I thought I had imagined it all. I must have fallen back to sleep." She shook her head vigorously as though trying to snap out of a daze. "What can I do?" she asked.

Adams could see the robe she was wearing begin to tremble. He was glad she hadn't asked anything more specific about Ben. "I was just about to send Kevin over to your house while I took care of matters here. It seems—"

He couldn't finish. He finally pulled as much strength back into himself as he possibly could.

Kevin looked up at his father with question marks in his eyes. "I'm staying with you," he said. "She's my sister!"

Adams came close to exploding. "You listen to me and you listen good. . . ." Suddenly he caught himself. He knelt down beside his son and held him tightly in his arms.

"I'm sorry," he said. "But this is something that I have to take care of on my own. It could be dangerous. You go on over to Betty's house and stay there until I get back. Okay?"

Kevin stood back from him when Adams rose to his feet again. The question marks that had earlier been in his eyes now turned to tiny darts of pent-up anger. He pulled his lips in tightly and began breathing heavily. "She's my sister," he said. "And I'm the only one who can save her."

Adams and Betty watched in amazement as the boy stormed out of the house without his coat. Through the living room window they saw him march directly to Betty's house and close the door behind him. His footprints in the snow crossed those that Betty had made just moments before.

Adams went over to the closet and pulled out his own over-and-under-double-barreled shotgun. He didn't want to waste any time going over to the office for a better one. As he loaded it he spoke hastily to Betty.

"When you get back home call the state for me. Ask for Jerry Malone in the lieutenant governor's office. Tell him about what's happened here—as much as you know of it. He'll know what to do from there." He loaded the gun and jammed about a dozen more live cartridges into his pocket. "And please don't let Kevin out of your sight. I've never seen him like this. He's liable to do anything."

And, as though to punctuate the words Adams had just spoken while loading his gun, once outside, neither he nor Betty noticed the tiny trail of footprints that led from behind Betty's house to the old Peugeot.

On the floor of the back seat, Kevin stroked the hatchet in the loop of his belt as Adams climbed in behind the wheel and shot out of the driveway and down the hill at full speed.

Adams knew exactly where he was headed.

CHAPTER THIRTY-ONE

If one were to look down upon the cabin from a great height, it would appear to be a scene from the inside of a glass snowball that had not been shaken for a while; the artificially suspended snow now settled at the bottom where it peacefully awaited someone to come and shake it all up again.

A thick carpet of white covered the roof of the cabin, as well as the fallen barn that was off to the side. The branches of the pines were bent with snow, and out behind the cabin the soft mounds that covered the murdered children could hardly be distinguished from the rest of the sloping ground.

There were trails through the snow. Down a steep embankment there was an overturned pickup. It had landed within fifty yards of the police cruiser, which had suffered a similar fate. The embankment was littered with fallen trees, and deep gouges scarred the earth and rocks. A trail of footprints led from the pickup to the cabin. They went straight up the embankment from the wreckage and cut through a small stand of pines that led to a clearing where the mounds were. The footprints were not the neat impressions of someone's idle stroll through the early hours of a snow-filled dawn. They zigged and zagged, stumbled and crawled, and sometimes fell in huge round splotches—indicating that whoever made them had slipped and fallen, many times, before reaching the isolated cabin at the end of the old logging trail.

There was something different about the cabin today. A wispy plume of white smoke rose from the stone chimney. There hadn't been a fire in its fireplace in almost a hundred years. Emma Prescott had risked it. Today was special. Besides, she had told herself, it was still dark when she started it. The thick black smoke that first rose from its disused flue went into the darkness. And now that the dawn was beginning to light the sky, the smoke had thinned and turned wispy-white. Even if folks in the valley below did see it, she had thought they'd think it was the normal rising of vapor thrown off from the moisture of the snow-ladened trees.

After having started the fire upon arriving at the cabin, Emma had removed Kathy's nightdress and washed her down with warm water made in the fireplace from a large kettle of snow. There were clothes around, too, those she had been in the process of creating for her dolls. When Kathy was warm and dry, Emma dressed her in the best of the clothing that was available—shoes, socks, skirt, blouse, and sweater. The old woman had even combed her hair and prettied her face before tying her to a ladder-back chair. Throughout it all the girl had been half unconscious.

Emma had worked so frantically and with such single-minded purpose to revive the girl that she had not thought of lighting the thick candles that surrounded the dolls in their individual boxes. The only scene that greeted Kathy's eyes whenever they would flutter open for a moment or two was the nightmarish view of the crazed librarian, scuttling about through shadows of the cabin, her form only occasionally being revealed by the dim light of the dancing flames in the fireplace. She hobbled about like a hunchback because of the pain of her dislocated shoulder.

Emma slept now. She didn't mean to. It happened not long after she lit the kerosene lantern that was on a crate by the door. Maybe it was the fumes from it, she didn't know. But after having washed the girl and changed her clothes, she was exhausted. She sat on the heap of pepper sacks that had been piled against a wall—just for a minute to catch her breath, she told herself—and stared into the yellow-blue butterfly of light that fluttered inside the lantern. The cabin had never been so warm. Her body had never ached so much. And her eyes had never felt heavier. The sacks made a comfortable bed. She had positioned herself in such a way that her shoulder was supported by the bulge of one of them, and another made a good pillow to settle her head on.

The paleness of dawn filtered in through the only window of the cabin and cast its light on the workbench. On it were the tools and paints and swatches of fabric with which Emma had made and clothed her dolls. The fire in the fireplace was almost out, and the little girl who was tied to the ladder-back chair facing it was asleep, too. Her tiny chin rested on the thick rope that bound her shoulders to the back of the chair. She looked like a limp Raggedy Ann. There were no dreams in her mind, only blackness. The ordeal of almost drowning, facedown in the icy brook, had offered her dreams enough to last a lifetime. While she had gasped for air, she saw a vision of her mother in a dazzling brillance that was unlike any light she had ever seen before. Her mother had been dressed in a soft summer dress, and there was a gentle breeze parting the tall grasses of a rolling field in which she was standing. Kathy had been about to abandon herself to the vision and to the icy chill of death itself, when Emma had reached out and pulled her from the brook.

Emma woke with a start. She sat upright on the pile of sacks. Her eyes showed a heavy line of redness about the edges. There was also pain in them. She tried to straighten her back but couldn't. She winced. My God! she thought. What if she couldn't get done all the things that she had planned that day? The thought sent a cold shudder through her that was stronger than the hammering pain in her shoulder.

She rose from the sacks and looked at the girl who was still sleeping before the died-down fire. The sight filled her with a curious joy. It eased the pain she felt. I'll light the candles before waking her up, she thought. It'll be a great surprise!

Emma hobbled to the low wooden table that was before the collection of dolls and removed a long wax taper from its drawer. She then returned to the kerosene lantern by the door and slid the taper beneath the lantern's sooted hood to get it lit. That done, she carried the taper back and lit every candle in the cabin with it. There were dozens of them. Most were gathered about the barn-wood boxes in which the dolls were standing. Their carefully carved faces appeared to glare out at her through the sheets of glass that covered the boxes. The movement of the candlelight made it seem as though they had life in them.

There, now, she thought after finishing. That's better. I should have lit them long ago.

She looked out the window at the increasing brightness of dawn. There was no time to waste.

Emma went to the girl, and because she was hunched over with the pain of her shoulder, her eyes were level with those of the child's. "Wake up," she called sweetly. Ol' Emma's got a surprise for you."

It was as though all the air had gone out of Kathy's lungs. At the sound of the crazed woman's voice it started to gush back in. With it came the realization of all the terror she had been through—of all that was yet to come. Her eyes opened on Emma's wrinkled face. It was so close to hers that the child could smell the badness of it.

"That's a good little girl," Emma cooed. "You're gonna like this."

And with those words the mad librarian dragged the child's chair to the front of the cabin where Kathy could see the dolls.

The child's face went pale. In the center of the collection was the doll of the girl who used to be her very best friend, Jennifer Lineham. The doll she had seen earlier of herself and the lifelike replica of her own brother, Kevin, stood there too, in their own boxes. She tried to scream but couldn't.

Emma was delighted. She began to ramble incoherently about the dolls that used to be in her mother's forbidden collection. "*They* had no life in them!" she said. "That's why I burned them up. Mother never knew how to make the spirit go into them like I do. *My* dolls have a life to them. Can't you see it? Can't you feel it?"

She pointed to Jennifer's doll. "She has the spirit in her, just like yours is going to have. Just like your brother's is, too."

This time when she tried, Kathy was able to scream. There was no form or definition to it—only a loud, uncontrolled screech it seemed would never stop.

Emma thought it was funny and mimicked her, soundlessly moving her lips and wagging her head from side to side, just like the child.

"Go ahead," she finally said. "The woods are deep with snow. No one beyond the dooryard will ever hear you!"

She slowly turned Kathy's chair away from the dolls so that it now faced the low wooden table. Just beyond it was the only door to the cabin. There was no more pain in Emma's shoulder. She skipped like a little child to the cupboard by the workbench and removed her special knife from it. Skipping back to the table she planted its blade into the center of it.

Kathy focused on the carved wooden handle as it wobbled. When it finally stopped, she saw that it was made in the image of the demented old woman herself.

Emma laughed. "That's right," she said. "It's me. Made it myself! Just like all the dolls behind ya."

The pride and madness in Emma's voice chilled the child. She stared at the door and screamed as loud as she could. "Daddy! Daddy! Help me!"

Emma Prescott did a small dance before the frightened girl. "That's right!" she cackled. "Get your daddy up here, too. I got a big surprise for *him!*"

She quickly went to the door and pulled a wooden

box away from the wall beside it. Standing on it, she reached her good arm up into the darkness of the rafters and made sure she had remembered to set the booby trap. She hadn't! The iron rod that held back the heavy broadaxe was still in the grove of the J-shaped bracket she had mounted on the rafter.

"Well, I'll be!" she said in a disbelieving tone. She looked down at Kathy and smiled. "If you hadn't gone screaming at the door like that, I might never have known."

Emma removed the iron rod that held the heavy broadaxe in place. The booby trap was now fully armed, ready for the axe to plummet down into the head of anyone who now stepped through the door.

The old woman got down from the box and pointed to the axe above her head. Its razor-sharp blade picked up the light from the nearby kerosene lantern. "A nice rig, isn't it?" she said to the little girl. She then made a chopping motion with her hand to her forehead, indicating what would happen to anyone who now entered the cabin.

Kathy screamed as loud as she possibly could—and wouldn't stop.

CHAPTER THIRTY-TWO

He moved so swiftly along the main highway to get where the old logging trail snaked out of the woods that it was difficult for him to turn the Peugeot right into it. The snow truck had been around to plow the main road and it piled a foot of snow across the entrance to the disused trail. He quickly reduced his speed and turned the car around to try again. This time he went into it with a great thump. In the back, huddled to the floorboard, Kevin braced himself against the jerking movements of the car. The blade of the hatchet in the loop of his belt almost cut into his side.

Adams felt an immediate surge of assurance as he began to follow the old trail. There were fresh tire tracks before him. It confirmed what Kevin had said. Emma *had* taken Kathy to the old Turner place at the end of the trail. He didn't know how her pickup could make it all the way up there with such snow on the ground. He wasn't even sure he would be able to make it himself. The only thought he had was to find them—and that Kathy would still be alive.

He was almost all the way there when he came to the spot where the tire tracks he had been following swerved and disappeared over the edge of the embankment that ran beside the narrow trail. Adams stopped the car and climbed out. He held his breath and peered down over the steep edge. At the bottom he saw Emma Prescott's overturned pickup. He could see that no one was inside. There were footprints all about it. A trail of them skidded and scampered up the other side of the embankment from where he was. It looked as though there had been a tremendous struggle of some sort.

Not far away from the pickup was the wreckage of the police cruiser. The front door was open. Arthur was not there. A glimmer of hope that his deputy might still be alive was dispelled by the sight of the overturned pickup. Something about it was too brutal, too savage.

Kathy! he thought. He had to find her!

He reached in through the open door of the Peugeot and pulled out the shotgun that had been lying across the front seat. His breath caught like a cataract of frozen stillness in the air as he raced toward the wreckage. The wide swatch of freshly turned earth that the pickup had created on its way to the bottom of the ravine made easy footholds for him.

In the midst of his skidding and jogging down the slope, a memory flashed through his mind. It was as abstract and out of place as any he had ever had. He remembered the first trout he had ever caught. It was in the very brook he now raced toward at full speed. He had cleaned and cooked it on a flat slate stone not far from where he was. It had been no more than a mouthful but he was as stuffed with it as the pride that had surged through his young blood. He had never told anyone about it, not even his own father. He was about

Kevin's age at the time, and he wondered if his own son would ever have such a secret of his own.

At the bottom, Adams walked right into the brook and circled the overturned pickup. He checked to make sure that no one was inside. There was no blood, either. He examined the trail of footprints that went up the other side of the embankment. There seemed to be no doubt in his mind that the sooner he followed them, the sooner he'd find Kathy.

Then, as though in response to his concern over whether or not his daughter were still alive, he heard a long, continuous scream. It came down to him along the surface of the brook and was amplified by the slate rocks that towered from different parts of the ravine. It conjured up an image that was far more ghostly than anything he had ever imagined. It was his own daughter screaming! The only solace it offered was that it meant she was still alive—and that he still had a chance to save her.

The early light of dawn fell through the branches of the snow-burdened trees and covered the footprints on the opposite embankment in a torrent of pure silence. Adams shot across the brook and headed up the slope toward the sound of his daughter's screaming. He didn't pay any attention to the footprints in the snow. He blazed his own trail—one that he knew would lead more directly to the old cabin.

As he raced ahead, something suddenly caught in one of his legs like the fangs of an angry wolf. Then he heard the muffled explosion that had caused it. He had slipped on a snow-covered log that was half buried in the ground and had unloaded a chamber of shot into his leg! The pain was immediately followed by dizziness and a blazing throbbing in his leg.

The gun flew out of his hand as he cartwheeled down the embankment. The trees, the sky, the earth all merged into an agonizing swirl of pain. Consciousness came to him as mere fragments of light scattered through the darkness of a long, unending tunnel. Through it there was only silence. His daughter had stopped screaming at the sound of the blast.

Adams landed in the brook and sunk like a ship whose hull had suddenly been ripped out on a jagged reef. He went down into the icy, almost comforting chill of it. Blood bubbled up and snaked along the surface of the brook, leaving a thin band of red wherever it touched the snow along the embankment. Adams struggled to climb back to the surface of his own wavering consciousness, but he couldn't hold on. He found himself slipping deeper and deeper into a dark haze of agonizing defeat.

The sound of the shotgun going off had stopped Kathy's screaming. It had also stopped Emma from prancing about like a possessed demon. Together they focused their attention on the front door of the cabin. Emma's eyes were lit with a wicked joy. Kathy's were wide in horror. If her father were to come charging through the door at that moment, he would be struck in the head by the broadaxe falling from the rafters. The girl was about to shout a warning when Emma produced a cloth from the pocket of her sweater and stuffed it into her opened mouth, all in one smooth motion.

"He's on his way," she said. "Isn't he?"

Kathy tried to push the cloth out of her mouth with her tongue. Her weary body struggled against the ropes that bound her to the chair. Tears burst from the corners of her eyes.

Emma laughed at the child's futile attempts to shout a warning to her approaching father. She quickly went to the low wooden table that stood before the dolls like a sacrificial altar and removed a wide roll of tape from its only drawer. She ripped off a fresh swatch of it with her teeth and slapped it across Kathy's mouth, before the child had a chance to work the cloth free with her busy tongue.

"That should hold you quiet," she said. "You can go'n say anything you want now!"

Emma Prescott cackled and laughed as she resumed her demented dance before the struggling child. She hobbled about like a dwarfed fiend, stomping her high-topped shoes against the wide floorboards of the dingy cabin until a cloud of dust, thick as a fog, was suspended in the air. Whenever she passed beneath the axe that was up in the darkness of the rafters, she would raise her one good arm and point to it. "Yeeeeee!" she'd scream, slapping her hand down hard against her hip with a loud whop. "Yippeeeee!"

The thought of having come so close to achieving her ultimate ambition in life—a collection of real live dolls of her very own—filled her with an all-consuming sense of triumph.

"I'm the doll keeper now!" she shrieked, as though she were entirely alone. "Do you hear that, Mamma? Me! Not you!"

Kathy struggled fiercely against the ropes that bound her to the chair. Her young body appeared to have been infused with an unaccountable surge of strength. But all that came of it was a pitiful wobbling of the chair to which she was tied. That, and the muffled cries that were uttered in the silence of her throat because of the gag.

Emma thought it was the most humorous thing she had ever seen. "Look at her, Mamma! What'cha think? Think she's gonna make me a good little doll?"

She suddenly huddled over and convulsed in a fit of demented laughter. The sound of it was as dark and chilling as the quiet isolation of the cabin itself. The dust had gotten to her throat. Between fits of choking laughter she addressed the inner turmoil of her own dark consciousness.

"We're all in it now! Ain't we, Mother? You and me. Grandpa too. Goin' for broke, like the cowboys say."

She tried to straighten herself up but couldn't. It didn't seem to matter. The pain of her dislocated shoulder was replaced by the joy of her total madness.

"Like the cowboys used to say!" she bellowed in the mocking tones of what she imagined a western range-hand would utter. "Yippee-ei-ooo! Yippee-ei-aaa!" she crooned as she galloped about the cabin on an imaginary bucking horse. "Ride 'em, ride 'em, ride 'em!"

The pounding of her boots on the floorboards sounded like an army of stampeding horses to the terrified child. Her body twisted with less and less force against the tightness of the ropes. A thin trail of mucus oozed from her nostrils as they flared with heavy breathing. She thought that plain and simple death would be better than anything she was feeling. And there was the thought of that gunshot blast, too. Was her father going to come through the door to rescue her, only to have his head chopped open by the axe?

As though she had read the child's thoughts, Emma stopped her wild galloping about. She almost stumbled over her own two feet with the exhilaration she felt. "This is gonna be the best yet," she uttered, exhausted and out of breath as she ambled to the front door and leaned her body against the wall beside it. She looked up at the axe. "Your daddy's got a big surprise coming to him," she said. "Just you wait and see."

Kathy closed her eyes. She didn't want to see. She didn't want to think. In her mind she said one word, *mommy*. She was ready to die and go to that place where her mother was—to that smiling lady who stood in that blazing field of golden sunlight.

Emma suddenly cocked her ear to the door. Someone was coming.

When Adams lost consciousness in the brook, Kevin was right there. The boy had heard the gunshot blast and saw his father go cartwheeling down the slope and into the frigid waters. He did his own cartwheeling and stumbling down his side of the embankment to reach him as quickly as he could. Kevin stood waist-high in the icy brook as he reached down into it for his father's shoulders. He got to him only moments after Adams had passed out.

Kevin managed to drag his father out of the water. He rested him on the snowy embankment beside the brook and examined the wound, where a trail of blood leaked from below the knee of his dad's torn trousers. Adams opened his eyes as the boy tore the rest of the pants leg away and began to prepare a tourniquet with it.

"What—?" Adams couldn't finish. He let his head back down into the snow.

"You shot yourself," Kevin said, working as fast as he could. His voice was as calm and as matter-of-fact as any emergency ambulance medic Adams had ever heard. "As soon as I get a tourniquet fixed it'll stop the bleeding."

Adams tried to recall what had happened. The scream, the shot, the pain, the fall, and the final drift into unconsciousness.

"How did you get—?"

"On the floor in the back seat of the car," Kevin responded to his father's unfinished question. "I didn't stay at Betty's."

The boy looped a strip of his father's torn pants about the wounded thigh and knotted it. Then he found a thick twig to use for tightening. Everything was done according to the first aid lessons his own father had taught him; everything was done with lightning speed.

When he twisted the hurriedly made tourniquet the flow of blood slowed immediately. Adams lifted himself on his elbows to see. His face showed signs of relief. It might not be as bad as he had imagined.

"Hold it like that," Kevin said, placing the twist of cloth and twig into his father's hand. "I want to get something."

As Adams held the tourniquet, Kevin raced to the wrecked police cruiser he had seen from the top of the embankment. He was gone only seconds before he reappeared with a first aid box.

"Did you try the radio?" Adams asked as his son tore the box open.

"Dead," the boy answered. "It's loose and hanging from its empty space. I couldn't get it to work."

Kevin then poured the whole bottle of Betadine on the wound in his father's leg. The boy winced. His father did not. The pain was already there and stung more than any iodine could.

Adams tried to lift himself to his feet but couldn't. Kevin saw what needed to be done. He placed himself beneath his father's shoulder and helped. The boy was strong and quite tall for his age. Adams was able to stand with his son's support, but there was more pain in his leg than he had ever felt—more than he had ever imagined he'd be able to tolerate. But it was nothing compared to the torture of not hearing Kathy's screaming anymore. While it lasted, he had at least known she was still alive. Now . . .

He looked at the trail of footprints that led from the overturned pickup to the top of the embankment. It was an easier route than the one he had attempted to blaze for himself.

"You stay here," he told the boy.

"Not this time, Dad," Kevin immediately snapped back. "I'm going with you, no matter what. Back home you can sorry me good all you want. I don't care. Besides . . . you need me." He pointed to the wound his father was trying to keep from bleeding with the tourniquet.

Adams looked up the embankment. He knew it was foolish of him to think he could make it up there without being helped. If he fell again, that would be it. He was lucky the boy had been there in the first place.

He looked at his son as though he suddenly realized something—something very special. "You saved my life," he said. "If you weren't here, I would have drowned."

Kevin hugged him tightly about the waist and pulled his father's arm across his shoulder. "Let's go," he said.

Together they began to limp and shove and pull themselves up the slope. The boy stopped once and, while Adams supported himself against a young elm, ran to the spot where his dad's shotgun had landed. There was still one live round in the chamber. It was dry—not like the shells that were in his father's drenched coat pocket.

Adams lifted his arm for the boy to slip beneath when he hurried back. "Just one shot left," he said, handing the gun to his father. "Let's make it good."

Adams swallowed the pain he was feeling. "We will," he said softly. There were other things he would have liked to have said to his son: things that any father plans to tell his children before they are fully grown; things that tend to ease a father's troubled thoughts about his not having been as good a parent as he could have been and about how proud he felt to be his father. And, as they continued to make their way up the embankment—looking like a pair of wounded deer racing against their last breath—Adams prayed that he would one day be able to speak such thoughts to both his children.

Emma had cocked her ear to the door when she heard what she thought was the sound of footsteps racing toward the cabin. She smiled and calculated that the hurried footfall was just about twenty yards off.

She now stood herself clear of the door so as to avoid the heavy broadaxe when it fell. Looking at Kathy, who was tied to the chair in the center of the cabin, Emma quietly laughed. The child's eyes were tightly closed. The first—and last—thing to be seen by anyone who came rushing through the door would be the girl. Behind her were the dolls. The flickering candlelight made them look like a band of floating children who had somehow gotten lost in the vast darkness of death that filled the gloomy cabin. They were so lifelike that Emma thought they might one day be taught to talk and move about—just like real children! The thought almost made her forget the rushing footsteps that approached the door. By the sound of it, she now estimated the footsteps to be no more than twenty-five or thirty feet away.

"Open your eyes, Miss Sweetie Pie!" she called out to Kathy. "Don't 'cha want to see your daddy get the axe?" The demented woman chuckled quietly as a muffled cry came from beneath the tape that sealed the child's lips.

Kathy kept her eyes closed. Tears poured down her cheeks. And, once again, she began to struggle with the ropes that circled her body and pinned her to the high-backed wooden chair.

Emma wiped a bead of perspiration from her upper lip. As the footfalls grew closer, she couldn't figure what it was. It didn't sound like any one man; as a matter of fact, it didn't sound like anything she had ever heard before. The uncertainty of who or what it was racing toward the cabin got the better of her. She quickly stepped in front of the door and peeked through a crack in the weathered boards.

It was the boy. Kevin. Something had gone wrong. He was almost to the door with a hatchet in his hand. His father was nowhere in sight. She didn't want the boy! Not now. She had something *special* planned for him! She wasn't ready yet!

Emma tried to slide the bolt in place to lock the boy outside, but she was too late. He came crashing through the door. Emma was pushed aside. Kathy opened her eyes.

Out of the darkness of the rafters, just like the birdlike object that had rushed toward his head in the nightmare, the broadaxe now hurtled toward him like a gleaming buzz saw. But he was too short for it. It whooshed right over his head and caught Emma Prescott squarely between the eyes as she attempted to reach out and pull him away from it.

Kathy almost swallowed the gag in her mouth as her eyes followed the wicked killer's contorted fall to the floor.

Kevin was stunned. He stood there motionless for a moment before he could take his eyes off the fallen woman. She landed on her back with the axe buried deeply into her forehead. Blood gushed from the wound and filled the sockets of her startled eyes before it spilled like thick red paint onto the wide floorboards of the cabin.

Emma's blood wasn't the only thing that began to spread itself along the old wooden floorboards of the cabin. When she reached for Kevin, the hatchet he had raised above his head flew out of his hand and struck the lantern that was on a crate beside the door. A wall of fire now spread itself along the floorboards from the spilled kerosene. It quickly separated the boy from his sister.

"KATHY!" he screamed, taking a step back.

The fire ate its way quickly into the old timbers. It licked at them like lightning in a hay barn and began to twist and turn toward the paints and thinners at the workbench.

"KATHY!" he screamed again.

The only response he got from her was the wobbling of her chair as she struggled to free herself.

Kevin hurried out to the porch to look for something he could grapple her chair with. But there was nothing. He had been taught never to jump into a river or lake to rescue anyone; you first looked for something to toss to them. They were sure to drag you under with them if you didn't.

This was different.

He looked at the snow-covered ground, hurling himself from the porch and into it. When he landed he thrashed about in it like a wild hog that's had a red-hot poker shoved into it. As he pitched about he frantically pulled his sweat shirt off and stuffed it with as much snow as it would hold. When he was sopping wet, he hurriedly rose and put the shirt right back on over his head, snow and all. Racing back up to the porch of the cabin, he rubbed whatever snow fell from it into his hair.

"Hold on!" he cried to his sister when he reached the door. "I'm coming in."

The boy filled his lungs with a long gulp of cold air before he plunged himself through the door of the cabin. It was as though he had dived into an open sea of flame.

CHAPTER THIRTY-THREE

When Betty Lineham returned to her house she called Jerry Malone at the state capital, as Adams had asked her to, and told him what had happened. He kept her on the phone a long time, asking her as many questions as she could answer, and many more that she could not. He did not know he was speaking to the mother of one of the murder victims, and she did not know how to tell him it was her own daughter he was asking all those questions about. Malone concluded by telling her that he would contact the appropriate people and have someone get there as soon as possible. He thought a state trooper from the Rutland area might possibly be able to make it there in less than thirty minutes—sooner if a car was out that way patrolling the interstate highway.

Betty had become so distracted and upset with having to respond to all the questions Malone had asked about the murder of her own daughter that all she could think of doing after the call was to go into the kitchen and sit down with a cup of tea—and try to forget Jennifer's death all over again.

She didn't know how long she had been sitting there

by the window when the stillness of the house did something to her. She realized that she had been crying. Her face was still wet with tears. It was the first time anything like that had ever happened to her. It was as though everything that had been stored up in her since Jennifer's brutal abduction and murder had poured out of her. Inside, she felt as empty and limp as something that had all the air let out of it. She dried her eyes with a tissue from her pocket and refocused them on the wall clock across the kitchen. About half an hour had elapsed since she first arrived back home and made the call to Malone. It had seemed an eternity.

She was about to go to the front of the house to see if a state trooper had already arrived at Adams's house when a sudden realization bolted into her mind. Kevin! she thought. She'd forgotten all about him. The house was so quiet she wondered if he had fallen asleep. If he had, she'd probably find him where the children sometimes played on a rainy afternoon, at the top of the stairs that led to the attic. There was a wide carpeted space up there, and shelves of books and magazines. She knew it was one of Kevin's favorite places in the whole house. He often went there to read or do his homework while his sister and Jennifer played in her daughter's downstairs bedroom.

"Kevin?" she called from the foot of the stairs. "Are you up there?"

The only response that came to her was the soft ticking of the old grandfather clock beside the door in the vestibule.

"Kevin!" she called again, this time louder and more firmly—just in case he *had* fallen asleep and didn't hear her the first time.

When there was no answer, she quickly climbed the stairs to see for herself. She even opened the attic door to see if he might be there. He wasn't. She went back down to the main part of the house and looked in every room. She couldn't find him anywhere.

It was then that she thought he might have disobeyed his father. She remembered how angry he had been when Adams told him to stay with her, and how he had stormed out of the house. But he *had* gone to her house. That much she knew. From Adams's living room window she had seen him enter the front door. She couldn't imagine where he might be.

She pulled her coat on and went out to the front of the house. She was relieved to see a state trooper's cruiser parked in Adams's driveway. If the boy had gone back home for any reason, he would be with the trooper. She was about to walk across the dooryard to find out when she saw the trail of small footprints that left her house from the back.

Oh, my God! she thought. The boy had gone in the front door, so we could see him, then he went right out the back. But where to? she asked herself.

She followed the trail of prints with her eyes and saw that they ended at the same spot where Adams had had his car parked. The prints disappeared in the area just before the markings of the rear tire. Her heart began to pound.

He sneaked in with his father, she thought. Then she remembered the boy's words to Adams. *She's my sister,* he had said. *And I'm the only one who can save her.*

She raced across the dooryard and met the trooper at the door. His face was pale, as though he had seen a ghost. He had just discovered Ben's body and was on his way to the cruiser to use the emergency police frequency. Seeing a dead police officer had unsettled him.

"Is there a boy in there?" she asked.

The trooper looked at her as though her words had startled him. "No," he finally answered, closing the black leather-bound notebook in his hand. "Are you the next-door neighbor who called this in?" he asked as she followed him down the steps to the cruiser.

Betty shook her head yes and quickly told him what she was troubled about.

"No," the trooper repeated, reaching for the radio phone. "I went all through the house, cellar to attic. There's no boy inside that house."

She turned her head to the side for a moment to think. She was on the brink of panic. What could she tell him?

For some reason her eyes scanned the nearby hills, as though in their snow-covered steeps there might possibly be a clue to the boy's whereabouts.

The expression on the trooper's face changed to one of alarm when he saw her eyes suddenly go large. With the radio phone still in his hand, he felt compelled to follow her line of sight to find out what she was looking at. He saw it immediately. Billows of dark smoke belched from a wall of white trees just below the peak of one of the nearby hills.

"Who lives up there?" the trooper asked, ready to use the phone in his hand for emergency assistance.

Betty didn't know, but she was willing to bet anything in the world that that's where Adams and Kevin were—and where Emma Prescott, the insane child-killer, had taken Kathy.

She didn't know where it came from, or what made her speak the words, but she pointed to the billowing cloud of dark smoke that hung above the snow-covered treetops of Tweed Hill and said, "That's where you'll find the killer. That's where the sheriff and the boy have gone."

She felt badly that her feelings did not extend to the possibility that Kathy might still be alive.

CHAPTER THIRTY-FOUR

Kevin's fingers worked frantically at the ropes that bound his sister to the chair. The flames were all about him now and he didn't know if he could get her out of the blazing cabin before the roof collapsed. Above his head the tinder-dry old roof boards had already begun to crawl with twisting fingers of cherry-red flame.

He had just managed to free her hands and the upper part of her body, and was about to begin working on the ropes that still bound her legs and ankles to the bottom rung of the chair, when he saw the knife that Emma Prescott had earlier rammed into the top of the low wooden table. The handle she had carved and painted to represent herself was smouldering and on the brink of bursting into flame. Its blade glittered with the fire that danced along the tabletop. It was only several feet farther into the cabin behind his sister. If he could only reach it, he could cut her loose in a second. He decided to go for it. He could grasp the handle with the sleeve of his sweat shirt. It was still wet from the snow he had stuffed into it—snow he had rubbed on Kathy's face and hair the moment he reached her. He even peeled the tape from her mouth and had her eat some snow to moisten her parched mouth.

When he rose to his feet he saw something behind the table that in his frenzy he hadn't seen earlier. The dolls! He froze in his tracks.

"Kevin!" Kathy shouted hoarsely. Melted snow splattered from her lips. "Don't just stand there. Get me loose!" She tried to reach the ropes that were knotted to the chair about her ankles, but her arms were too short.

"Kevin!" she screamed again when she saw that her brother was still frozen to the spot. "Wake up! We have to get out of here!"

The boy's eyes didn't register anything but the abstract bewilderment he felt as he stared at the dolls. The heat had melted down the candles to oozing puddles of ignited wax that slithered along the sides of the burning boxes in which the dolls stood. As he watched, the glass that covered them shattered, exposing the features and characteristics of the individual dolls in all their perfect clarity. The doll upon which his attention had fallen, and the one that had caused him to remain rooted to the spot beside his sister's chair, was the doll of himself. It stood between Jennifer's and his own little sister's doll. Dream fused with reality in such a chaotic mix that he wasn't sure if this was just another one of the horrible nightmares he had been having lately.

A white-hot spark suddenly exploded from a blazing rafter and shot past him like a flare. Another loud snap and a fiery coal sizzled along the floor and bounced like a stone skipping across a pond. Kathy followed it with her eyes as it headed toward the workbench where the paints and thinners were. It came to rest on a pile of cloths on the floor beside the leg of the workbench. Flames immediately sprang from them and began to set the bench on fire. Kathy saw how close it was to a can that was marked: "Paint Thinner—Keep Away From Heat." She began to scream. "Kevin!" she choked. "It's going to blow up. Get us out of here!"

Kevin finally began to move, but it wasn't what the girl had expected. Her brother simply lifted one foot above the other and paced in place without going anywhere. It was almost the same as when he had frozen in front of Jennifer in their kitchen, the same day she was killed. Kathy screamed hysterically. She had come so close to being rescued, and now it seemed that wasn't going to be.

Her cries and choking sobs spilled out into the cold white dawn and blended with the noisy chewing of the fire, eating its way through the heavy timbers of the cabin.

Kathy slumped forward in the chair, giving in to the weakness and exhaustion of the long and fruitless struggle she had been through. Oh, Kevin, she thought. I love you anyway.

The trooper that Betty Lineham had been speaking to called for emergency assistance on the radio phone. A small army of townspeople with chain saws and shovels now cleared the opening of the trail so that the fire truck and ambulance that he had called for could get up to where all that black smoke was coming from.

It wasn't easy. For every foot the fire truck went

forward, it skidded back two. Some of the volunteer firemen had already begun to climb the trail on foot. Every one of them had an axe, a pick, or a coil of heavy rope slung across his shoulder. They faced about three miles of steep trail ahead of them.

The snowmobiles arrived too late; the head of the trail had already been blocked with the fire truck, ambulance, and a state emergency vehicle. They couldn't pass. The trees on either side of the narrow trail were too thick. A few of the snowmobiles buzzed about like angry hornets as their drivers looked for the slightest opening in the snow-covered armor that surrounded the clogged trail. One or two managed to squeeze through some of the thinner spaces but quickly buried themselves in the powdery snow that had not yet been packed down enough for a snowmobile to function.

And through all this, there suddenly emerged the sound of crashing trees being snapped in two and rooted up. Everyone's chain saw stopped. Even the snowmobile drivers heard it above the roar of their engines. Everyone focused their attention up the trail, toward where the crashing noise was coming from. It sounded as though a giant were pushing his way through the woods toward them. When they finally saw who it was and what he was doing, a cheer went up.

It was Les Knowel, the backwoods recluse. Before his wife died he had been an excavator, and nothing was ever going to make him give up his John Deere bulldozer, not while he still lived up in those hills. Roads were going out on him all the time, and with a bulldozer all you had to do was put in one of your own.

He had the snowplow rigged up and was blazing a wide trail right down toward the fire truck. When he got to it he spun the bulldozer around on one of its steel caterpillar tracks and placed its rear end right in front of the red fire truck.

He hadn't seen the fire, nor did he know anything about what was going on. All he knew was that the sound of chain saws, sirens, and fire bells meant trouble. He had come out of the woods, ready to offer any help he could.

After the initial cheer of his arrival, a momentary silence fell upon the crowd as the old recluse, still seated atop his John Deere, opened his coat and pulled out a bottle of whiskey. He took a long swig and put it right back in where it had come from. Aside from the twinkle in his eyes, there was an odd question in them, too. He looked at the knot of volunteer firemen that had gathered about him. He wrinkled up his weathered old brow and shot a glance over his shoulder to the front of the fire truck.

"What's the matter?" he asked. "Don't 'cha know how to hook up a cable?"

The firemen leaped to and ran it out like a greased snake in a pond. As soon as the cable was connected to the bulldozer, Les pulled out and began to tow the fire truck up the trail.

"Where to?" he asked the chief who had climbed up and taken a seat beside him. "What's on fire?"

"Someone told me it was the old Turner place," the chief answered. "Know it?"

Les Knowel didn't have to respond. Not only did he know it, but he guessed the rest of it as well: the children, the killer, the old isolated cabin at the end of the trail! Jesus, he thought. He lived just a few miles away, on the other side of Bannion Hill. He could have gone up to that old abandoned cabin a thousand times during the past year, anytime he wanted. But he respected other people's land, just the same as he wanted folks to respect his. The land wasn't his, and he wasn't going to trespass—even if no one had lived on the Turner land since almost before he was born. He now suspected what that shooting was the other day. Arthur Winston, he thought. The deputy was probably trying to signal for help!

He leaned heavily on the forward accelerator and munched the snow beneath the tracks of his bulldozer until the trail seemed to run out as smooth as the main highway. By the time he finished with it, he thought, every vehicle in the state would be able to pass.

Right behind the fire truck, Betty Lineham sat in the front seat of the ambulance. She was never one given to prayer, but her mind went through every one she had ever learned. If we can only get there in time, she thought as they joggled steadily up the trail behind the truck. If we can only get there in time!

Kevin stood in the heat of the blazing cabin, still staring at his doll as though he were in a trance. He had come face to face with the nightmare that had been plaguing his dreams for the past several nights—ever since Jennifer was killed. And now there she was, too. Her doll, smouldering in the heat and about to burst into flame, stood to the side of his. On the other side, there was the one of his baby sister.

Something deep within him wanted to scream. He was rooted to the spot where he stood, unable to move. Vapor rose from his shirt as the moisture from the snow he had packed into it evaporated in the heat of the blaze. Beside him, his sister was slumped over in the chair. Vapor rose from her hunched shoulders. She appeared to be on the brink of losing consciousness.

He gave no thought to death or to the fire in which he was about to be consumed. The loud roar of the timbers being chewed into by the flames hardly penetrated his state of dreamlike consciousness. He knew the danger of it, yet it didn't matter. It was as though he were living in a dream from which he would shortly wake to find that all was as it had been before—before the killings, before the nightmares, before his mom had ever died.

"KEVIN!" someone shouted from the door of the cabin. "SNAP OUT OF IT!"

It was his father.

Adams leaned heavily on the doorjamb, exhausted from having dragged himself the remaining distance from where his son had bolted away and raced to the cabin. His leg was bleeding more heavily than it was before. In his haste the tourniquet had come loose and gotten lost. A trail of blood stained the snow from where he had crawled out of the woods and through the clearing to the cabin.

"KEVIN!" he screamed to the boy inside the roaring inferno. "GET KATHY OUT OF THERE! NOW!"

It came to the boy as a distant cry of someone calling

to him. The louder the shouts, the clearer the message became.

"KEVIN!"

His father's voice was shrill. In it there was a warning of danger. He must wake up. He'd be late for school. The children were already there, standing before him, waiting for the bell to ring, waiting for the town librarian to come and . . .

"Kevin!" This time it was Kathy who called out to him. "Wake up!" she cried. "It's Daddy! It's Daddy! He's here!"

The boy's eyes snapped open like those of a startled owl. It took less than a second for him to realize he was not dreaming. Coils of sooty black smoke wove about him and his sister like angry pythons. The heat had now completely dried his shirt, and the clothing that his sister wore was beginning to smoulder—just like those of the dolls only moments before they would burst into flame. There was no time to waste. He had to be quick! But there was no way to get Kathy out of the cabin without having to go through the wall of fire that separated them from their father at the door.

Adams took a step into the blazing cabin at precisely the same moment that the can of paint thinner exploded on the workbench. A jumble of arms, legs, and heads—all belonging to the dolls—hurtled about the cabin in a macabre dance of fiery undulations. Another explosion, this time from the remaining cans of paints and oils, sent flames shooting about like a flamethrower he had once seen tested in Vietnam. His knee buckled and he fell, landing on the body of Emma Prescott that was just inside the door. Her hair was on fire, and the blood in her eyes boiled. As he feebly struggled to lift himself from her dead body, her face—frozen into an eerie grin the moment the axe blade had sunk into her forehead—appeared to mock his futile efforts.

From inside the cabin, beyond the wall of bright flame where he had last glimpsed his children, Adams heard a rumbling noise that sounded as though the thick old timbers of the cabin had finally given in to the raging fire.

"No!" he cried, beating Emma Prescott's dead body with his fists. "NO!"

Adams pulled the broadaxe from the dead woman's forehead and swung it into the wall beside the doorjamb. He used it as a support to pull himself up to his feet. It took all the strength he had left. The pain in his leg had spread to the rest of his body and was so intense that he had to catch himself from blacking out. He spun to face the fire that separated him from his children and lunged forward. But the moment he put his weight on the wounded leg it buckled and he collapsed in a disjointed heap.

Adams tried to pull himself up again but couldn't. He had lost too much blood. He was dying. God! he thought, crawling and inching his way closer and closer to the wall of fire. Please don't let us die like this. Please!

He pressed his cheek to the floor, where there was still air enough to breathe, and heard the rumbling sound again. Something suddenly barreled out of the flames and hurtled past him. It sounded as though part of the roof had collapsed—the part that was above his children. He lifted his head from the floorboards to see. The roof was still there, blazing cherry-red with flame.

He turned to the door. It was Kevin! He had dragged his sister, chair and all, right through the fire and out onto the porch.

"Thank you," Adams muttered to himself as his face hit the floor again. With his children out of the cabin, he could accept death more peacefully.

Outside, Kevin flung himself, along with his sister, right off the porch and into a deep drift of snow. They sizzled and smouldered until the flames that had ignited their clothing were extinguished. The girl was black with soot and there were burn-blisters on her face and arms. Kevin was no better.

"Daddy's in there!" Kathy screamed and choked. "Get him! Get him! Get him!"

The moment her brother disappeared into the burning cabin Kathy heard the sound of something crashing through the woods at the edge of the clearing. When she turned, she saw Les Knowel's bulldozer parting the trees. It was headed directly toward the cabin. Behind him was the fire truck, and just behind that, Betty Lineham came racing toward her from the door of the ambulance. Kathy's eyes were as large as they had ever been in her entire life when she turned back to the cabin and saw her brother pulling their dad out onto the porch by the shoulders.

Almost before Kathy could blink her eyes, Betty Lineham was on her knees beside the girl—holding her, gingerly washing the burn-blisters on her face and arms with snow while she whispered soothing words close to the child's ear. She untied the knots that still bound her ankles to what remained of the wooden chair and held her tightly. But the thing that made Kathy feel best of all was the sight of the men from the ambulance. They now swarmed about her father and brother, helping them to safety from the steps of the porch as the cabin's roof finally toppled into the raging blaze.

One of the firemen looked up at Kathy and winked. There was a smile on his face. Kathy would remember that gesture for the rest of her life. It told her that her dad and her brother were going to be all right.

EPILOGUE

On the following morning, the first person Adams saw when he opened his eyes was Betty Lineham. She was sitting on the hospital bed beside him, gently running her fingers across the top of his hand where an IV needle was inserted into a vein. The transfusions of blood he received the day before had saved his life. He was weak, but on the mend. A winding bandage of heavy gauze covered the wound in his leg, which was elevated in a hanging sling. The doctors said he would only have to remain in the hospital for another day or so.

Across the room, where there was an empty bed, Kevin and Kathy sat in chairs by the window and watched a program on the wall-mounted television set. There were patches of shiny salves on the burns and bruises that covered their arms and faces. Other than that, they appeared to be perfectly normal. Outside the window, the snow looked as deep and white as anything that had ever appeared in a painted picture.

Adams lifted his head from the pillow. "How long have I been like this?" he asked, examining himself. When he saw his children, he asked, "Are they all right?"

Betty shook her head. His children were indeed all right, and so was he. She quickly told him what the doctors had said about him being able to leave in a another day or so. She had taken care of the children the night before and would continue to do so until he got back on his feet.

Someone then entered the room. At first, Adams didn't recognize who it was. It took him a moment to realize it was Dr. York, the state psychologist he had spoken to at the capital. York smiled and walked briskly to the head of Adams's bed. He was carrying a small pile of newspapers.

Without saying a word, the psychologist held up, one at a time, the front page of each paper for him to read.

HATCHER DENOUNCES LOCAL SHERIFF AS FRAUD IN COVER-UP OF SHODDY INVESTIGATION! the first one read.

LOCAL SHERIFF FINDS CHILD-KILLER WHO HAS TERRORIZED TWEED VALLEY FOR ALMOST A YEAR. CASE SOLVED AS SHERIFF AND HIS TWO CHILDREN COME CLOSE TO DEATH IN KILLER'S BURNING LAIR! read the second.

But it was the third headline that brought the widest grin to Adams's face.

HATCHER RESIGNS POST AMID THREATS OF LIBEL AND SLANDER SUITS BY OFFICE OF LIEUTENANT GOVERNOR. BID FOR ELECTION TO STATE SENATE NOW DOUBTFUL.

Adams motioned with his free hand for York to

come and sit beside him in the empty chair opposite Betty.

"How are the children?" he quietly asked.

"Fine," the psychologist responded. "I was here at the hospital on business when you were all brought in yesterday. Their wounds are superficial and will be completely healed in about a week."

Adams shook his head. "It was their mental state I was worried about," he said. "How's that going to be?"

York leaned back for a moment before speaking. "You have two very extraordinary children," he began. "I spent a lot of time with Kevin. He told me everything he could remember about that ESP thing . . . about how he was able to somehow *see* the cabin where the killer had taken his sister. He was worried by that, and a bit frightened, to say the least. I told him nobody really knew what caused such things to happen, but there seemed to be good evidence to suggest that such things do happen and that it appears to be a temporary phenomenon, especially with children." He paused a moment as though he were considering something. "I don't think there's anything to worry about," he finally said. "Besides, Kevin told me he wanted to be a sheriff when he grew up, just like his dad. If he doesn't lose that curious ability to sometimes *see*, he should make one of the best investigators this state had ever had!"

The children couldn't help themselves. They had turned their attention away from the TV and focused on York's words as he spoke. They now laughed. Kevin's face was as bright as a beam.

"Go hush yourselves up," Betty said to the children. There was a bright grin on her own face too.

They smiled and turned back to the TV. Kathy giggled something in Kevin's ear and they both looked back at Betty. When their eyes met hers they quickly turned back to the television program. There had been an expression in their fleeting glance that made Betty's heart skip. It was as though they might have been her own children.

"And Kathy?" Adams asked the psychologist. "How is she?"

York looked at him and smiled. "I've never seen a stronger child," he said. "At first I thought she was going to need a lot of psychological counseling after what had happened. She will need *some*—Kevin too—and I'll be around to help arrange it. Unless I'm mistaken, it doesn't look as though either of them are going to require any long-term psychological assistance. They're two very rock-ribbed kids and I'm sure they're going to be fine. All they need right now is some time to forget, together with the warmth and caring of two loving—"

York had been about to say "parents" when he remembered that Adams's wife was no longer alive. He looked at Betty before returning his attention to Adams. His accidental slip of words had affected them in an unexpected way. Something close and warm suddenly revealed itself in their eyes. York felt sheepish. "Well, you know what I mean," he concluded.

The psychologist cleared his throat. He had a message for Adams. "I spoke to Jerry Malone just before I got here," he began. "Now that Hatcher is out of the show, the governor himself was wondering if you'd like to move up to the capital. He has a good job waiting there for you."

The news didn't seem to have the punch to it that York thought it might. But he wasn't surprised. Betty stared off at the children across the room. Adams appeared to be thinking about something other than the job offer.

"Take your time with a decision," York finally said as he rose from the chair to leave. "Get in touch with Malone when you decide. I don't think there's any rush."

The way the psychologist looked at the children and then at Adams and Betty before he left the room caused a gentle smile to cross Adams's lips.

"Do you think you're going to do it?" Betty asked after the psychologist left. "Move to the capital?" She knew there were many other things she could have said that would tend to make him change his mind about ever leaving Tweed Valley, but she didn't want to influence his decision in any way. It was too great a responsibility. If he decided to stay because of anything she said, he might later resent her for it. It had to be his own clean thought. Her mind was already made up in either case. If he decided to move to the capital, she'd go too, period.

Adams looked at her for what seemed an eternity. "No," he finally answered. "I'm not moving anywhere. I guess—"

He didn't finish. The quiet that then passed between them spoke of a bridge, one that two hurt and lonely people would build across the void in their lives to join one another. It promised to be a strong one.

Betty fought with the tears that welled up in her eyes. There was no anguish in them. Only joy.

Adams reached out with the arm that didn't have the IV plugged into it and pulled her down to him. They kissed, gently. There was more to it than their first awkward kiss the night he had to leave for the capital. "It's going to be all right," he whispered close to her ear. "Things will never be the same again—not for me, not for you, not for the kids. Healing is going to take a while, for all of us. But we can work it out. I'm sure of it."

Across the room, Kevin and Kathy had long ago given up their interest in the TV. They sat like two ponies in a paddock waiting for the pasture gate to open. Betty saw them when she finally looked up, and she stretched her arm out to them. They came racing to the bed where they were warmly embraced by Betty and their father in a bundle of hugs and kisses.

"Yes," Betty said, struggling to keep her emotions from spilling out like a spring tide. "It's going to be all right."